CW00702593

A Street Café Named Desire

R J Gould

Published by Accent Press Ltd 2014

ISBN 9781783752577

Copyright © **R J Gould** 2014

The right of **R J Gould** to be identified as the author of this work has been asserted by the author in accordance with the Copyright, Designs and Patents Act 1988.

The story contained within this book is a work of fiction. Names and characters are the product of the author's imagination and any resemblance to actual persons, living or dead, is entirely coincidental.

All rights reserved. No part of this book may be reproduced, stored in a retrieval system, or transmitted in any form or by any means, electronic, electrostatic, magnetic tape, mechanical, photocopying, recording or otherwise, without the written permission of the publishers: Accent Press Ltd, Ty Cynon House, Navigation Park, Abercynon, CF45 4SN

Chapter One

He was forty-three. Autumn shouldn't be such a surprise any more, but the annual explosion of colour never ceased to amaze him.

Here they were at their twenty-five year school reunion, crowded around the bar area of the upmarket Hotel Marlborough in Henley. Huge sash windows provided a magnificent view of a fast-flowing, grey River Thames. Rowers were flying downstream. Beyond the river was a steep bank with a dramatic display of early autumn trees.

'David. You're David!'

Turning, he was clamped in a bear hug by a woman whose strong grip took his breath away. A face with two scarlet lips came hurtling towards him. His desperate attempt to avoid impact failed and their lips collided.

'Well, well. David. Incredible – just incredible.'

What did this 'incredible' mean? That he'd hardly changed? That he'd transformed beyond imagination? She stepped back and her vice-like grip transferred to his shoulders.

'David, David.'

How long would this continue – wasn't she going to advance the conversation? He knew he was David. Obviously she did too. Unfortunately he couldn't assist because his natural response – hello Alice, hello Barbara, Clare, Diane, Elizabeth, Fiona, or whatever – was impossible. He had no idea who she was.

'You do remember me, don't you?'

'Yes.'

'That field trip!' She had released her grip, but the physical assault continued with a punch on his upper left arm. It was no more than a prod really, but right on the spot where the flu vaccination had been applied.

David winced. She noticed.

'You're much too tough to worry about a little tap like that. Well you certainly were back then,' she continued, her face contorting into a grotesque smirk. She gave him another slightly harder punch in the same place.

'Helen, darling!' The boxer turned to acknowledge the greeting as another unrecognisable ex-schoolmate approached. Now he had her name and with that a distant memory of teenage groping with a lithe blonde girl during the fourth form field trip to the French Alps. He noted the dramatic change in size and shape since her school days.

'It's, let me see now, don't tell me. It's … it's Sharon!' Helen screamed and the two women jumped up and down before regressing into adolescent reminiscences about their poor behaviour in various lessons at school. If he closed his eyes he could be listening to his own teenage children. But he didn't close his eyes because a shaft of late afternoon sun had burst through the voluminous clouds and now the trees beyond the bank were ablaze in their full glory.

A week or so ago the leaves would have been green. Now they were dazzling reds, yellows, oranges, and browns.

'Are you listening, David? You agree with me, don't you?' Sharon asked.

'Yes, I do. Absolutely.' Of course green wasn't one colour, he reflected. There were shades – light to dark, and variations like sage and jade.

'That's not true. It wasn't like that, was it, David?' It was Helen.

'No it wasn't. Absolutely not.'

'But a minute ago you said it was,' Sharon countered.

'It's all to do with perception,' David mumbled, eager not to disrupt his train of thought. Without doubt there was a wider range of colours when it came to the reds, oranges, yellows, and browns. Bronze, sienna, ochre, and sand for starters. Chocolate. Copper. Mahogany. Rust.

'Are you with us, David?' Helen delivered a punch to precisely the same spot. Her accuracy was uncanny.

'He always was a dreamer, drifting off into his own little world,' Sharon added, her voice high-pitched and piercing. The two women were giggling, making it hard for him to concentrate on colours.

He was ill at ease because there was a frustrating gap, a missing one on the tip of his tongue. Then it came to him, perhaps the dominant colour out there across the river. 'Russet,' he announced.

'David, what on earth are you going on about?' He turned away from the autumn beauty; both women were frowning at him.

'Rush it, you said. Rush what?'

David remained silent as Helen continued. 'We were remembering how Mr Strickland used to take the piss out of you in Geography.'

'Highlight of the week, that was.' Helen laughed coarsely as Sharon took over, speaking with a deep voice in an attempt to impersonate the teacher.

'And where are we now, David? I hope in the Australian outback with the rest of us.'

'Toss-er' Helen added in teenage-speak.

'I rather liked him,' David announced to the gap between the two women. 'Excuse me ladies, must circulate.' He turned and headed towards the bar.

'Well, look who we've got here.' The voice of Bill Thatcher hadn't changed

'It's our little David,' another unchanged voice, this was Ben Carpenter.

An overzealous slap landed on David's back. 'You buying the drinks, mate?' Ben asked.

David realised he was no longer scared of them. How

could you be, looking at the two pot-bellied, balding, greying men with sallow puffy faces? They had lost their menacing edge. Also, he was prepared to admit when he'd had time to reflect, he wasn't scared because he didn't much care what happened, not after what he had been subjected to over the past few weeks.

He eyed Ben. 'Why don't you get me one?'

Ben looked aghast. 'What?'

'I'll have a bottle of Bud, thank you.'

'Is little David acting tough?' Bill enquired.

'I think he is,' added Ben.

'It's not a case of acting tough, it's about growing up. And I seem to have made a better job of it than you two. I suppose keeping fit helps, the judo.'

'You do judo?' sneered Bill.

'Yes. And not drinking as much beer as you has assisted.' With that, David gave Bill a generous whack on his pot belly. When he analysed his action afterwards, readily admitting it had been a step too far, he wondered whether the annoying physical maltreatment by Helen might have been part of the reason for his own mild assault. But probably it all came down to his profound unhappiness – he couldn't care less about the outcome of his actions. Not at that instant at any rate. But he did care a few nanoseconds later when Bill floored him with a right hook to the chin.

Bill looked down at him with contempt. 'You gonna try your judo on me, little David?'

Of course there never had been any judo, only badminton which had kept him in reasonable shape but clearly hadn't prepared him for fighting. David gazed up at a gathering of his ex-classmates in a circle around him, some with a look of concern, but most smiling. Helen and Sharon were in the smiling group, but at least Helen did have the decency to tell Bill and Ben to lay off as it was a festive occasion. The crowd dispersed and David stood gingerly. He made his way to a chair by the window. In the short interval between boredom and humiliation dusk had enveloped the trees. Now they stood as forlorn grey silhouettes. Despite there no longer being anything of interest to see, he chose to stare out the window rather than look inside the room at the alcohol-fuelled gathering.

'One Bud coming up.'

He turned. The woman handed over the bottle and sat next to him, a glass of white wine in her other hand. 'You OK?'

'Just my pride hurt a bit. Well my chin, too.'

'Poor you. Those two were appalling twenty-five years ago and they haven't improved by the look of things.'

David recognised the voice, the engaging Scottish lilt from all those years ago.

'I'm Titless,' the woman added.

He glanced from her face to her upper body and saw shapely curves. When he looked up she was smiling and he reddened.

'Not anymore, but I was then. I took a while to develop. Too long for Bill and Ben, so that was their nickname for me.'

'I remember you. Bridget.'

'Congratulations. You're the first to know my name tonight, not that I've spoken to many.'

'Well, you've changed beyond all recognition.'

Like every parent, David had told his children the story of the ugly duckling that turned into a beautiful white swan, and while he appreciated the moral symbolism, he had never seen such a transformation in real life until now. Bridget had been an unsociable, awkward girl, liable to blush the instant someone addressed her. She had appeared friendless and was known as 'Spotty Swot' amongst his circle of friends. He hadn't been aware of the 'Titless' nickname, not surprising as he kept well away from the gang. Her legs, he remembered, had looked too spindly to support her. He'd felt sorry for Bridget, a rather sad-looking loner, but he'd been too shy to do anything about it.

The woman by his side was divine – a goddess. Not in a garishly sexy way – just downright beautiful. Every facial feature of textbook perfection. A narrow face with high cheekbones; a little, upturned nose; pouting lips; soft, powder blue eyes. Eyes that were now smiling at him.

'I feel like I'm being inspected. Do you approve?'

'Yes, yes. You look lovely, if you don't mind me saying.'

'Thank you, I never say no to a compliment. I was wondering though – what on earth made you come along to this awful reunion?'

'It's a long story.'

'It's a long evening.'

Chapter Two

Two weeks ago. That's when David had made the decision to attend the reunion. And that was just two weeks after Jane had told him she was leaving. Not only Jane, but Jim was there too. His best friend Jim.

It was a sunny Saturday and David was sitting in the garden with a mug of tea, flicking through the *Daily Mail*. According to the newspaper there was a lot wrong with the world. He had never been able to understand why this was Jane's newspaper of choice.

David was addicted to perusing and mocking the content. One article covered a new drama about vampires which was, claimed the journalist, 'sucking the innocence out of our children with a shocking tale of depravity that has become the norm on television'. His daughter Rachel loved the programme. David couldn't gauge the extent of her innocence; she was probably the same as most other sixteen-year-olds in keeping her feelings very much to herself, but there was no evidence of anything being sucked out by what she watched.

On the same page a woman's life of drink and one-night stands had left her feeling hollow. But then she found the answer: 'I'm going to become a nun.' Two photographs showed the before and after. The first, a smiling woman with a rather low cut top holding up a glass of red wine. The second a dour woman, her mane of jet black hair now covered or possibly even discarded, replaced by a nun's customary headgear. David smiled self-righteously, the writer's implied preference for the nun at odds with the saucy underwear display 'to capture your man' on the previous page.

What a contrast between the women featured on these pages and sensible, practical, lovable Jane – he was lucky to have such a wonderful wife.

He read on, reaching the finance articles. The stock market was continuing its downward trend, with the companies he had a few shares in doing particularly badly.

All in all it had been a satisfying afternoon. He'd pruned the roses, taken the dead heads off the geraniums, and swept up the first wave of fallen leaves. The garden waste had been deposited in the green recycling bin ready for the Monday collection. It was his turn to cook tonight. The lamb was out the freezer and a bottle of Pinot Grigio, Jane's favourite, was chilling in the fridge.

His wife was out shopping, a regular Saturday pursuit. She favoured going to Brent Cross over the local precinct despite the distance and the queue of drivers battling to get into one of the substantial, but still inadequate, car parks. Inside the mall there were two vast walkways to trek around, as big as athletics tracks. At least in a race everybody was going the same way, but here a stream of determined shoppers struggled to pass those travelling in the opposite direction. For years David had kept his dislike of these trips to himself and selflessly accompanied Jane on her expeditions. But a while back she must have sensed that David hated the experience and volunteered to go alone. She seemed happy window shopping, for despite being away for hours she rarely came back with a purchase.

He didn't hear the front door open and only looked up when she called his name.

There was an urgency to her tone. 'David,' she repeated.

Smiling, he turned to face her. 'Hello, Jane. Have you had a good time? Oh, hello there, Jim. How are things with you?'

Jim stood by her side, his face serious. Then as David

glanced down he saw they were holding hands. Instantly his heart was pounding, his skin itching with prickly heat, his mouth dry. He couldn't speak. His mind raced, searching for an explanation beyond the one that he knew had to be true. As he awaited the awful inevitability of what was to come, the few seconds' interval stretched on endlessly.

It was Jane who spoke first, getting straight to the point. 'Jim and I are in love, David. We've been in a relationship for a couple of months and we both know we can't live apart. We've tried to fight it, but it isn't possible. I've decided to move in with him.'

There was a pause, perhaps inviting a reaction from David, but he remained speechless. Unexpected tears welled up, blurring his vision, and a single tear trickled down his right cheek. He trapped the salty moisture with his tongue.

Now Jim was speaking in a this-is-the-sensible-way-forward-for-mature-adults manner. David caught phrases like 'I'm sure we can do this amicably', 'we hope a divorce can go through as smoothly as possible', and worst of all, 'we must remain friends after a healing period'.

It was Jane's turn to add some unemotional sound bites. 'It's not as if we have shared interests any more'; 'all the children do is hear us argue'.

He didn't think they argued much at all. Admittedly they didn't chat or laugh as they used to, but there was no conflict, not in his opinion anyway. The reference to the children took him out of his numb state. How on earth were they going to cope with this? Was Jane intending to take them with her, to live with the person they knew as Uncle Jim, or were they to remain with him? Did lawyers settle that?

'What about the kids?' he blurted out.

Lawyers would not be needed in this case since Jane had already made the decision. 'I think the children should stay here. After all, this is their family home. I've written a letter for you to give them and I'll be back tomorrow morning to chat once they know what's what.'

Now there was anger to mix with his self-pity. 'So it's my job to tell them? "Rachel, Sam. Come here a minute. Just to let you know mum has left, she's gone to live with Jim." All right with that?'

'There's no need for sarcasm, David. I can't face them today, it's too difficult for me,' Jane said in an actually-I-feel-tough-enough-to-face-anything voice.

'Surely you understand how poor Jane feels, David,' Jim added. 'Show some compassion, for God's sake.'

Jane took over. 'I think we should go now, but as I said, I'll see them tomorrow.'

She turned to leave. Jim remained facing him. 'You take care of yourself now, David.' He extended his arm for a handshake which sent David into such a state of shock that he sat down, his mouth agape.

And with that Jim turned and followed Jane out through the kitchen, towards the front door.

David was still in shock, sitting on the white plastic chair with the mildew-covered orange and brown striped cushion when Sam came home. He couldn't have missed Jane by more than a couple of minutes. With great excitement Sam began to recount how he'd been testing out his friend Adrian's new radio controlled car in the local park. While David fretted about what to say, Sam talked about the speed of the Lamborghini model, how it was something he'd love to own so that he could race against his friend.

'It's only £69.99 at Argos, Dad.'

This pause for his dad to consider the proposition was the opportunity David needed.

'Sam, listen, something terrible has happened. It's your mother.'

'She's not had an accident, has she?' asked Sam with

an expression suggesting surprisingly little concern.

'No, not an accident,' replied David, for an instant wishing she had.

'Good, that's alright then. Dad, what about an advance Christmas present? If I had to wait until then I wouldn't be able to use it for ages, with the mud and snow and stuff. But it would be brilliant for now. What do you reckon?'

'Maybe, but listen. Your mother.'

'Yes?' Sam enquired impatiently.

'She's leaving us. Well, me, to be more precise, although I suppose also you because she doesn't intend to live here. She's going to live with Jim.'

'Uncle Jim?'

'Yes, Uncle Jim.' As he spoke there was a sudden gust of wind and a medley of early falling leaves swirled down from the cherry tree.

'They're just friends, Dad. Mum's always going on about how helpless he is since his wife died. She goes round loads to check he's OK, but they're only visits.'

'I'm afraid not, Sam.'

'Dad, you must have misheard.'

There was a pause as David weighed up the value of convincing Sam that he was indeed right.

'Who's going to cook dinner then?' said the boy, whose calm, practical outlook on life had always been in such sharp contrast to his sister's frequent emotional outbursts.

'What?'

'If Mum leaves, who's going to cook dinner?'

'Well tonight's my turn, it's Saturday,' David mumbled, disturbed by the way the conversation was progressing.

'But what about other days?'

'Sam, I haven't given it a lot of thought. Me again, I suppose.'

'Oh. It's just that Mum's a better cook than you. It's

OK to say that, isn't it, Dad?'

'Yes, it's fine to say that,' said David reassuringly, wondering whether this was Sam's way of dealing with the traumatic news.

'What are we eating tonight?' Sam persevered.

'We've got lamb.'

'I like the taste, but when you see lambs jumping about outside in the fresh air it does make you think.'

'We live in the middle of London. When did you last see a frolicking lamb?'

'Last week. Not live, on TV.' Sam returned to the big issue. 'I'm sure everything will turn out OK, about Mum, I mean. She'll stay with us, just you see.'

David was not so sure, it had seemed pretty final to him.

'Dad, will you have a good think about the car?'

'Yes, I will,' David replied. Although he was pleased the news hadn't made Sam distraught, there was a degree of despondency that his son was indifferent to his feelings. Perhaps it was too much to expect a thirteen-year-old boy to have overt sympathy for an adult.

'See you later,' Sam said as he turned and headed indoors. His once white trainers were caked in mud though the luminous green Nike tick was as prominent as ever. He was wearing faded jeans and a black T-shirt with an appropriate skeleton cartoon over his painfully thin frame. A good boy, David reflected.

'Take your trainers off before you go upstairs,' he called after Sam.

David went into the kitchen, opened the wine, and poured himself a generous glass. He rarely drank before dinner but this was no ordinary day. During his conversation with Sam his distress, mixed with anger, had waned. Sitting down at the kitchen table the shock resurfaced, but there was little time to think things through.

‘Hello, I’m back.’ It was Rachel.

‘In the kitchen,’ David called out.

There was the sound of the light brisk walk that he loved.

‘Hello, Dad.’ Rachel kissed him on the cheek and he could smell the stale tobacco on her clothes. He’d confronted her about the danger of smoking several times over the past few months, but to no avail. Jane hadn’t helped. ‘She’s sixteen, David, she needs to experiment. You can’t expect her to listen to an old fart like you,’ she had said. David hadn’t taken the ‘old fart’ description as a fact, but it was probably what she believed.

‘You OK, Dad? Lost in thought?’

‘It’s your mother.’ Rachel stepped back with a look of concern. At least this was a better start than the conversation with Sam. ‘She visited this afternoon.’

She gave him an impatient teenager look implying a questioning of sanity. ‘Dad, what do you mean ‘visited’?’ *She has such an expressive face*, David reflected as she continued. ‘She lives here.’

‘Jim was with her.’

‘I love Uncle Jim. It’s like we’re friends, he’s so easy to talk to.’

That statement made David contemplate the danger of continuing. Maybe she would be pleased her mother was moving on from an old fart to such a nice man. But there was no option other than to persevere. ‘She, well actually they … look, straight to the point because you’re old enough to understand,’ he blurted out. ‘They’re having a relationship and now Mum is leaving me and going to live with him.’

Rachel was stunned into silence, an unusual event. Her face reddened with anger.

David pressed on. ‘They came round this afternoon together, hand in hand, and told me.’

‘God, I’m an idiot. That explains things.’

'What do you mean, Rachel?'

'Lately whenever you call to tell us you'll be late home from work she's off as quick as a flash to see him. Says he needs support since his wife died. I bet she gives him support all right.'

'Obviously things were going on that I had no idea about. Maybe there'll be an explanation when she's back tomorrow morning to talk to both of you.'

'Great. She's pissing off and didn't even have the guts to tell us herself. She's left you to do her dirty work.'

Rachel went to the fridge, took out the orange juice, and drank straight from the carton.

'I'm sure it's not easy for her. Anyway, she's written you a letter,' David said as he handed her the envelope Jane had left on the table.

'Not easy! How can you defend her, are you mad? What about us?' She was right, it was a daft thing to say and David was all set to agree.

'Fucking bitch!' Rachel continued as she ripped the unopened letter and let the resulting little squares drop to the floor. 'Well I won't be seeing her.' She was holding back tears. 'I'm going round to Hannah's.'

She turned and strode out the kitchen then turned back. 'Are you OK, Dad?'

'Yes, don't worry about me. You go.'

A few seconds later there was the slam of the front door.

David finished his first glass of wine and poured a second. He switched on the oven and began to prepare the lamb, potatoes, and carrots for the dinner for either two or three – depending on when Rachel decided to return.

Chapter Three

David's conversation with Bridget was interrupted by an ex-classmate.

'Eating time,' she announced with a piercing screech. The woman was insecurely balanced on a chair, dressed in adult school uniform – short skirt, fishnet stockings, tight white shirt, and a kipper tie. Like everyone else at the reunion she was in her mid-forties and she looked ridiculous.

She appeared unable to speak like a normal grown up. 'It's bad bad news, you'll need to leave the bar. Sorreee. I know that's gonna be hard, but it is yummy yum yum buffet food. Just take the first door on the right.' Like an air hostess demonstrating emergency procedures she waved her arm in the appropriate direction, the clumsy motion sending her tumbling into the arms of the man standing by her side. They both ended up sprawled across the floor but the brave man had at least cushioned her fall, preventing injury to anything beyond pride.

'I'm glad I'm a grown-up,' Bridget said. 'Let's eat.'

'Yes, good idea,' David agreed.

They entered a grand room with dark wood panelling, rich golden velvet drapes, and ornate chandeliers. There was a glass vase with a single white rose on each of the round tables. The tablecloths were the maroon of their old school blazer with matching serviettes neatly folded into the wine glasses. They made their way towards the food, laid out on trestle tables at the far end.

'I love roast lamb, don't you?' David exclaimed as he looked at what was on offer. 'What a wonderful smell.'

'Actually I'm a vegetarian.'

‘Oh, I am sorry.’

‘I’m not.’

They joined the short queue and Helen and Sharon stood behind them.

‘Hello again, David. Recovered?’ It was Helen.

‘Yes, thank you.’

‘And who are you?’ Helen asked, looking at his companion.

‘Bridget.’

‘Were you in our year?’

‘Yes.’

‘Bridget who?’

‘Bridget Wilkinson.’

‘Well I don’t remember you. Sharon, do you remember Bridget?’

‘No, I don’t.’ With that, Helen and Sharon lost interest and turned away to chat with the man behind them in the queue.

David handed Bridget a plate. She walked past the large silver platter of meat garnished with strong smelling rosemary, past the roast potatoes and the broccoli too, stopping at a small bowl. There was an untidily written note on a folded piece of grey-brown cardboard behind it. *For vegetarians only*. She took a spoonful of the pasta dish, added salad, and then turned to wait for David, who had paused by the lamb.

‘I don’t think I’ll have this,’ he said as much to himself as to Bridget.

‘No need to do that for me,’ she said cheerfully.

‘It’s not that. I haven’t had lamb since the night Jane left and it’s brought back a flood of unpleasant memories.’ He moved on to the pasta and was about to put some on his plate when he saw the notice banning consumption by meat eaters. He placed the serving spoon back in the bowl.

‘Don’t be silly, David. Take some. I’ve hardly had any so you’d be sharing my portion.’

He dropped a small pile of the sticky, cheese-saturated offering onto his plate. 'Mm, looks lovely,' he said unconvincingly. He lifted it up towards his nose. 'Smells good too.'

They sat at a table in the far corner of the room, Bridget eating while David stirred his food with a fork. Other tables filled with their groups of six, but no one joined them until the queue had almost disappeared. Then a man and woman approached, each holding a plate of food piled high.

'Aren't you David Willoughby?' asked the man, smartly dressed in suit and tie. 'I'm George, George Pickford.' He extended his arm and David shook his hand. 'And this is my wife, Patricia. Patricia Thwaites she was then, weren't you darling? We married soon after leaving school.'

'Hello, David. Nice to see you after all this time. You're looking well.'

Patricia, dressed in a long emerald green gown, bent down and pecked him on the cheek. 'Is this your wife?' she asked, looking across to Bridget.

'No, this is Bridget. She was in our year. Bridget Wilkinson.'

Patricia looked down at her with curiosity. 'That's odd, I don't remember that name and I'm known for my memory. Do you recall her, George?'

'No, I don't.' George peered down and examined her face intently. 'Are you sure you were in our year?'

'Well, I think I was,' Bridget replied, the sarcasm missed by the questioners.

'Anyway,' George continued, 'do you mind if we take a couple of chairs and some cutlery? We want to join Samantha's table, rather a lot of catching up to do.'

The move was already commencing as he spoke, George and Patricia edging backwards, each with chair in one hand and plate with cutlery in the other.

‘Go ahead, you won’t find any interesting conversation here,’ Bridget muttered.

She smiled at David. ‘I made a lasting impression, didn’t I? Actually I’m glad we aren’t being bothered, I’m dying to find out more about what happened. Only if you don’t mind telling, of course. In fact, I’m being absurdly nosy, aren’t I?’

‘No, you’re not. I don’t mind at all. I think I was up to when Rachel stormed out. I was all set to tell her off for swearing, but then I thought considering the circumstances it was best not to. Anyway, when she left I carried on cooking, and drinking rather too much wine. After a while Sam came downstairs.’

‘Dad, Adrian’s invited me round. He’s got the new Wii football game, you can be any team you want and pick your own players. Can I go? He said I could stay over.’

‘Well, I suppose so. Have your dinner then I’ll drive you there. No, actually, it’s best I don’t drive. I’ll call a taxi.’

‘No need, he said I can eat there and his dad can pick me up. He’s on his way back from something and has to pass this way.’ As if on cue there was a ring at the doorbell. ‘That’ll be him now. Bye Dad, see you in the morning.’

And Sam was gone. As the front door closed the phone rang and David lifted the receiver.

‘Dad, I’m staying at Hannah’s tonight. Will you call me tomorrow? But only when Mum’s gone. I don’t want to see her.’ There was a pause. ‘Are you OK?’

‘Yes, I am. Thanks.’

‘Good, see you tomorrow then. Must go, bye.’

David served up and sat in uncomfortable silence in the kitchen, picking at the lamb, potatoes, and carrots.

On the fridge there was a photo of the four of them – mother, father, and two children – smiling during their summer holiday in Brittany. It had rained for much of the two weeks, but that day the sun had burst through. They'd rushed down to the beach and the kids had splashed around in the sea. David had enjoyed watching them play, for once without the inhibiting need to be seen as cool that teenagehood usually brought. Jane had sat reading a novel. She looked happy enough those few months earlier, but now he knew that wasn't the case. Why hadn't she tried to talk things through rather than deceive him? A young English couple staying at their hotel had walked by just as David was about to take a photo of the two dripping children, one each side of their mother. All smiles.

'Join the others,' the man had said, so David handed over the camera and there was the result on the fridge. Four beaming faces. The backdrop of the sea and to the left, the edge of a craggy low cliff. A bright blue sky. Others running around on the sand behind them. A multi-coloured ball on its way down into a bikini clad woman's outstretched hands. And a seagull, top corner right. Funny what you can see when you look closely. Until that lonely dinner he had only been aware of the four of them. Smiling.

David poured out the last dregs from the wine bottle and lifted the glass to his lips. Dizzily, he tilted his head back to drink. Now the wine tasted rough and acidic. He stumbled upstairs and still clothed, dropped down onto his double bed for one.

He slept intermittently, dreaming of being in a hurry and having to do something with great urgency. He was unclear what that something was. He knew action was required but he couldn't engage in it. He struggled to get the unknown task accomplished as the ringing and knocking persisted and grew louder. Now awake he sat up unsteadily to the sound of continued banging coming from below. He stood, made his way downstairs, and opened the front door.

It was Jane. 'I've been standing here for more than five minutes ringing the sodding bell. I left the bloody house keys at Jim's.'

'Come in. Fancy a coffee?'

'No, not now thank you. To be truthful I'm nervous about talking to the kids, but I appreciate I have to do it. Are they upstairs?'

'No, they're out.'

'What do you mean "out"?'

'Rachel's at Hannah's and Sam's with Adrian.'

'But you knew I was coming over to speak to them this morning. How could you do this, David?'

'They decided last night and just went. I was …'

'You were what? Spiteful? Vindictive? I suppose you're going to tell me you tried to stop them but they pushed past you.'

'I was. I was a little drunk, I wasn't thinking properly.'

'I can't believe how selfish you are, getting drunk when this is so important. When are they due back?'

'No idea. Actually, Rachel said she didn't want to see you.'

'And I suppose you let her get away with it. Your attitude's appalling.' Jane strode into the kitchen. 'Maybe I will have a coffee.'

As she walked she disturbed the uneven squares of paper scattered across the floor. She stopped abruptly and peered down. 'My letter. How dare you! You tore up my letter!'

'It wasn't me, it …' David began as Jane swivelled round to face him. But then he had second thoughts. Why should he betray Rachel? A rare surge of anger sent his heart racing as he shouted, 'Perhaps if you'd waited yesterday and had a conversation with them there and then, it would have been more sensible than a letter!'

'I'm not going to listen to this.' Jane headed into the hall and opened the front door. She turned, exuding hate from her eyes, in her voice, and via the index finger pointing at him. 'How dare you tell me what I should be doing! You can't imagine what I'm going through, you inconsiderate bastard.'

David had known her for over twenty years. It struck him now for the first time that she had never been able to admit she was the one in the wrong. And it was happening again. According to Jane he was the one who was selfish, inconsiderate, and spiteful, when it was she who was walking out on him.

'And now you're smiling!' she shrieked.

'You have their mobile numbers, I suggest you phone them. Oh, and Jane …'

'What?'

'I hope things don't work out for you.'

He sensed surprise and perhaps even a little fear in her eyes before she turned and slammed the door.

Chapter Four

'You said that. Good for you,' Bridget declared.

'Well, I did feel rather guilty after she'd gone, but at the time it was like a release of tension.'

'I can understand that.'

The woman dressed in adult schoolwear was making another announcement. She had climbed onto one of the table tops and was swaying perilously, stiletto heels and alcohol not helping her to maintain balance. 'It's time for the music! A back to the 80s disco in the bar. Non-stop hits so let's rock, rock, rock.' She started to dance on the table and sent the vase with its solitary rose crashing to the floor. 'Roger, where's Roger? Help me down, will you, it's not safe up here.'

Bridget stood. 'I suppose we'd better mingle a bit. Shall we dance?' She took hold of David's hand and pulled him towards the music. 'Ghostbusters' was blaring out and those already dancing were lifting their arms into the air and chanting 'Ghostbusters' at approximately appropriate times.

'Not this one, Bridget, I can't stand it,' David pleaded.

'OK, let's see what's next.'

'This is better,' David said as Madonna's 'Like a Virgin' began. They moved to the centre of the room and leapt about in similar fashion to the other partygoers. The dance floor got crowded and every so often there was a 'Sorry. Oh, hello, David' as they bumped into another couple. Eurythmics and Thompson Twins hits followed Madonna.

'Now let's slow it down for all you lovers out there,' the DJ announced. 'It's from 1984, it's Cars performing

"Drive".' There were sighs and screams of 'I love this!' as the first sad chords were struck. Bridget put her arms round David's neck and he responded by placing his hands on her waist, lightheaded with the warmth of her body against his. He wanted the closeness to linger but she pulled away at the end of the song.

'Let's get a drink,' she suggested.

Together they walked to the bar. David ordered another Bud and a glass of house white which he handed to Bridget as Bill Thatcher approached them.

'Well, if it isn't me old mate David again. And who's this? A neat-looking bird for someone like you to be hanging around with.'

'I'd rather not be defined as a bird, most people stopped using that term about twenty years ago. My name's Bridget and will you get out of the way so we can get past?'

'You what?'

'Just piss off out the way, will you, or else I might accidentally spill my wine all over your ugly face.'

'You what?' he repeated, standing his ground.

'Or does your repertoire extend to hitting females?'

Bill had a puzzled look on his face, unsure how to react.

'You look confused, Bill. Oh, it must be because "repertoire" is rather a difficult word for you to understand. It comes from the Latin, *repertorium*, but of course you were far too thick to be in the Latin class at school. Well let me put it another way. Either hit me now or fuck off out of it.'

With that, she turned and walked past Bill with David following her.

'Bloody hell, Bridget. There I was thinking you were an exceptionally delicate and polite woman, but then you manage to intimidate the school bully. Rather high-risk, but well done.'

‘I’ve had years of practice.’

‘What do you mean?’

‘It’s a long story.’

‘As you said a while back, it’s a long evening.’

‘Not now, maybe another time. But I’d love to hear more about what happened to you. Let’s go somewhere quieter.’ Led by Bridget they left the bar and reached the reception area. ‘We can sit down over there,’ she suggested, pointing towards two vast red leather armchairs. They sank into them and placed their drinks on a smoked glass coffee table littered with back copies of *Country Life*.

Bridget continued. ‘You still haven’t answered my original question. How come you ended up here tonight?’

David glanced back towards the room they had come from, expecting Bill, Ben, and a lynching party of their associates to arrive at any moment. But the other guests remained at the bar or on the dance floor. A Culture Club song was playing, he couldn’t remember the title. ‘Good idea sitting here,’ he joked, looking across to the muscular night porter with shaved head and beefy arms covered in tattoos. ‘He’ll protect us when Bill arrives.’

Bridget smiled, one of those smiles that encourage you to smile back. ‘You were up to when you told Jane you hoped she ended up unhappy, or something like that.’

David paused. He took a gulp of beer to give himself time to consider what next to tell Bridget. She seemed genuinely interested, even concerned, with his plight. But he had only just met her, well since childhood anyway. How much should he be relating about personal matters that were still painful to think about?

‘It was not a happy time, for me or the children. Sam was convinced everything would end up fine and Rachel was threatening to murder her mother. It was a mess and to a large extent, still is. If you don’t mind I’ll leave it at that for now. Suffice to say it was clear that Jane wasn’t going to change her mind. She'd already packed suitcases to take to Jim's and she'd even lifted some of what she wanted from the house, including a painting we'd bought soon after we married which I'm very fond of. I was annoyed that she thought she could take whatever she felt like without even asking.'

Bill, Ben, and five other men came into the reception area. David tensed up but the group walked past without making eye contact, cigarettes at the ready to be lit as soon as they stepped outside.

'And Jane still hadn't sat down with the kids to explain what was going on. She should have tried harder. Even though Rachel rejected her approaches, she should have persevered.'

Bridget nodded. Her sympathetic face was as beautiful as her smiling one. David had succumbed to teenage-esque passion together with the angst that invariably goes with it. He was an adolescent again, the twenty-five years since being at school washed away by this chance meeting.

'I'll tell you what's odd though,' he continued. 'I was unhappy, I still am. But just a few weeks on I'm not nearly as unhappy as I thought I would or even should be. It's made me realise the relationship between Jane and me had become distant; her walking out brought the reality home. My anger's pretty well gone because I recognise that at least in part I'm responsible for what happened.'

Bridget interrupted. 'Wait a minute. It's good of you to think that, but you weren't the one who ran off with someone else without any discussion.'

'No, true enough. Thanks for saying so, Bridget. And I must admit the shock was huge. Luckily, friends and work colleagues rallied round. I was invited to the cinema, bowling, clubbing, dinner parties. Some of them suggested strategies for getting a new partner, but that was the last thing on my mind. In fact I haven't taken up any offers because I feel the pressure of being responsible for looking after the kids.'

'So how come you came to this reunion?' Bridget persevered.

David wanted to impress her with light and witty patter. Instead it was like being in a counselling session. 'Another drink first?' he asked.

'No, I'm fine, thanks. Carry on.'

With reluctance he did so. 'Well, one evening I was watching some TV drama and there was a young girl who looked the spitting image of Marianne Dunnell. Do you remember her?'

'I certainly do.'

'We used to call her Marianne Faithfull. She looked just like the singer – all the boys thought she was an absolute stunner.'

'Us girls called her Marianne Unfaithful. She hopped from boyfriend to boyfriend every day and her girlfriends didn't last much longer.'

'Oh, I didn't know that. Anyway, I had a sudden impulse to contact her even though she'd had little to do with me at school. My Rachel uses Facebook, for far too long I tell her, but I wondered whether it could help me get in touch with Marianne. The next evening Rachel showed me how it all worked. I set up a profile and went on the search for friends. When I typed in the name, up came one Marianne Dunnell. She listed Dunnell as her maiden name as well as Peters as her married one. She was located in Oxford, Boars Hill to be exact. I was pretty sure it had to be her, bearing in mind the unusual surname and where she lives. I sent a message asking her to be my friend and the next day I had a reply. Do you use Facebook?'

'No, my kids do but I can't be bothered with it. My two say they've got about three thousand friends. Or is it three million? But they only recognise about five of them.'

Bill, Ben, and their entourage came back into reception, laughing loudly. 'You fuckin' didn't?' one of them enquired. 'I fuckin' did' another responded. 'Fuckin' hell' a third piped in, their voices so alike it was hard to tell who was doing the talking. This time they did notice Bridget and David. Bill, who was at the front of the group, stopped and looked down at Bridget. The other men formed a row behind him, facing her.

'Bitch,' he declared and the others thought this was highly amusing.

'Yeah, bitch' another of the faceless nobodies muttered as he followed Bill back into the bar.

'They are …' David began.

'Never mind them, they aren't worth thinking about. What happened with Marianne?'

'Initially very little. She wrote a brief hello, not much more than a 'yes, I do remember you'. I wasn't going to let her get away with that so I wrote back, rather a long message that I soon discovered was being read by all her friends and their friends. Apparently she was teased about this long-lost admirer of hers. It was highly embarrassing as I'd written how much everyone at school had fancied her and asked if she wanted to meet up for old times' sake.'

'How did she reply?'

'She started off with advice about how to send a personal message on Facebook. Then she gave an update. To cut a long story short, she got married to a man training to be a cleric soon after leaving school. Now she has five teenage children, two dogs, and a hamster, and works as a librarian in the law department at the university.'

'Marianne a librarian! Hard to believe. In fact, being married to a vicar and with loads of kids presumably from the same father is also a revelation.'

'Well, in our short flurry of messaging she mentioned the reunion and gave me the email address of the organiser, that woman who likes standing on tables. Marianne intended to come along herself but emailed me with only a couple of days to go. Her husband had organised a surprise weekend away to celebrate their wedding anniversary and she had to cancel. I'd signed up for the reunion and booked the hotel by then so I thought why not.'

Bridget glanced at her watch then across to the night porter who was leaning over the reception counter reading a newspaper. He yawned, she yawned too. The 1980s hits were still blasting out.

'Well, I'm glad you made it, David. But I'm afraid I'm done for the night, if you don't mind.'

'No, I've had enough too. Well, I don't mean enough of you, just that if you're heading off then I don't feel like mixing with anyone else.'

They stood and took the wide staircase, with its plush red carpet and ivory and gold striped wallpaper, up to the fire door on the first floor landing.

'I'm this way,' Bridget announced.

'Me too.'

They walked along the corridor glancing at the prints of hunting scenes until Bridget stopped at Room 134. 'This is mine.'

'I'm next door. 136.'

'Coincidence. Hey, it's been nice chatting, David, I've enjoyed this evening loads. Maybe see you at breakfast.'

David didn't reply. He was too busy thinking of something to say to prolong their time together, the closeness of their bedrooms a nagging contributory factor. Possibilities crossed his mind.

Fancy a coffee before bed?
Would you like to see if the décor in my bedroom is the same as yours?
Shall we share a bed tonight?

She took hold of his shoulder and planted a kiss on his

cheek. 'Goodnight,' she said, key in hand, and he was left thinking of the elusive one-liner after she had closed her door and left him standing alone in the corridor.

Chapter Five

The days after that dreadful Saturday when Jane walked out, the days he hadn't wanted to tell Bridget about, had been hell. The Sunday morning meeting with Jane had hardly been a good start. He fluctuated between guilt and a questioning of sanity that he should even be considering an apology. Three times he lifted the phone then replaced it before guilt won at 12.07 p.m. and he called her.

Jim answered her mobile. 'What do you want, David?' he snapped.

'To speak with Jane, if you don't mind.'

'I'm not letting you.'

'I want to speak to my wife.'

'Not after what you said. She wants nothing to do with you.' Before David could respond, Jim launched into a severe tirade covering decency, loyalty, compassion, morality, and quite possibly much more, but David hung up before the end of the monologue.

He walked round to the newsagent to buy the *Sunday Times*. Everything on the short journey was the same as ever – Isobel pushing the pram in a vain attempt to stop her baby crying, Lawrence washing his BMW, Mrs Grant nurturing her flowers and plants with care beyond the call of duty. It was only his life that was different.

'Hello, Mr Willoughby, and how are you today?' asked Stanley Entwhistle, the newsagent and postmaster who had been around since David had first moved to the area. He had a wild mop of white hair with matching strands leaping up from his eyebrows and out his ears. Stanley had seen David's children progress from infancy to adolescence and now he would be seeing his marriage go from ceremony to cessation.

'Fine, thanks.'

David dropped the newspaper onto the counter and took out his wallet.

'What about your *Mail on Sunday*?'

'Not today, thanks.'

Back at home David half-heartedly read the newspaper, vaguely acknowledging that economic freefall, terrorist threats, and post-accident motorway mayhem perhaps were more significant than his own crisis. He skipped lunch.

He was in the hall en route from kitchen to downstairs toilet when the first of his children returned. Rachel opened the front door, cigarette in hand.

'Put that thing out,' David ordered.

'OK,' she said, throwing the stub behind her onto the small tidy front lawn, 'but I smoke. I won't inside the house, but that's all I'm agreeing to.'

Still somewhat hung-over, David didn't have the energy to argue.

'And have I missed my fucking bitch of a mother?' Rachel continued.

The previous day's anger might be acceptable, but David was not prepared to tolerate habitual use of that word from his sixteen-year-old daughter. 'There is no need to swear, thank you very much.'

'Fucking bitch, fucking bitch, fucking bitch,' Rachel chanted as she brushed past him and headed up to her room. A minute later Rihanna was belting out of her music system.

David stood in the hall trying to remember why he'd left the kitchen in the first place.

The phone rang. It was Sam. 'Dad, could you pick me up? Now, please. Adrian and I have had a bit of a bust-up. He's blaming me for running his car into a skirting board, but he didn't tell me it had a turbo accelerator. Anyway it's only the bumper that's broken and his dad says a bit of glue will sort it.'

David agreed to set off immediately. He called up to Rachel to let her know he was popping out. He left without keys; rang the doorbell to get back in to collect them; rang it again when a Rihanna track ended and Rachel had a chance of hearing; picked them up; went out and unlocked the car; recalled that the original reason for leaving the kitchen was to go to the toilet; went back inside to do so; and finally departed. 'I can't think clearly anymore,' he uttered as he started the engine.

He drove through the comfortable streets of suburban Mill Hill with a surge of feeling sorry for himself, jealous that for those in the immaculately ordered houses he was passing, life would no doubt be as secure as the day before. Well maybe not, he reconsidered, his mind now racing with what ifs. Perhaps the loss of a job or a death in the family. Or conceivably like him, a wife leaving, leaving to live with a so-called best friend. A wave of self-disgust added to his concoction of emotions when for a split second he hoped others were facing similar grief.

He turned into the gravelled drive of Adrian's impressive Totteridge house, an ornate structure with classical pillars at the front door. Armless marble Romanesque statues stood on each side, a naked man and woman facing each other. The doorbell chimed 'La Marseillaise' – Adrian's mother was French. David knew the father dealt in property sales in Europe and rumour had it he was struggling to cope with the severe economic recession on top of changed Spanish laws about foreign ownership. Clearly he wasn't struggling sufficiently to have to vacate this palace or trade in the Porsche and Daimler on the drive.

Mrs Grainger came to the door. 'I am so sorry to hear your news.' She took hold of him. 'You poor, poor, poor thing,' each 'poor' accompanied by a consoling pat on the back. He hardly knew the woman but if there was anything she could do to help, all he had to do was ask.

She stepped back and looked him in the eye. 'I know exactly how you feel,' she uttered with compassion. David sensed that Mr Grainger had been guilty of transgressions.

Sam was a few paces behind her, mouthing, 'Can we go, Dad?'

Just as David felt he had an opportunity to exit with Mrs Grainger in silent mode, Mr Grainger came racing downstairs. The conversation was pretty well repeated though with three differences – no hugging, Mr Grainger far cheerier than his wife, and the 'I know exactly how you feel' statement omitted.

'I want to leave,' Sam uttered when there was a pause in the conversation.

Declining Mrs Grainger's offer of a cup of tea or coffee and Mr Grainger's additional option of something a little stiffer, David and his son edged out of the door with a promise that if help was needed they would ask.

Back at home, Sunday stretched on endlessly for all three of them. Rachel listened to music while plodding through French and Science revision for school tests on Monday. Sam played Wii golf in between racing through Maths and History homework that he found insultingly easy. David resumed reading the newspaper without taking anything in. He shuddered at the thought of Jane and Jim in bed together with reading the last thing on their minds.

Intermittently throughout the day he heard the children's phones ringing, Rachel letting her Lady Gaga tune go without answering and Sam engaging in whispered dialogue after a brief *Star Wars* burst.

'Was it Mum you were speaking to?' David asked Sam as they were eating the leftover lamb that evening.

'Yes,' Sam admitted.

'Well you're an idiot then,' Rachel attacked.

Sam didn't rise to the bait and didn't indicate what had

been said.

Monday, the first day back at work and school for the decimated family, brought new problems. As usual David needed to leave home ahead of Rachel and Sam, but now there was no Jane to get the children on their way. She'd always been on hand for last-minute panics associated with making packed lunches, signing school letters, and searching for PE kit. Rachel assured him that she could take care of things and he was prepared to trust his daughter, a trust only countered by the packet of Marlboro Lights resting inside her school bag.

Without enthusiasm David drove into the underground car park of the concrete 1960s block that accommodated the complex web of local authority services. He was an accountant in the social welfare department, responsible for allocating funding to family members who had power of attorney over older relatives residing in care homes. It didn't take Jane's words for him to acknowledge that he was a boring old fart as a result of doing this work for far too long. Over the last three years or so he'd applied for more interesting and higher-paid positions. He'd answered internal adverts in Hospital Capital Projects; Policing in the Community; Roads, Highways and Transportation; and top of his list, Parks, Open Spaces and Countryside. In each case he'd been short-listed and interviewed and had then received a near identical rejection letter.

It was frustrating and recently he had considered giving up on the local authority and trying to move into the private sector. But the seemingly endless recession made such a step difficult, plus the fact that the longer he stayed where he was, the less sense it made to leave as his final salary pension benefit accumulated. He did have a remote dream – to open an arts café – but the likelihood of that was more improbable than Jane returning.

He was in a rut, tied to the local authority with the evident futility of trying for internal promotion. By nature he was conscientious and keen to succeed, but it was becoming impossible to please the public who blamed him personally for the diminishing government funding available to support the aged.

David took the concrete staircase to the ground floor and entered the café. Ownership had transferred recently from the local authority to a franchised chain, but this had brought no improvement in quality. He purchased a so-called cappuccino and took his first sip of the powdery synthetic liquid in the polystyrene container as he made his way to the lift.

He nodded greetings to fellow employees as they travelled in silence to the fourth floor. He got out, chucked the near full beaker of coffee into a bin, and made his way to his office. Perhaps his frustration with work had impacted on his relationship with Jane; maybe it was his fault that she had left him.

He'd hoped for an easy day that first Monday, but he didn't get it. One of the junior staff had made promises to support more care home places than there was funding for. It was David who was left to deal with irate callers who had been offered assistance during a telephone conversation only to see it rejected by letter. And it was David who was confronted by the head of service accusing him of reckless decision making. When he explained that it wasn't his mistake, the allegation shifted to poor line management of his team.

A little over six months ago he'd applied for the post of head of service and after that debacle he decided he was done with seeking promotion. He lost out to an external candidate with no experience in this field. The staff newsletter issued the month after her appointment had profiled Mary Dyer as the 'high-flyer' with a first class honours degree in Accounting and Finance from the London School of Economics. She had been 'snapped up' by Price Waterhouse Coopers, working first as an auditor and then in the management consultancy division. Now, tired of the commercial sector, she wanted 'to give something back to the community'. What the article failed to mention was that she thought the local authority was rife with inefficiency and full of lazy staff, and her new mission in life was to shake things up.

'I'm at meetings most of the day, David,' Mary said during the brief telephone conversation soon after he reached the office. 'I should be back by four o'clock. We can sort out your over-generous promises then.'

'I've already told you, Mary. They were not my promises.'

'Well in that case we'll sort out how you can better control your reckless staff.'

Four o'clock turned out to be gone five. She came in with a pile of large folders of case notes and dumped them on his desk, then sat down in the chair facing him.

Office gossip centred on what Mary wore. She was suspected of possessing vast wardrobes housing an eclectic collection of clothes. Female colleagues claimed she never wore the same outfit twice. Some of the men, though not David amongst them, devised titles and sent out emails to inform others of their choices. Today she was 'Eastern European Peasant' with flowing skirt and brightly coloured layers of T-shirt, blouse, cardigan, and jacket.

As per usual his attempt to be friendly was instantly quashed as she attacked him for wasting her valuable time. She then proceeded to waste *his* time by plodding through each case at pedestrian pace.

'Mrs Thornton next. I can't find the date when she was moved out the hospital ward and into the convalescence unit. Do you have that information?'

'No, it wasn't my case.'

'And who advised that she should go into residential care rather than back home?'

'I don't know. I've already told you, it wasn't my case.'

'Did we get involved in the discussion?'

'I'm not sure.'

'Have we had access to her financial records?'

'I expect so.'

And so it went on, until 6.00 when David apologised for terminating the meeting as he had to pick up Rachel. Mary gave him a look rather like the one men have been giving working mothers for many years when they're faced with the need to juggle work and family. With reluctance she agreed to delay further castigation until the next morning. She picked up her pile of folders and left.

A disgruntled David shut down his computer. When he came out his office Jabulani was waiting for him in the corridor.

'What's going on? She's been on the warpath all day.'

'Mary thinks we're wasting money because we're supporting old people on low incomes.'

Jabulani had been working at the local authority for only a few months, but had already developed a sound grasp of the office politics. 'We know she's after a departmental deficit of zero and at last she's found a way of achieving it. No income and no expenditure.'

David appreciated his sense of humour and would have moaned about his meeting with Mary if he'd had the time. 'More tomorrow, Jabulani. I've got to dash to collect Rachel.'

He rushed down to the car park then made his way to Rachel's school. Turning on the radio, he was confronted by worsening financial difficulties in the European Union; renewed civil war in an African state; declining UK league table position for literacy and numeracy; and flood warnings across West Yorkshire. He switched off.

Rachel had a good voice and loved drama. She'd been selected to perform in the annual play since her first year at secondary school. This year's choice, *Fiddler on the Roof*, was ideal as it gave her the opportunity to both sing and act. Rehearsals were on Mondays after school and as usual on that Monday, David picked her up on the way back from work. Owing to his meeting and the roads being even more congested than usual, he was late. By the time he arrived dusk was descending and Rachel was sitting alone on a low brick wall in front of the school gates. When she saw him approach she dropped her cigarette, stamped on it, and walked towards the car.

David decided not to complain. He hoped smoking might be no more than an angry reaction to her mother's decision and would soon cease.

He chose to be light and cheery. 'Hello, Rachel, sorry I'm a bit late. Had a good day?'

'No. I'm fed up with the musical.'

'Rehearsals don't always go well. That's why you have them, to iron things out.'

'Yeah, but I'm only in the chorus and I'm better than some of the so-called stars who are acting like prima donnas.'

'Well maybe …'

'Maybe nothing.'

They sat in silence, progressing slowly through the rush hour traffic.

Suddenly Rachel broke into song.

'*If I were a fucking bitch,*
Yubby dibby dibby dibby dibby dibby dibby dum,
All day long I'd biddy biddy bum,
If I were a fucking bitch.'

'Stop that! Now!' David ordered and Rachel reverted to humming the *Fiddler on the Roof* melody until they reached home. On arrival she got out the car without speaking, opened the front door, walked past Sam, and marched upstairs.

'What's up with her?' Sam asked.

'Just upset about Mum,' David replied. 'How was school?'

‘Fine. Me and Adrian have made up. Dad, you know that car I told you about on Saturday, I’d really like it. Have you had time to decide? I promise if I get it I won’t ask for anything else for Christmas.’

‘There’s over three months to go before Christmas.’

‘I know. What about lending me the money and giving me money as my Christmas present and I can pay it straight back?’

‘Let me think it over, Sam. I’m going to make dinner now. Have you got homework to do?’

‘Yeah, some. What are we eating?’

‘Pasta. Is that OK?’

‘I suppose so. Your cooking isn’t bad, it’s just that Mum’s is much better.’

‘You keep telling me that! I’m doing my best.’

‘Sorry.’ And with that Sam turned and headed upstairs.

David was left to make spaghetti Bolognese, with little chance of it being a popular choice since Rachel wasn’t keen on cooked tomatoes and Sam had already given his verdict.

An hour later as they sat in silence eating, David wondered how he could cope. There was so much that needed doing – fitting in shopping for food around work, extending the range of what he could cook, helping the two of them with homework, being a chauffeur, handling discipline – generally everything associated with a single parent bringing up two teenage children.

Chapter Six

Alone in his bedroom at the Hotel Marlborough, having said goodnight to Bridget, David was unable to completely dismiss these memories of the traumatic days after Jane had left.

However, he now had something competing for his attention. He undressed then lay in bed thinking rather obsessively about the slow dance with Bridget. Having relieved his erection he planned how to manipulate a further meeting with her. Infatuation had kicked in big time after one short meeting. Lust, love, friendship, acquaintance, any of these would do, but lust was top of his wish list. Unable to sleep he wondered whether he had ever had such an intense feeling for Jane, even during their early years together. Maybe Jane knew something was missing all along and had found it at last with Jim.

One thing was clear – he had to see Bridget again. In devising a strategy to engineer this he mulled over the fact that she had acquired all sorts of information about him, but he knew very little about her beyond name. Why had she come to the reunion? She'd mentioned having children, but how many and how old were they? Since she had children, did that mean she was married? He'd noted the absence of a wedding ring. Where did she live? And work? It was highly likely she had a husband she was devoted to, as he was to her. With five adorable children, they lived blissfully in a dreamy thatched cottage which Bridget took great delight in returning to at the end of the day, having toiled selflessly in a job she was passionate about. Probably a charity supporting the nation's or the world's most needy.

The thought that he might never see Bridget again filled him with despair. Angst waned then resurfaced with renewed intensity as he lay restless in bed. There was no point even trying to sleep. He put on the bedside light and made himself a cup of tea which he drank with one of the complimentary custard creams.

For a foolhardy instant he contemplated knocking on Bridget's bedroom door there and then. But then what? 'I'm making tea, care to join me?' 'I was making tea but there aren't any milk cartons. Do you have one I could borrow?' 'I know we've only just met, well as adults, but I've fallen helplessly in love and want to spend the night with you.'

No, not a sensible idea barging in at 2.49 a.m. however good an excuse he could think up. Instead he'd make sure he was up early the next morning in case she was one of the first to have breakfast. He'd hover outside the dining room until she appeared then pretend it was a coincidence they had arrived together. With the plan established he returned to bed and set his mobile for a 7.30 a.m. alarm call. Still, he couldn't relax. Besotted with thoughts of Bridget, he rehearsed the conversation.

'What a coincidence being down at the same time for breakfast.'

'Shall we sit together?'

'If you give me your phone number I'll call and we can reminisce about this awful reunion.'

'Let's not wait another twenty-five years before we meet up again.'

'Do you by any chance live in a thatched cottage?'

All sensible thought was blurred by exhaustion.

He tossed and turned throughout the rest of the night, sleeping intermittently until the alarm sounded. He stretched across to the bedside cabinet and switched it off. The dream that followed was of he and Bridget lying on a sun soaked tropical beach, engaged in conversation that was generating much laughter. Then a dark cloud rolled in from the sea and deafening cracks of thunder disturbed their peace. Bang! Bang! Bang! Then again. Bang! Bang! Bang! But it wasn't a dream – someone was knocking at the door.

'Coming!' he shouted as he glanced at his phone. He'd gone back to sleep and it was now 9.30. He rushed to the door and flung it open.

'Hello, Bridget.'

She looked startled. 'David, perhaps … erm'

'Yes?'

'Perhaps you should put on trousers or something.'

David had taken off his pyjama bottoms in the night. 'My God,' he exclaimed, looking down to double-check Bridget's observation. 'Just a minute,' he stammered before slamming the door shut. He immediately re-opened it a fraction and edged his head around the small gap. 'Sorry, didn't mean to slam it in your face, I'll leave it ajar.' He gently pushed the door to, then raced to the side of the bed and pulled on his jeans.

'Just another minute,' he called out as he darted into the bathroom to clean his teeth on the off-chance that Bridget would be prepared to kiss a lunatic answering the door naked from waist down. He had never been so embarrassed in his life, although getting drunk at the Christmas lunch the first time he met Jane's parents was a close call. On reflection, even worse was fainting in the delivery room when Jane was giving birth to Rachel.

He opened the door. 'I'm ever so sorry, Bridget.'

She seemed unperturbed. 'That's OK, at least you were partly dressed. I usually don't wear anything when I sleep.'

This created a stirring between David's legs and he was grateful he now had something on to disguise the movement.

'Did you sleep well?' she enquired.

‘What made you ask?’

Bridget frowned. ‘Well, I was being polite, I suppose. I slept like a log.’

‘Me too.’

‘Anyway, I wanted to say goodbye and thank you for a fun evening,’ she continued. ‘Without you it would have been an absolute nightmare.’

Bridget’s comment left room for interpretation. What she said didn’t necessarily imply she had enjoyed their time together, merely that it prevented the nightmare. ‘I had a wonderful time,’ he countered.

‘Your chin’s come up with a massive bruise, Bill must have hit you pretty hard. Does it hurt?’

‘It was great to see you after all these years.’

‘Poor you, what a terrible few weeks you’ve had.’

‘I loved the dancing.’

‘I still can’t believe what you told me about Marianne Dunnell.’

‘Bridget!’

‘Yes?’

‘Are you married?’

‘What?’

‘Are you married?’

‘No, why?’

‘I just wondered. You have children, don’t you?’

‘Yes, two. Kay’s twelve and Andy’s sixteen.’

‘Where do you live?’

‘Lots of questions, David.’

‘Well, I was thinking in the night that I didn’t ask anything about you, we only talked about me.’

‘That’s not your fault. If you remember I was keen to hear about you, there was no time to discover anything about my boring existence.’

‘Maybe we can meet again, then I can be the judge?’

‘Yes, I’d like to. Got a pen and paper?’

David walked across to the table and took a sheet of the

hotel's headed paper. He tore it in half, wrote down his name and number, and handed it to Bridget with the pen and other half. He watched as she jotted down her number and email address. Large swirls adorned her writing; she added a smiley face.

'I left my name off, I'm assuming you'll remember who I am,' she said as she handed it over. 'Well, I'd best be going home.'

'Where is home?'

'London. I live in Muswell Hill.'

'I'm London, too. Mill Hill.'

'Almost neighbours. OK, well, you take care, David, and I look forward to hearing from you.' She kissed him on each cheek French style then took a step back, lifted her hand for a small wave, picked up the lime green canvas bag on the floor beside her, then headed off down the corridor. David watched, hoping she would turn round for a final acknowledgment, but she didn't.

It was gone 9.45, barely time to get downstairs before breakfast ended. The dining room was near deserted, the one reunion member remaining was the loud-mouthed woman who had made the announcements the night before. Her school uniform had been replaced by the much more appropriate jeans and blouse. She gave him a watery smile of acknowledgement as he entered so he had little choice but to join her.

'One of the few,' she commented as he sat down.

'What do you mean?'

'I think most people gave up on breakfast, too hungover. I'm in the hungover category too, but since I woke up ridiculously early I thought I might as well come down. How come you made it?'

'I probably didn't drink as much as most.'

'You were with Bridget, weren't you? She still upstairs?'

'No, she's headed off home.'

‘Us over-aged teenagers. You getting off with Bridget, me with Roger. I wouldn’t have gone anywhere near him when I was at school and now I get so pissed I end up in bed with him. It was his snoring that woke me up. Panic and guilt too, my husband would kill me if he found out. Hopefully Roger’ll be gone by the time I get back upstairs.’ She cut a piece of bacon, lifted it to her mouth, and rather ungraciously chewed. ‘You or Bridget married?’ she asked, her mouth still full.

‘I am, though separated. I don’t know much about Bridget. But before any rumours start to fly, we didn’t spend the night together.’

The woman took a slurp of coffee. ‘Why not?’

‘That’s a daft question. Why should we, we were chatting?’

‘Oh,’ she replied, looking at David in puzzlement. ‘You seemed to be getting on well enough.’

‘But that doesn’t mean we end up sleeping together,’ David retorted, with a degree of admiration for this woman’s black and white decision making process. No principles, just doing what you fancy at that moment. And of course he would have loved to have spent the night with Bridget. ‘There is such a thing as morality,’ he stated with false conviction.

‘Sor-ree,’ she replied.

‘No, I’m sorry, I didn’t mean to lecture. And I’m afraid I don’t even know your name.’

‘Penny Tratton. I know you’re David because I handled the bookings, but we were in different classes in school. I don’t think our paths crossed much.’

‘Penny Tratton? No, I can’t say I remember your name.’

‘The boys changed it, of course. Penny Tration they called me.’

‘Penny Tration. Why?’

‘Penny Tration, penetration. I lived up to the nickname

a bit, I'm afraid. And I did it again last night so that's going to do my reputation a power of good.'

She burst into tears. David stood, walked to the other side of the table, and put an arm around her shoulders. 'Come on, don't be upset. You can walk away from today and forget all about it. And you did organise a great reunion.'

'Thank you, you're very kind,' she said, the tears disappearing as quickly as they had arrived. 'I'm going to wake Roger up and tell him to get to his own room if he's still there, then I'll pack and head off to my lovely family.' She stood, sobbing again as she dramatically strode out the room.

David stood too, and walked to the buffet table. A disinterested waitress was clearing away the plates.

'Sorry sir, it's gone ten, we're closed for breakfast.'

'Can I at least have a coffee?'

''Fraid not, but there is a Starbucks round the corner.'

Chapter Seven

David decided against a Starbucks coffee and set off from the reunion immediately after his Sunday morning conversation with Penny Tratton. He was tired and irritable and had no enthusiasm about returning home. The very word 'home' had a cosy ring to it but any link with cosiness was shattered.

The Tuesday after Jane left had been even worse than the Monday. Rachel had come downstairs for breakfast with a new song to insult her mother, this one based on the Queen hit 'We Are the Champions'.

She is a fucking bitch
She is a fucking bitch
No time for losers
'Cause she is the biggest bitch – in the world

It was a song David had always liked and he had to admit Rachel sang the updated version perfectly; she had a lovely voice. Half-heartedly he acted out the enraged parent, but for the rest of the day he couldn't get the tune or words out of his head.

He was humming it as he entered the car park underneath the local authority offices. It had been constructed for tiny vehicles, the concrete columns demanding preposterously tight turns. David failed to negotiate carefully enough and the front passenger side of his car donated a Tornado Red streak to the multi-coloured assortment of scraped paints on the pillar. The parking bays were so small it was difficult to open a door without knocking against a neighbour's car. His door no more than tapped against a Honda Civic, but it was enough to set off the alarm. He made a run for it.

He paused at the mid-point between stairwell and lifts, weighing up the pros and cons of purchasing a coffee at the dismal café. He took the lift, having resolved never to go there again.

Work began with a continuation of the meeting with Mary Dyer to discuss overspend on residential care home support. Today the office gossips had described her attire as 'Ms Footsie 100 CEO'. She was wearing a tailored navy pinstripe suit with a crisp white blouse buttoned to the neck and shiny patent shoes with large black bows.

There was no welcoming smile, not even a greeting, as he entered her office. He was on time but she made a point of looking at her watch before gesturing for him to sit down opposite her.

'I'm pushed for time this morning, David, but we need to get this done. We're already £350,000 over budget and that's with half the financial year to go. Before we start I want to make it clear that you're the one who should be sorting it, it's within your remit.'

David was prepared. At home the previous evening he had constructed water-tight counter arguments. 'A couple of points before you continue, Mary. Did you know that –'

'Don't interrupt, David. Let me finish.' She paused and made steely eye contact before continuing. 'Some questions. Are you double-checking how many assets these old people have before we start dishing out money? Do we ask if their children can contribute? And are we pushing them to consider having their parents move in with them?'

'Yes to all those things. Applicants have to complete Form F43-H27/B and attach evidence and then …' He looked up. Mary was sifting through files and it was evident she wasn't listening. She didn't even notice that he'd stopped speaking mid-sentence.

'I've been doing some checking and I can tell you, this division is out of control.' She pulled out an invoice.

‘Even the stationery budget is way over. You spent £286 on Post-its last month. Why on earth would you want £286-worth of Post-its?’

‘That was a mistake. Dorothy was asked to get 400 but she mistook the instruction and ordered 400 packs and there are ten sets of Post-its in each pack.’

‘So now you’ve got 4,000 little booklets. How many pieces of paper in each, a hundred? That’s 400,000 Post-its.’

‘I don’t think there are a hundred in each booklet, I could get Dorothy to count.’

‘Hardly the point, David. David? Are you listening?’

‘No time for losers, ’cause she is the biggest bitch – in the world’ he was thinking, dividing his anger between Jane and Mary.

‘Well, that’s an aside, I think we should get back to the main issue, don’t you?’ Mary continued, her tone implying it was he who had raised the Post-its controversy.

There was a timid knock on the door. It was Dorothy. ‘There’s a phone call for you, David.’

‘Not now, Dorothy. I’ll call whoever it is after this meeting.’

‘I think you should take this one.’ Dorothy was frowning and nodding intently.

‘Excuse me, Mary, I’ll be back very soon.’

David returned a couple of minutes later. ‘Mary, I’m ever so sorry, I’m going to have to pop out. Something’s cropped up with one of my children at school. I’m sure it won’t take long, can we meet this afternoon?’

Mary looked at him in disbelief. ‘I appreciate family concerns can be important, but you can’t constantly put them ahead of work matters.’

‘She is a fucking bitch ... ’ he hummed inside his head. What a cheek, twice hardly constituted constantly. Over his many years of service at the local authority he had rarely missed a day’s work. ‘Yes, you’re quite right and I

do apologise,' he said as he edged out of the door.

When he arrived at Rachel's school the receptionist escorted him to the Head's office. It had a relaxed and welcoming feel to it with the walls jam packed with children's art work. Oriental and African artefacts were strewn across two coffee tables, one in the middle of the room, and one by a window overlooking a neat quadrangle with sturdy wooden benches and tables. A white dish on the nearest table caught David's eye. Across its centre was a brightly coloured dragon, the tail extending beyond the edge of the plate and running on underneath. David recognised these items from the termly school newsletters which had photos of teachers being presented with gifts by foreign dignitaries during the annual exchange visits to an English speaking college in China and a school in rural Madagascar.

David rather liked the Head. John Edwards was a tall, lean man with a sweep of sandy brown hair across his brow. He wore horn-rimmed spectacles that made him look full of wisdom. He was tapping his fingers on a large desk covered with papers. As David walked towards him, Mr Edwards sprang up and strode across the room to greet his visitor with a firm handshake.

'Do sit down,' he said, directing David to a drab beige armchair that had seen better days. Mr Edwards sat next to him on a matching seat. On the coffee table between them were three delicate enamelled boxes adorned with colourful paintings of pagodas and trees with twisted branches.

David looked up and Mr Edwards began. 'We have a problem with Rachel. She was caught smoking this morning when she should have been in class and that's the second time within a few days. When Miss Franks told her off she called her a f… ing bitch. It's unacceptable and I see no option but to suspend her.'

'I agree that sort of behaviour is disgraceful, Mr

Edwards, but there are extenuating circumstances. You see, my wife walked out on us last Saturday and Rachel has reacted with considerable anger. That's no excuse for her smoking or her rudeness, but I'm sure you accept it at least to some extent explains things.'

'I'm sorry to hear your news, Mr Willoughby, and yes, of course something like that is going to affect behaviour.' He looked down at a sheet of paper with handwritten notes. 'However, the first smoking incident took place before last weekend and my staff have been complaining about her insolence for quite a while. Apparently today she announced she's quitting the musical, too.'

'Well, she hasn't mentioned that to me. Look, I accept your dissatisfaction, but I'm worried about the effect a suspension might have on Rachel. The situation with my wife is particularly severe. She's in a relationship with a family friend, someone we've known for years. And Rachel was very fond of Jim Wainwright, she trusted him implicitly.' David was surprised to see the headmaster reddening, obviously a sensitive soul. He pressed on, sensing the chance of a rethink. 'Surely you appreciate my point, Mr Edwards?'

'I'm not in a position to comment on the personal details, Mr Willoughby. However perhaps I should mention that Jim Wainwright is one of our governors, a highly valued member of the team. It would have been better not to have known the name. I suggest we focus on Rachel's behaviour.'

'It's a tough time for her. Would you put the suspension on hold?'

Mr Edwards paused, took off his glasses, and placed them on the table. He looked across at David, who for a brief instant felt as if he was a pupil himself.

Finally the headmaster responded. 'Yes, I'll agree to probation instead of suspension, though with conditions. I want Rachel to apologise to Miss Franks and to write me an action plan to set out how she intends to improve her behaviour and performance. She's an able girl, Mr Willoughby, and she's in danger of substantial underachievement.'

'Thank you, Mr Edwards, I appreciate your decision. I'll make sure she does both things you've asked for.'

'One other point though. She needs to be made aware that if she steps out of line, however slightly, that will be it and she'll be suspended.'

'Fair enough, I'll make sure she behaves properly.'

The headmaster stood and David did likewise. 'You might want to help her put together her plan of action,' Edwards suggested. 'I want to see something that sets out how she intends to make a sustained effort to improve.'

'I'll do that too.'

The headmaster shook hands with David while making uncompromising eye contact. 'She's by reception, I'll take you there. She can't go back to classes today but we'll see her and her plan tomorrow.'

David glanced at his watch on their way out. It was 11.56. He'd told Mary he'd be back by 1.00 at the latest and he might still make it. Mr Edwards led him to a tiny windowless room, as near as a school could get to having a cell. There were two plastic chairs, one occupied by Rachel and another by a teacher who was marking exercise books on his lap. 'You can go home now, Rachel,' the Head said before David had a chance to speak. 'If you do what your father and I have discussed, we'll see you tomorrow.' He turned and left without waiting for a reply.

'Hello, Rachel, shall we go?' She nodded and followed David out to the car.

The journey home was silent until David turned into their street. Then Rachel spoke. 'I'm sorry, Dad. Things must be hard for you and it's not fair for me to make it worse.' David glanced to his side and saw tears rolling down Rachel's cheeks. He pulled into the drive and switched off.

'We need each other to get through this, Rachel, but whatever happens you know I'm here to support you.' They leant across the handbrake to cuddle and Rachel shook as she sobbed. He couldn't leave her at home alone in this state. Mary would have to wait.

He made ham sandwiches for lunch and while they were eating, outlined his conversation with Mr Edwards. The key messages were the need for an apology and an action plan. As soon as she'd finished eating Rachel opened her bag, took out a pad of paper and a pen, and got going.

'This is easy,' she said as she wrote.

1. No smoking in school or nearby
2. Polite attitude towards all teachers
3. Work as hard as possible
4. Give in homework on time

She tore out the piece of paper and handed it to David. 'Done it.'

'Well, if you stick with these that would be great, but they're a bit open-ended.' He'd attended countless meetings to set SMART objectives and decided not to burden his daughter with a process that she would probably encounter far too often in the future. He chose an intermediate path. 'Perhaps you could give an indication of how you intend to reach these actions.'

'What do you mean?' Rachel replied, a glimmer of outraged teenager reappearing. 'I've said I won't smoke, will be polite and work hard. What more do they want?'

'Break them up a bit. For instance, which subject will you have to work hardest in to be successful? Who do you need to be polite to? Is there a teacher you've been particularly rude to, maybe the one you swore at today?'

'Yeah, the fucking bitch.'

'Rachel!'

'Only joking, Dad. OK, back to the drawing board. I'll

take it upstairs if that's all right.' She stood and planted a kiss on David's forehead.

It was gone 3.00 and he'd forgotten to call work to apologise to Mary. A difficult conversation was now needed. Luckily a friendly voice answered the phone. 'Hello, Dorothy. Would you track down Mary and apologise for me, I'm not going to make it back in this afternoon … Yes, everything's fine now, just a spot of bother at Rachel's school … Tell her I'm in all day tomorrow so we can meet whenever is good for her … No, I don't need to speak to her now … Oh, and Dorothy, out of interest could you let me know how many Post-its there are in one of those little packs?'

Chapter Eight

Driving home from the reunion, David's thoughts raced between Bridget, Rachel, Jane, and Mary – anticipation, concern, rage, and animosity. On arrival he parked the car and needing to stretch his legs and get some fresh air, walked round to the newsagent ahead of going indoors.

Everything was the same as ever – Isobel pushing the pram in a vain attempt to stop her baby crying, Lawrence washing his BMW, Mrs Grant nurturing her flowers and plants with care beyond the call of duty.

'Hello, Mr Willoughby, and how are you today?' asked Stanley Entwhistle.

'I'm fine, thanks.'

David put the *Sunday Times* on the counter and took out his wallet.

'No *Mail on Sunday* again?'

David wondered whether the Jane and Jim news had got around. It must have done by now. Perhaps Stanley was seeking confirmation of the gossip.

'I don't think I'll be buying it anymore,' David announced.

This Sunday turned out to be identical to the previous post-Jane ones. On their return from stay-overs at friends, the children embarked on half-hearted homework while David ploughed through the newspaper. A near silent evening meal was followed by television viewing as all three did little more than hang around waiting for the new week to begin.

Back at work on the Monday, David was glad the uncomfortable sessions with Mary had come to an end. He was tackling her strategy for restoring the finances of his department. His staff were devising new rules, codes of conduct, terms and conditions, information booklets, and application forms. At the regular Monday morning meeting, a committed young member of his team expressed concern that the complexity of applying for financial support would result in people giving up. While this might address the problem of over-budgeted expenditure, the cost would be great hardship for many families. He was right and David was dismayed by his own indifference to the fact.

Lunch provided a pleasant break from work. It was Jabulani's second autumn in England and like the first, the weather was awful. He read from a Bill Bryson book that he'd brought in. Bryson described his arrival in England as feeling like he was now living inside a Tupperware box.

'When I first read it I thought it was funny, now I realise it's true.' Jabulani went on to describe the contrast to the sun and heat of Zimbabwe, with such passion that David could feel the warmth. The conversation gave him the energy to return to his challenging afternoon tasks.

Rachel was back in *Fiddler on the Roof* so David collected her after the rehearsal. 'Go well today?' he asked.

'Rubbish.'

'Why?'

'The director's making the musical into a comedy. A whole community is being persecuted and that idiot is going for cheap laughs. It's like a pantomime. He'll probably do the Holocaust next year.'

'He's your drama teacher, isn't he?'

'Yes.'

'Well, he has a lot of experience of what works. Maybe you should go with the flow.'

'He's wrong, I'm right.'

The journey was completed in silence. Rachel announced she was going for a walk and headed off straight from the car, stopping a short distance away to extract a cigarette from her school bag.

David went indoors and picked up the post from the hall floor. There was a letter from Rachel's headteacher, Mr Edwards, which he opened with trepidation. Since the meeting at her school over three weeks ago David had been unable to get Rachel to talk about progress beyond a perfunctory statement that everything was fine.

Dear Mr Willoughby

I am pleased to report that there has been a remarkable improvement in Rachel's attitude and performance in school over the past few weeks. The action plan she presented to me was realistic and well thought out, and she has tackled the points listed with gusto.

In particular she has worked hard in those subjects that until recently she has shown no interest in, with her marks in Biology and French rising significantly. Teachers now report on a polite, well-mannered girl. She has returned to the cast of Fiddler on the Roof *and much to my staff's amusement, she is frequently heard humming 'If I Were a Rich Man' with an engaging smile as she walks along the corridors. Another song too by all accounts, a Queen hit, the one about champions.*

Thank you for your support. Let's hope she maintains the progress, but you are welcome to tell her that we are delighted to note the upturn.

Yours sincerely
John Edwards
Headmaster

That's one worry out the way, David reflected, despite the reference to the humming. Behaviour at home had improved, too. Although she had yet to see Jane, they had spoken a couple of times and her mother's name could now be mentioned without the swearing.

When they were sitting together for dinner David announced the arrival of the letter and read it out. There was the standard teenage dismissive response to praise.

The meal turned out to be another culinary failure.

'Eat up, Sam. I thought you liked fish and chips,' David urged when he saw his son looking down at the plate, knife and fork stationary in his hands.

'But what's this?' Sam asked, stabbing with his fork.

'What do you mean what is it? It's fish.'

'I mean what type of fish?'

'Sea bass.'

'I only like fish with breadcrumbs, cod or plaice.'

'I thought it would be nice to try something different.'

Rachel intervened. 'Stop being so bloody fussy, Sam.'

'OK, I'll try it.'

'Thank you. I'll stick to what you like best next time. What about you, Rachel? You've hardly touched yours either.'

'I don't want everyone to think I'm fat on stage.'

'That's not likely.'

The pair of them picked at their food, only the moving of chairs as they got up breaking the silence.

'Hang on a minute please, Rachel,' David said.

Sam left and Rachel sat with her arms folded, impatient, anticipating a telling off.

'You know what you said earlier, that you were right and the drama teacher was wrong …'

'Yes?'

'I've been thinking about it. Sometimes in life you just have to do what you're told, you can't always have things your own way.'

'Why not?'

'Don't be silly. The world is what it is, not what you'd like it to be.'

'That's pathetic dad. What about people like Nelson Mandela and Martin Luther King? Or Bill Gates and Mark

Zuckerberg. They didn't think that, they changed things.'

'So did Hitler and Attila the Hun,' David added, regretting his put down as he spoke.

Rather than ridiculing his choices, Rachel was prepared to out-debate her father. 'Of course there have been evil people. But the world is a better place now than ever before, so on balance the effect of the people who have tried to change things must have been positive.'

Checkmate.

It was evident Rachel knew she had won hands down. 'Good discussion, Dad. Thanks,' she said with the tone of a victor. She stood up. 'I'd like to carry on, but I must do homework so I can earn some brownie points on that list of mine.'

With both children upstairs, David disposed of the high volume of leftovers, cleared the table, and loaded the dishwasher. Bridget had been on his mind all day and now he imagined her in the kitchen with him, sharing a bottle of wine, chatting as they tidied up. All good clean fun until he fantasised about removing each other's clothes and making love on the kitchen table.

The reunion aside, he'd done nothing to start his new life without Jane. There were fair enough reasons for inactivity – shopping, cooking, cleaning, chauffeuring, and generally supporting his children – but he was well aware these were self-imposed barriers. There were times when both children were out, including sleepovers at friends, when he could have done something for himself. Now there was Bridget, an opportunity he must not let slip. They'd met only two days ago. Was it too soon to call her?

As he carried saucepans from draining board to cupboard, he glanced at the letter from Rachel's headteacher. It was smeared with a streak of tomato sauce. Her improvement had been guided by an action plan so perhaps that was what *he* needed. Just maybe, Rachel's view, the one he had been so dismissive of, was correct.

An individual did have the power to change things, perhaps in his case not the whole world, but certainly his own.

An action plan to change his world! Daft, but with an hour or more to kill and nothing better to do, he'd develop something for the fun of it. A plan with SMART objectives.

Sitting down with paper and pen he decided the SMAR was of value, but not the T for Time. So rather than being specific, he wrote 'short term' at the top of the page to cover things best done within the next month or so, then 'medium/long term' half way down the sheet.

He put on a Fleet Foxes CD. He'd loved it at first but now it seemed bland. For this exercise he wanted music with a bit of a punch. He ejected Fleet Foxes and inserted The Maccabees. Satisfied with this choice he looked at the sheet in front of him. Jane had been amused by his handwriting. She claimed it was like a young schoolboy's – tiny, the letters not quite joined up. She was right.

But it was the content that counted and short term objective number one was easy. He had yet to tell his mother about the separation from Jane. Rachel and Sam had been instructed not to mention it. They'd spoken on the telephone several times over the past month and he'd replied to her standard 'How are things with you?' with the usual 'Everything's fine thank you, Mother.' He was wary of the danger of causing distress; after all she did have a weak heart. He needed to tell her in person rather than over the phone. He'd arrange a trip up to Birmingham one Saturday within the next month to break the news.

Number two was about Jabulani. He had fled from Zimbabwe approaching two years ago. Although a qualified accountant, he couldn't get employment that matched his experience. Over the last few months they'd developed a strong bond and most days met up for lunchtime chats. It was evident Jabulani knew more about English history and culture than David did, picked up during his school days. His knowledge extended to the names and locations of the major London stores and he had a particular obsession with Harrods. Jabulani's birthday was coming up. David would take him out for tea at the Ladurée café one Saturday within the next month.

Jane had made it clear she wanted a quick divorce. She intended to marry Jim as soon as possible, which did make David wonder how long their clandestine relationship had been going on. In a scribbled note found on the kitchen table when he'd returned from work one evening the previous week, she had stated her target was a divorce by March so they could get married in early summer. The following day he'd received a letter from her solicitor suggesting that the first step, the financial settlement, could be tackled immediately. David decided it was reasonable to put this as a short term objective since the process was to begin in the near future, even though completion would take a while.

Next he turned his attention to Bridget. He really had to concentrate on her – she should be right at the top of the list. He'd call her over the next day or so to ask if she'd like to meet up. Who could predict what would happen, she might well say no? On the other hand it might mark the start of a wonderful relationship. A no was more likely, David reckoned. Or even worse, the dreaded 'I do like you but I just want us to be friends'.

The Maccabees album had ended and it was approaching ten o'clock. He considered this a good time to stop, with the first part of his action plan complete and the evening news programme about to start.

Short term

1. Inform mother about separation
2. Take Jabulani to Harrods for tea
3. Start process to obtain an amicable divorce from

Jane

4. Call Bridget to arrange a meet up

Self-mockery surfaced as David read over what he had written. It had taken an hour to put down merely twenty-six words. In terms of priority, number four should have come first, but he'd listed it last. Why? Cowardice probably, fear of rejection. It was too late to call Bridget that evening and anyway, he wanted time to plan what to say. But it wasn't too late to make a call to a long established night owl. He dialled.

'Hello, Mother.'

'Who is it?'

That was her standard infuriating reply. She would have recognised his voice and it could only be her single son who was addressing her as 'Mother'.

'It's me, David.' He knew what would follow.

'Oh, David,' she said in a tone implying surprise. 'I was wondering when I'd hear from you. I suppose you're too busy to call an old lady. Mind you, I'm not complaining. How are you?'

He ignored her implicit accusation of neglect. 'Everything's fine, thanks. And you?'

'I suppose I shouldn't make a fuss. My bones are creaking a bit, par for the course as soon as it gets cold.'

'I'd like to visit on Saturday if it's convenient.'

'Of course it's convenient. It's not as if I have a busy social life. Who's coming with you?'

'Just me. Rachel's got a rehearsal for *Fiddler on the Roof* and Sam's playing football.' He hoped she wouldn't pick up on the lack of explanation for Jane's non-attendance. 'But that's good because I need to talk to you about a couple of things.'

'I hardly ever get to see your children now they're grown up. No time for their old grandmother, too many more important things to do.'

'Mother, you saw them about five weeks ago and they

phoned you last week.’

‘I suppose I should be grateful for small mercies. Well, I’ll see you when I see you,’ she muttered in the dour Brummie accent David had tried hard to lose.

Chapter Nine

He set off early on Saturday, a pleasant morning with a golden autumn sun struggling to make the M1 a little less unattractive than usual. Almost the whole trip from home to his mother's house in the Birmingham suburb of Edgbaston was along two motorways, the M1 and the M6. Always a stressful drive, with the high volume of traffic whatever time of day or night he travelled. But today he didn't care how slow the journey was because he was happy, more than happy, ecstatic, following last night's conversation with Bridget. Being stuck in traffic would give him time to daydream about what might be. And less time to spend with his mother, too.

He'd been nervous dialling, but right from her greeting Bridget made the conversation easy. She had joked about events at the reunion before accepting his invitation to meet up the following Wednesday evening after work for a drink at The Greyhound. He was a teenager again, his heart racing as he asked her, then mumbling incoherently after she had accepted.

He passed Junction 14, the Milton Keynes turnoff. This was almost halfway and so far so good. After listening to 'From Our Own Correspondent' on Radio 4 he switched it off. He needed to concentrate on how best to tell his mother about the disintegration of his marriage. She would be devastated; she was very fond of Jane. She was from the generation of female stay-at-homes whose lives were devoted to supporting their husbands and children, and for her a closely knit family was paramount.

David had been her favourite. She'd made no attempt to hide this and it had created considerable tension between him and his sister Charlotte. Day in, day out, as they stepped through the front door after school, the two children had been greeted enthusiastically with 'Tea, dears?' His routine reply of 'Yes please, Mum' was swiftly followed by her bringing a pot of tea and plate of biscuits into the lounge. Charlotte usually declined the offer to join them, intent on going straight to her bedroom to blast her punk music. They always sat on the same two armchairs. His mother then endeavoured to drag out any detail she could about his school day. She was proud of even the smallest achievements. The older he got the less he revealed and now, approaching thirty years on, there was a tinge of guilt about how he had shunned her, particularly when she most needed his support and affection.

He could still visualise the ashen-faced, swollen-eyed mother who met him at the front door on the day his father died. A policewoman was supporting her. As he stepped in she rushed up and squeezed him with extraordinary force.

'Daddy's dead,' she wailed. 'Daddy's dead,' over and over again. 'My poor Cyril.'

A heart attack at work. No warning and no second chance. Dead on arrival at hospital. David was seventeen and Charlotte two years older.

His mother struggled to cope and considerable responsibility was placed on Charlotte's and his own young shoulders. Between tears she would reminisce about family times together. The same stories over and over again. Journeys to the seaside in their Ford Capri. Competitions for who would be the first to spot the sea as they reached the summit of the South Downs. Breaking into a refrain of 'Oh I do like to be beside the seaside!' Striped windbreakers providing protection from the harsh breeze. Thick, grey clouds filling the sky, obliterating the blue. A rapid collection of possessions and a dash back to the car. Then the slow journey home, stretched out and exhausted, the two children falling asleep in the back seat. He was unsure which parts of the stories were genuine memories and which were family mythologies.

A few months after his father's death he left for university, a planned exodus to far-away Exeter with the strong intention never to return home to live. 'The Great Escape' Charlotte had called it, resenting David for the resulting additional responsibility she had to endure. She didn't go to university; she worked as a secretary in a local estate agent's office. From there she plotted her own getaway, achieved four years after their father's death when she married one of the estate agents.

It was many years later when they found out that the official account of their father's death at work wasn't quite the truth. He was having an affair with a colleague and died astride her on her bed. That morning over breakfast he'd informed his family he was going to be late home. 'I'm rushed off my feet,' he'd said. His mother knew the truth all along of course because the emergency team were called to the distraught woman's flat. The cause of death was recorded as a heart attack brought on by physical exertion. Their mother had protected them from the facts until an uncle got drunk one Christmas and relayed what had happened in lurid detail to the full extended family. Later, upstairs in Charlotte's bedroom and now far removed from the tragedy of the event, they had laughed at the irony. He was rushed off his feet well enough, but he wouldn't have expected to be off his feet for ever more.

David was approaching the Junction 18 exit to Daventry, just a few minutes away from the turnoff onto the M6. He was making excellent progress and could be able to get home by early evening if he escaped within a timeframe that wouldn't offend his mother.

Her intense bitterness had taken root from the time of his father's death, only later did he appreciate that the circumstances of it were the cause. Living alone in the same house she never made an attempt to socialise beyond the family, with few friends or interests to keep her occupied. Bearing in mind the betrayal by her own husband, how would she react to Jane's infidelity? He would need to choose his words carefully.

David drove onto the M6. Even at this horrendous motorway merging point it was devoid of congestion.

He'd decided long ago that he didn't much like his mother. After all these years there was still a pang of guilt about his escape to university because he could have carried on living at home and commuted to Birmingham or Warwick or even Aston. But how much of the guilt was justified and how much was fostered by his mother's words? There was always that hint of admonishment in her tone when he visited, implying insufficient interest in her well-being. And the truth was that the more she behaved like that, the more he backed away.

He reached Junction 4 at Lichfield to be confronted by the flashing lights of an overhead sign alerting drivers to reduce speed to 50mph. This was superfluous because ahead there was a complete standstill. He braked sharply. He was less than ten miles from his destination and it was anybody's guess how long it would take.

It was Jane who had first made him aware of his mother's deviousness and she refused to tolerate such behaviour.

'Are you sure it's not too much bother visiting me? Have you got the time?' his mother would ask Jane during a telephone call.

'You're right, we are busy this weekend. That's very understanding, Glenda, we appreciate it. Perhaps some time next month,' came Jane's reply, smiling broadly and giving David a thumbs-up sign. Jane did have a nice smile and he would miss it.

The traffic was moving again and David edged past a stationary lorry on the middle lane with its warning lights flashing. While studying Maths at university there had been a lecture on how traffic congestion occurred even when there hadn't been an accident. It was something to do with declining rates of acceleration, he recalled. Partial differentiation was needed for the calculation. He cast his mind back to the manic lecturer with wild ginger hair and thick, black plastic glasses frames. He wrote formulae at great speed on a blackboard covering the full width of the auditorium. He had a high-pitched, squeaky voice that students imitated at the pub. David tried to remember the maths he learned but it was way beyond him now.

Once past the lorry the congestion ceased and soon he was turning off the motorway and embarking on the last short stretch of journey. A flutter of nervousness rose in his stomach as he pulled into the street with its two lines of solid Edwardian houses. He stepped out of the car and picked up the bunch of dusty pink roses he'd bought at the garage when filling up.

He rang the bell and heard the shuffling movement towards the front door before it was opened. 'Hello, Mother, some flowers,' he said with an encouraging smile as he held them out in front of him.

She frowned as she took hold of them. 'Flowers, what am I going to do with them? You needn't have bothered.'

Here we go again, David thought. He contemplated snatching them back but instead maintained his attempt at warmth. 'They're to cheer you up. Let's get a vase.'

'No need to cheer me up, I'm not miserable,' she snapped grumpily. Together they walked into the kitchen and then descended into a timewarp from his school days.

'Tea, dear?'

'Yes please, Mum.'

'Well, you go into the lounge and I'll bring it in.'

The two armchairs of thirty years ago were gone, replaced by near-clones; high, wing-backed, sage green Dralon monstrosities with little squares of matching fabric over the backs and arms. He peered round the room. The sideboard was crammed with pictures of him and Charlotte as children and as adults with their families. Unframed and leaning against an empty cut glass vase was a copy of the photo from his summer holiday in Brittany, the one still pinned to his fridge. Jane, Rachel, and Sam with him – all smiles. His mother entered carrying a tray with matching Royal Albert china teapot, milk jug, two cups and saucers, and a plate of biscuits. She noticed him looking at the photograph.

'Lovely photo, that.'

'Mother, I have to tell you something.'

'If it's about Jane leaving you, David, I already know.'

'How do you know?'

'Jane telephoned to tell me. The poor dear, she's finding it all rather difficult to cope with.'

'She's finding it difficult! What about me? Don't forget it was her who –'

'I know what you're going to say, David, but it takes two to tango. She's a lovely girl, I can understand how she feels.'

'You what!'

'No doubt she has her reasons. Let's face it, you aren't the easiest person to live with.'

David was flabbergasted, speechless. He snatched a digestive biscuit and shovelled half of it in, but his mouth was so dry he was unable to swallow the fragments.

He stood. 'Wug a munnet.'

'What?'

'Wait a minute!' he managed to enunciate, showering crumbs out in front of him.

In the bathroom he spat out the remains into the sink, cupped his hand to collect some water, and washed down the residue. With both hands he gathered more water and threw it against his face. He looked in the mirror. His face was red from choking and with rage. He took four deep breaths before returning to the lounge where his mother was calmly pouring tea. She looked up and smiled.

'Perhaps Jane leaving will give you the opportunity to make something of your life,' she suggested. 'You can start afresh.'

Thoughts about how to respond raced through his mind. 'Do you realise that raising the children has been left to me?', 'Actually, Mother, I do have an action plan – I'm seeing a wonderful woman on Wednesday.', 'You're a fine one to talk, you've had years and years to make a fresh start since the death of your two-timing husband and you've done bugger all.'

But he said none of these things and the conversation turned to small talk about Rachel and Sam; Charlotte and her family; Mr and Mrs Andrews, her next door neighbours to the left; and Mr and Mrs Gupta, the new neighbours to her right.

Forty-two minutes on, when there was a lull in the conversation, he stood and announced his departure.

'That's a short visit. Still, I expect you've got more important things to do than sit and chat with your old mother.'

He was close to saying 'yes' but instead reverted to one of his old faithful excuses.

'I've got to get back in time to collect Sam.'

On the slow traffic-congested drive home he tried to lighten his mood by thinking about the forthcoming date with Bridget. Well, hardly a date. For all he knew she'd be as polite as last time, they'd talk pleasantly, then that would be it. He remained downhearted despite listening to Coldplay, Kaiser Chiefs, and The Decemberists on the long, long journey home.

Chapter Ten

Wednesday came at last – the first day of his new life. APSTO1 (action plan short-term objective number one) had been achieved and APSTO4 was about to be accomplished.

David arrived early and sat near the entrance inside The Greyhound, at a scuffed table with initials crudely carved into the dark wooden surface. The pub was a popular after-work venue and was filled with young men talking loudly, laughing, and swigging from bottles of lager. Music videos blared out from two giant, wall-mounted TV screens – conversation would not be easy.

He struggled to fight off the negativity brought on by another awful day at work. Mary wasn't giving him enough time to implement the expenditure-reducing strategies established during their recent meetings. She continued to blame him for insufficient control of his subordinates despite having issued a policy directive urging managers to delegate more responsibility to junior team members. As soon as he'd settled down with a mug of coffee and a ginger nut biscuit, she had stormed in, demanding the matter be resolved immediately.

'What matter?' he'd asked.

'You don't even know, do you?'

'Know what?'

'The Head of Finance has published a league table and our department is bottom in terms of deviance from budget.'

She was free all evening and expected him to be available to assist her in developing a cost-cutting strategy. However long it took. There was no way he was going to cancel on Bridget. On informing Mary he had a family commitment he couldn't miss, he was subjected to a tirade of abuse centred on his inability to set priorities.

While waiting for Bridget, David practiced his greeting smile. He stopped when he noticed a group at the bar pointing at him and laughing. He transformed his smile into an expression of deep thought with a frown and a look up towards the ceiling. He then rested his elbow on the table and placed his clenched fist on his forehead in a Socratic pose. He let out a long, audible sigh.

'David, are you all right?'

Bugger, it was Bridget standing by his side, staring down at him with a look of concern. He must have missed her enter the pub.

'Hello, Bridget. I'm fine, just a hard day at work,' he said as he reversed the facial contortions back towards the awkward welcoming smile. 'What would you like to drink?'

'I'll have a –'

'No, not here!' he blurted out.

'Oh.'

'It's too loud. Not that I have a problem with loudness, but if we want to talk it won't be any good.'

'OK, somewhere else is fine. Any ideas where?' Bridget consented.

David reddened with embarrassment. He had planned to mark the start of their meeting with easy-going charm and had failed. 'There's a Costa next door, unless you're desperate for alcohol.'

'I'm not desperate, coffee's fine.'

They swapped venue. The café was near deserted with a winding-down-at-the-end-of-the-day feel. David left Bridget seated as he went to the counter to get drinks.

'Here we are,' he declared, setting down a latte and a double espresso on the table. 'Actually, their coffee isn't bad.'

‘Are you an expert then?’

‘Not at all, though I can taste the difference between good and awful. And I do think ambiance is important.’

‘What makes a place feel right?’

‘Ideally, not being part of a chain like this one. If you go to Europe there are lots of individually owned quirky cafes, places where it’s interesting to be, with things to see or listen to. I’ve been to some great ones.’

‘Interesting – actually I agree with you. At any rate, this coffee’s fine,’ Bridget said, having taken a sip of her espresso.

Things moved ahead nicely when they started talking about the trauma of raising teenagers. David outlined his concern about how things were changing for his two now Jane had left and Bridget admitted that having to set off to work before hers departed for school was something she worried about. She worked in a gallery selling mid-priced contemporary art. David gasped when, in response to his question, she indicated that mid-priced was between £20,000 and £50,000.

She smiled her beautiful smile. ‘And all I get is a measly annual salary, not much more than the cheapest painting I sell. Actually, a bonus too, so I shouldn’t grumble.’

She outlined why she’d ended up working at the gallery. After school she’d gone on to college and obtained a History of Art degree. That’s where she met her husband Roland, a sculptor who even as a student was acquiring a considerable reputation. His work was taken on by a dealer in Old Bond Street who was looking for new talent and by chance for an additional member of his sales team. Ahead of developing a long term career plan she decided to take the job. So her first employment included selling her husband’s works. A proper career never materialised, although she still had no idea what ‘proper’ constituted. She stayed on, even after Roland died.

'Died! I assumed you'd separated, I am sorry, how awful. How long ago?' David asked.

'A little over five years.'

'What happened?'

'An accident, but I'd rather not talk about it. Perhaps another time.'

'Of course, I understand,' David said with a degree of sincerity, but with some concern that she might still be in a sorrowful state following the death of her loved one. Maybe in permanent mourning like Queen Victoria after Prince Albert died. It would have been better for his chances if they had separated.

He was keen to pursue the questioning, appreciating the need for great delicacy and sensitivity. 'And what's happened since then?'

'In what way?'

'Have you found a replacement?'

She smiled. 'You make it sound like I'm on the lookout for a new plumber or electrician. But I suppose I know what you're getting at. Well I've had the odd fling, some of them very odd, but nothing serious.'

'Good.'

'What's good?'

David shuddered; his complete cock-up at the beginning of the meeting was in danger of being revived. He'd thought 'good' in relation to his chances, but with no intention of stating it, he said, 'I mean it's good of you to tell me a little bit about yourself because last time we met it was all about me.'

The conversation improved as they discussed art, music, films, and books. Both were avid cinema-goers and they shared many non-mainstream favourites.

David was thinking about how he could reach the next step, another meeting, when Bridget glanced at her watch then stood. 'I didn't realise the time. I'm going to have to leave, I promised the kids I wouldn't be late.'

He had to think fast. A film, a concert, a visit to an art gallery? He was struck by inspiration. 'Bridget, Thursday week is Guy Fawkes Day and we're going to have a few fireworks at home. Would you and your children like to join us?'

'We usually go to the big event in the park,' she replied.

'I've been trying to get my lot to do that for years, but they won't have it. They insist on a small display at home. We get snacky food like sausages. Why not join us for that, too.'

'We're all vegetarians.'

'Then we'll eat snacky veggie things, my kids won't mind.'

Bridget looked down at him and nodded. 'OK, I'd love to. What time would you like us there?'

David gave details of when they'd start and his address, then Bridget departed without the kiss he had hoped for.

The next morning at breakfast he announced the Guy Fawkes plan to Rachel and Sam.

'But Dad, we like the big event in the park,' Sam complained.

'I know, but this once we'll do it at home. Bridget's children prefer a quieter firework display.'

'How can you have a quiet firework display? What's the matter with them?' Rachel mocked.

'Scared of big rockets and all the people,' Sam added.

'No need to be like that. Be friendly, that's all I ask.'

At the dinner table the jokes continued.

'I've got a great idea Dad, we can get sparklers for those kids,' Rachel started.

Sam joined in. 'Yeah, but we'll need to provide extra thick gloves so they can hold them safely.'

David cleared away the half-eaten plates of ravioli. Rachel had opened up every parcel in search of tomato and Sam had cut the edges off each envelope in the same way he removed the crusts from slices of bread. Once he'd done that there wasn't much left to eat. David was running out of ideas for meals and decided a cookery course could be the first point if he was ever going to bother with a medium/long term action plan.

Rachel reappeared and helped him stack the dishwasher. 'How was Grandma when you said Mum had left us?'

'She already knew, Mum had told her.'

'But what did she think?'

'Well, I was disappointed. She implied it had to be as much my fault as hers.'

'Ridiculous.' Rachel ran hot water over the cloth, squeezed it, then began to wipe the table. 'Are you going to divorce Mum?'

'Yes, that's what she wants. I can't see the point of fighting it. She and Jim are going to get married.'

Rachel now had her back to him as she wiped the work surfaces. 'Do you like this Bridget? Are you going out with her?'

'I am fond of her, but we've only just met.'

Rachel was on her hands and knees sweeping the floor with the brush and pan. David had never seen such a display of cleaning from his daughter. 'You'll let me know if things develop, won't you? And who is Jabulani?'

'Rachel, have you been reading my stuff?'

'You read *my* action plan so why shouldn't I read yours?' She stood up. 'Anyway, if you don't want things read don't leave them lying around.'

She smiled, planted a kiss on his cheek.

'I can't wait to read your long term plan.'

Chapter Eleven

David found the piece of paper with his short term objectives on the table in the hall, next to the telephone. He must have left it there when he'd called Bridget so Rachel could hardly be accused of high level spying for spotting and reading it. However, he was irritated Rachel had done so, compounded by the fact that despite the worldly advice he had provided, his list was no more analytical than her original one that he'd insisted she revise.

Well aware of the banality of what he had so far written, he nevertheless decided to push ahead with the setting of longer term objectives. Writing the list would be meaningless, but at the very least an act of defiance against the expectation of rational behaviour that comes with adulthood. The exercise would also provide a time-killer ahead of *News at Ten*.

He sat at the kitchen table. The first point was easy, he'd already decided.

1. Take a cookery course

For a while he stared at the sheet of paper with the single objective, clueless what to put next.

He made himself a cup of tea.

He took out the rubbish.

Was that single point the sum of his ambition?

He emptied the washing machine.

He hung the clothes on the drier.

How creative could he be?

He took the sausages for tomorrow's dinner out the freezer and put them in the fridge.

Carrying out these mundane tasks brought about the

realisation that he had to confront his growing frustration at work – all the worse now that he was line managed by Mary. He had a tolerable job with a good pension, but in his mid-forties a pension couldn't be the main reason for staying on. Enough was enough he thought as he added the next point.

2. Quit my job and pack in accountancy

What new job could he take on? How bold could his decision making be because one thing had been on his mind for ages and he would love to put it down?

A café, an arts café like some of the ones he'd spent time at during holidays.

He could be his own boss, get away from sitting in front of a computer screen all day, meet new people, create something currently unavailable on the high street that he would be proud to provide.

3. Open an arts café

The list was taking shape.

Medium/Long term

1. Take a cookery course
2. Quit my job and pack in accountancy
3. Open an arts café

Now that boldness was on the agenda his pulse raced at the dare of what to write next. The Bridget statement.

He was finding it impossible to stop thinking about her, lustfully last thing at night and slightly less lustfully during the day. Infatuation had set in big time, perhaps it was a serious disorder. Was there such a thing as Manic Obsession? In the past he would be inclined to write something like 'develop a loving and long-lasting relationship with Bridget.' But now, light-headed with bravado, he wrote a rather more direct statement.

4. Have sex with Bridget.

He smiled at this frivolity. Of course he sought much

more than that, but at least he couldn't be faulted in terms of being well on the way to setting a SMART objective. What he had written was Specific, Measurable, Attainable (hopefully), and Relevant. Only Time was missing so he randomly picked his birthday, the twentieth of February.

4. Have sex with Bridget by February 20th

Now in flat out happy-go-lucky mode he added a number five for good measure.

5. Have more sex with Bridget by the first week of March

This sheet of paper must not be discovered by Rachel. He folded it into a tight rectangle and placed it inside his brown coat pocket. He'd take it to work and leave it there, locked in his filing cabinet. Or better still, he'd word process and password protect the document and shred the hard copy.

Jabulani didn't need reminding that the promise of being taken to tea at the Ladurée café in Harrods was imminent.

David now had a clear picture of Jabulani's distressing story. It had emerged bit by bit as their friendship developed. He had lived in Harare, working at senior level as an accountant in Zimbabwe's Ministry of Agriculture and Rural Development. He was a true patriot, proud of his country's independence but dismayed as the government's policies grew more extreme. The massive economic problems of hyperinflation, unemployment, and food shortages were resulting in intense poverty. Encouraged by his brother, a doctor, he signed up to a peaceful opposition coalition. Somehow the group members' details were being passed on to the government's security forces because intimidation began as soon as anyone joined. He lost his job in the ministry and his wife, Jestina, lost hers as a teacher.

His brother, Farai, was a more active member, much braver too, because he was demonstrating on the streets of the city. Three times over a couple of months he was taken in by the police, questioned, and beaten. One warm summer's evening Jabulani and his family were invited round to his brother's for a meal. As they turned the corner into his street they stopped the car and could do nothing but watch as Farai was led out handcuffed by four members of the Central Intelligence Organisation. Jabulani gazed in helpless silence as his brother was pushed into a sleek black SUV and driven off. There was no option but to return home; it would be far too dangerous to go to the CIO headquarters to enquire why he had been arrested.

Jabulani still had contacts within government departments. This included a friend who worked at the Ministry of State Security, a dissident who risked his life passing on information to foreign journalists. He spent the next day pressing him for news, finally to be informed that his brother would not be released. He had been murdered on the night of his capture. The contact advised Jabulani to flee and provided details of how to go about it.

Jabulani was devastated but realised for the sake of his family they had to leave. They gathered what possessions they could carry by hand, including some gold jewellery he had had the sense to purchase over the previous three years as a hedge against the diving value of the currency. They set off on an arduous and costly journey to England that took almost three months. They arrived as asylum seekers and were amongst the few lucky ones to be granted recognition as refugees. He reckoned his accountancy qualification had helped, together with his knowledge of and passion for all things British, which charmed the immigration officials. This passion had been somewhat dampened by his experiences since arrival, with endless forms to fill in and meetings to attend, plus the formidable struggle to get decent accommodation and a suitable job.

'I wouldn't be proud to invite you to my home, my

friend.'

'Where do you live, Jabulani?'

'Queensbury. Do you know it?'

'Vaguely, I've driven through once or twice.'

'I think the Queen would be embarrassed having her name associated with it if she knew what it was like there.' Jabulani had a broad grin as he said this, his smile was striking and infectious and David laughed.

'I'm sure she would. I bet it's not cheap either.'

'It takes most of my salary to pay the rent. Jestina's income has to cover pretty well everything else.'

'She's a teacher, isn't she?'

'Yes, but she can't teach here, her Zimbabwean qualification doesn't count and she'd have to retrain. So she works as a learning mentor for refugees like us.' He paused. 'David, I was going to ask you, though I don't wish to take a liberty. Would it be possible for my wife to join us on Saturday?'

'Of course she can, that would be lovely.'

'And do you think my children could come, too?'

'Sure. Bring them as well.'

This reply was greeted with another beaming smile. 'David Willoughby, you're a very good man, a very good man indeed.'

They made plans to meet outside Harrods at 3 p.m. that Saturday.

It was the last day of October and autumn had set in with a grey, chilling mist hanging over the city. Knightsbridge was bursting with affluent shoppers carrying designer label bags. The aged and infirm were in grave danger as the insensitive shoppers pushed past in their race to the next shop. There was a steady flow of customers in and out of Harrods.

Having agreed to include the children, David had scrapped the idea of going to the rather sedate Ladurée café. The plan now was to take them to what he considered to be a more suitable choice, Café Godiva.

Jabulani appeared at the exit to the Underground station, wife by his side and four young children behind them. The children had on matching red fleeces with motifs on the right breast. The men shook hands before Jabulani introduced his family.

'My wife, Jestina.' A handshake.

'My eldest, Chenzira.' A boy, about ten years old, extended his hand and David shook it.

The process was repeated as Maiba, Rufaro, and Sekayi were introduced – in all, two boys and two girls. Now that he was standing close to them David could examine the fleeces with their badges edged in blue and gold cannons below bold white lettering.

He must have looked aghast because Jabulani spoke with concern. 'What is it, my friend?'

'Oh, it's nothing.'

'But yes, something is bothering you.'

'The fleeces, they're Arsenal.'

'Yes, our team. The magic ones, they play the most beautiful football in the world.'

'I support Spurs.'

'Then may the Lord forgive you.'

David looked away from the badges to the faces, first the youngsters then up towards the adults. All were smiling broadly. 'Very funny,' he retorted. 'Well, I hope you lose today!'

He led them into Harrods and towards Café Godiva.

The children devoured chocolate drinks and chocolate cakes while the adults had coffee and tastes of what the children had chosen. Conversation was light, centred on the huge differences in lifestyle between London and Harare. There was much laughter, occasionally broken by sadness as Jabulani and Jestina recalled what they had left behind in their beloved country. Being in the company of this optimistic, closely knit family was uplifting. It was only after they had said their goodbyes that David was overcome by a wave of despondency with the realisation that his own family had disintegrated.

Chapter Twelve

Thursday, 5th of November. Bridget, Kay, and Andy were due to arrive around 5.30 for the veggie snacks, to be followed by the firework display. David had bought the fireworks the previous weekend and planned to take some of the afternoon off to pop into Waitrose to get the food. He'd decided it was only fair for all of them to refrain from meat and had searched online for hours to find appetising ready-mades or at the very least, easy to prepare dishes.

To simplify the shopping expedition he'd made a list. French bread. Couscous. Marinated tofu. Hummus. Various cheeses (make sure vegetarian). Pitta bread. Olives. Dolmades. Dried apricots. Mixed nuts. Tortilla crisps. Salsa dip. Fruit. Ice cream. Yoghurt.

A little after 3.00, as he was putting on his coat to leave the office, his phone rang. It was a teacher from Sam's school who informed him that there'd been an accident. Apparently it was nothing serious, but Sam was in A&E having his leg looked at.

David's first thought was of the effect this might have on Bridget's visit, but concern for Sam wasn't far behind. He explained his predicament to Dorothy, giving her details of how to cover for him should Mary enquire.

'OK, Dorothy. I'd better get going.'

'I hope he's OK,' Dorothy called out as David strode out the department's entrance. He looked behind to wave an acknowledgement, unaware Mary was about to pass him. She kept her balance as they collided, but the coffee she was carrying tipped over her tailored brown jacket.

'Look where you're going, for God's sake.'

‘Sorry, Mary. At least it’s brown.’

‘At least what’s brown?’

‘Your jacket, when it’s dry you’ll hardly be able to see a mark.’

She looked furious.

David continued. ‘I was joking. I’ll pay for the dry cleaning of course, it was completely my fault.’

‘Yes, it was.’

‘I already said it was.’ Her look of disdain remained ferocious, but David was learning how to cope with her tirades and gave her a defiant look.

‘Where are you going?’ she asked. ‘I have some cases I need to go through with you.’

‘Sorry, can’t now, Mary. My son’s in A&E.’

David didn’t wait to see or hear a reaction.

He drove to the hospital deep in thought, plotting how the evening’s rendezvous would be able to go ahead whatever Sam’s condition. When he arrived at the casualty department, Sam was in the waiting room wearing his shiny navy blue track suit and one trainer, the other foot bare. A teacher wearing similar sports gear was by his side. Both were reading tattered *Top Gear* magazines.

Sam looked up and smiled as he approached.

‘Hi, Dad.’

The teacher stood up. ‘Hello, Mr Willoughby, thank you for getting here so quickly. We were playing football and Sam went over heavily when he was tackled. His leg swelled up quite a bit. We put an ice pack on but thought it best to have it checked out.’

‘Sorry, Dad,’ Sam added.

‘It’s OK, Sam, it’s not your fault. Does it hurt a lot?’

‘Not really, but my leg’s got bigger.’ He pulled up his trouser leg. ‘Look.’

‘What did the doctor say?’

The teacher took over. ‘We’ve been here for over an

hour. A nurse had a preliminary look, but we're still waiting for a doctor. Apparently there's been a coach crash and they're busy dealing with that.'

'Well now I'm here there's no need for you to stay, Mr ...'

'Barnes, Noel Barnes.'

'You might as well head off, Noel. Thanks for bringing him.'

'Yes. Thank you, sir,' Sam added.

'I will go if that's all right with you. Good luck, Sam, hope to see you back in school tomorrow.'

The wait was a long one, almost another hour before the X-ray then a further thirty minutes before being seen by the enthusiastic, moon-faced doctor who looked far too young to be a medic. Fortunately there was no break, just a bad sprain, resulting in another wait until a nurse applied a bandage. David's concern grew as it got nearer and nearer to Bridget's arrival time. They got home well after 5 p.m. and it was clear he wouldn't have time to get food before she arrived.

There was a ring of the doorbell on the dot of 5.30, by which time Sam was sitting on the sofa in the lounge with his left leg propped up, watching TV. Rachel was in her bedroom, listening to Jay-Z and doing homework. David had searched kitchen cupboards in the futile hope that Jane, an ardent carnivore, had a hidden supply of vegetarian delights. A tin of baked beans and a packet of frozen chips was all he would be able to offer.

The guests stood in the hall while David called up to Rachel. At the third attempt she came downstairs to be introduced, disappointing David with an ice cold greeting. They trooped into the lounge to meet Sam who was cheerful enough in explaining what had happened. *Neighbours* was on and David suggested the children remain viewing while he and Bridget went to the kitchen to sort things out. Once alone with her, he explained the dilemma.

'Not a problem,' Bridget said. 'You stay here with the kids and I'll go and get the food.'

'But I'm meant to be the host.'

'Well you didn't count on Sam's accident. It's no big deal, we passed Waitrose round the corner. I'll nip out.'

'If you're sure you don't mind. I'll get some money.'

'No need. You got the fireworks so it's only fair I get the food.' She turned and headed out the room before he could protest.

He called after her as she stood by the front door. 'I've made a list, it's in my coat pocket by you there. The brown one.'

Bridget took the sheet of paper from his coat and dropped it into her handbag. 'Got it. Tell Andy and Kay I'll be back in a few minutes.'

David went into the lounge where stony faces and silence prevailed except for the piercing shrieks of the animals featured on *Michaela's Zoo Babies*. 'Bridget's popped out to get some food,' he informed them.

'What are we eating?' Sam asked.

'Hummus, couscous, pitta bread.'

Rachel reddened. 'I hate stuff like that. Why can't we have proper food?'

'What do you mean by proper food?' the until-now silent Andy asked.

'Stuff that tastes good and has lots of protein.'

'And you're the judge of that, are you?'

'Yes, I know what's good and what isn't.'

'Well, I don't think you do. Go on, define "good".'

If looks could kill, Andy was close to death as Rachel growled, 'Meat of course, sausages, bacon, ham, chicken satay, anything except bloody veggie stuff.'

Andy held his ground. 'Well isn't that a healthy diet. Before you know it you'll be as fat as the pigs you eat. And riddled with cancer, too.'

Rachel stood up. 'Fuck you, veggie boy,' she muttered as she exited.

A concerned David hoped Bridget would get back quickly. It was Kay who took on the role of peace maker, breaking the icy silence by chatting to Sam about his leg. She was a pretty girl, resembling her mother with high cheekbones, blue eyes, and light brown hair. It would be hard to identify Andy as from the same family. He was tall and thin with a narrow face, piercing eyes, and longish jet black hair that was wild and uncontrollably curly. Soon the three youngsters were chatting civilly and the crisis seemed over, at least until Rachel reappeared.

The doorbell rang and Bridget was back balancing cardboard boxes of pizzas in one hand and three plastic bags in the other.

'Here, let me help,' David offered. He took hold of the pizzas and they went into the kitchen, followed by Kay and Andy with Sam limping after them.

Rachel joined the group as the boxes were being opened. 'I thought I smelt pizzas. What happened to the Greek stuff?'

'I reckoned you'd all prefer pizzas,' Bridget said brightly. 'There's a roasted veg and a margarita for us, which you can share of course, and I've got a ham and a pepperoni for you lot. And there are crisps and Cokes in the bags.' She had gained an instant giant brownie point and before long the youngsters were tucking in.

'Can we watch *The Simpsons* before the fireworks?' Rachel asked as they munched the last slices of pizza.

'Yeah, I'd like to,' Andy added, the antagonism between the two children hopefully in remission.

'Is that OK with you, Bridget?' David asked. 'We could do a quick clear up then get started in about half an hour.'

The four youngsters headed back to the lounge, leaving the adults to dispose of empty cartons, load the dishwasher, and drink a glass of wine.

'That was a big hit,' David said. 'An inspiration to ignore my list.'

'I'm not sure I took the right piece of paper,' Bridget replied with an expression of absolute serenity. She opened her bag and handed David his now unfolded action plan, not altering her demeanour as David blushed more than he ever imagined would be possible.

Escape was the only thought on his mind. 'I need to check the fireworks,' he mumbled. Bridget was left standing alone in the kitchen as David fled out the back door and into the garden. Once inside the shed where they were stored he had little desire to ever step out again. But there was no choice because the audience was assembling outside.

'Can I light the first one, Dad?' Sam asked. He had a plastic bag over his slippered foot.

'OK, as long as you're careful. What do you want?'

'A rocket, of course.'

David went back in the shed to get one and brought it out together with an empty wine bottle and a box of extra-long matches.

Kay stood next to Sam as he placed the rocket inside the bottle, then lit the match and held it against the twist of paper until it caught. 'Quick. Run!' he called out to Kay as he hobbled towards the others. In her rush to escape, Kay's foot clipped the bottle, which fell to the ground. The resting position couldn't have been more accurate if she'd tried. The rocket took off at a shallow angle and with a piercing whistle and sparkles of red and green light, shot straight through the open shed door before bouncing around in a vain attempt to escape the confines of the building. There was a brief pause before the rat-tat-tat of bangers. Then the whole shed was illuminated by a shower of pastel pink sparks as a fountain ignited.

All this was happening in seconds, enough time for a

range of possible remedial actions to rush through David's mind, but insufficient time to get up and do anything. Finally he edged towards the shed. Before he had taken more than a few steps there was an almighty explosion as the whole collection of rockets was set off. One came flying through a window with an almighty crash, sending a shower of glass onto the lawn. Another shot out the shed door, staying low as it headed towards the spectators. They scattered to dodge the missile.

'Wick-ed!' Rachel yelled.

'This is so cool,' Andy added.

By now in addition to a cacophony of noise and an explosion of colour, the shed itself was alight.

'Have you got a hose, David?' Bridget called out.

'Yes.'

'Where is it?'

'In the shed, I'm afraid.'

'What about buckets?'

'There are a couple in the kitchen, under the sink.'

Rachel and Andy ran in to collect them, but their feeble attempts to throw water from too far a distance did little to diminish the flames, which were now coming through the roof. The last fireworks to go were jumping jacks which scuttled out the shed, bouncing along the lawn. A discussion ensued about whether to call the fire brigade, David deciding against it as the shed was well away from their own and their neighbours' houses so couldn't spread to other buildings. They watched transfixed as the fire waned and the light dimmed.

'Well, that was the best firework display I've ever seen,' Andy exclaimed as they made their way indoors.

'Good, I'm glad you enjoyed it. I never much liked that shed anyway,' David said, making light of the incident, but aware of the problem to come.

Chapter Thirteen

David and Jane were sitting at the kitchen table, looking out to the charred remains of the shed. It was Saturday.

'What made you decide on having fireworks here? We always used to go to the park.'

'I thought it would be nice for the children to have a quiet event at home,' David suggested.

Jane stood and walked across to the fridge where she took out a carton of milk. She inspected the label. 'Since when have you been drinking this?'

'It's called milk, you've seen it before.'

'Not red top.'

'It's healthier. And safer to go organic, too.'

'Have you got a heart problem?' she asked.

'Absolutely not, I'm fine.' He glanced at Jane. Did she look disappointed? He didn't like the way she came in as if she owned the place, though admittedly she did own half of the part not held by the mortgage company. On arrival, using the key without ringing the bell, she'd entered with the merest of nods to acknowledge his presence before walking into the kitchen and turning on the coffee machine.

She'd found out about the shed fire from Sam and had come to see the damage.

The day before this visit another letter from her solicitor had arrived, advising David that he needed to get an estate agent to value the house ahead of making any financial settlement. Jane was there to assess the impact of the accident ahead of the valuation. 'It's a complete wreck, you must have had a hell of a lot of fireworks.'

'It is wooden, Jane.'

'*Was* wooden, David. What else was in it, apart from fireworks?'

'Just the usual stuff.' David fought off panic.

'If insurance doesn't cover it you'll have to pay since you burnt it down. That's only fair.'

Jane tilted her head back to catch the last dregs of cappuccino. She replaced the cup on the saucer and looked across at him. There was a thin line of frothed milk above her upper lip. It made her appear less threatening, comical. She looked down at the cup. 'We've got four of these, haven't we? I think I'll take them, they're rather nice. You use mugs so they won't be missed.' She got up, opened the unit above the dishwasher, and removed the three remaining cups and saucers. She set them down on the table then opened a base unit to get a plastic bag.

'*The Times* now,' she remarked as she wrapped a cup using the travel section of the newspaper lying as yet unread on the kitchen table. She carefully placed it in the bag and began to wrap a saucer. '*Mail* not good enough for you?'

'I quite like a newspaper to have some news in it,' he sniped, watching with discomfort as she moved around the kitchen knowing where everything was. He resolved to rearrange things as soon as she'd left.

'I didn't just come over to see the burnt shed. I need to collect some warmer clothes now that the weather's turning.'

David's panic intensified. This was it.

She moved towards the hall. 'Are the kids upstairs?'

'Jane.'

'Yes?'

'I found it impossible to keep your clothes in our bedroom. The thought of them in the wardrobe near our – my – bed, was upsetting. So I took them out and bagged them up. I was going to let you know so you could come over to collect.'

‘Well, I’m here now so I’ll take them, but I wish you’d left it for me to pack. I could have sorted them out the way I wanted and made sure they were properly folded, which I’m sure you haven’t done. Where are they?’

‘I’m sure you can appreciate that I was pretty angry about what’s happened.’

‘I don’t want to go through all that again. Where are they?’

‘I didn’t want them in the house, I took them out. I put them in the shed.’

There’s often a moment of silence before an explosion, the calm before the storm. The streak of lightning before the clap of thunder. The release of the missile before the explosion on impact. The …

‘You absolute bastard, David!’ she shrieked. ‘You absolute fucking tosshead bastard.’

‘I didn’t burn them on purpose.’

‘You make me sick. You’re a pathetic creep, do you know that? A pathetic, moronic creep.’

Rachel was by the door. ‘Well I rather like him.’

Jane spun round. She managed to change tone. ‘Rachel, dear, it’s nice to see you. Do you know what your father’s done? He’s burned all my clothes.’

‘Oh dear, how sad,’ Rachel said with a broad grin.

‘And I can see that he’s completely corrupted you. You haven’t even tried to understand how I feel.’

‘How’s Uncle Jim, Mummy?’ she asked, emphasising the last word.

‘He’s fine, thank … you’re being sarcastic, aren’t you.’

‘Of course not, my sweet, considerate Mummy.’

Jane turned to face David. ‘Every penny of damage you’re going to pay for and more for the stress you’ve given me.’ She turned, ignoring Rachel as she stormed past her, heading towards the front door.

‘Don’t forget your cups and saucers, Jane,’ David called out. He adopted a calm and pleasant tone, one that might be used if he was suggesting it would be prudent to take an umbrella on the off chance that it could rain. He lifted the bag and lobbed it high in the air. It landed with an almighty crash on the wooden floor by her side.

Jane exited, slamming the front door shut.

Rachel was still smiling. 'Good for you, Dad. This calls for a song. What shall we do, Queen or *Fiddler*?'

'I think I'll go for Queen please, Rachel.'

Sam had avoided the conflict, but now downstairs he watched in wonder as the unlikely duet commenced.

That evening there was a knock on the front door soon after David had settled down with a novel and a mug of instant coffee.

'David, we need to speak.' It was Jim and David contemplated slamming the door in his face. 'May I come in please, just for a short while?'

Jim strode in before David had a chance to reply. He held up a bottle of red wine. 'It's a Prince de Courthezon 2007, rather special.' He made his way into the kitchen, took out two large glasses from the unit to the right of the hob, then opened the cutlery drawer to extract the bottle opener. *He knows where things are*, David realised. He's done this before with Jane.

David shuddered as he thought about their opportunities; perhaps the weekend last Easter when he and the children went up to Birmingham to stay with his mother. Jim invited him to sit down as if he was the host.

Jim. Such a good friend, always concerned about others, ever willing to offer advice or to help in a crisis. David had respected his serenity and wisdom. The devious bastard. Until now he'd never focused on Jim's looks, but as he watched him pour the wine he acknowledged the man had fine facial features that seemed to ooze wisdom. The most notable quality was his soft, blue, penetrating eyes. David felt inferior to this tall man looking down at him. He could appreciate Jane's choice.

'I always think a glass of wine helps break the ice at times like this,' Jim said as he lifted his and clinked it against David's glass which still rested on the table.

'Done this before have you?'

'What do you mean, David?'

'You said "always" and "at times like this". I was wondering whether you've made a habit of stealing other men's wives.'

'Don't be silly, Jane is very special. Unique. But never mind me. I want to find out how you're feeling. I'd like to think I can help in some way.'

'I can move on without your help.'

'Clearly not if it involves activities like burning Jane's clothes.'

'That was an accident.'

'I'm sure you're right, David.'

Jim was an expert at fostering conversation and was able to draw out an account of the fire. David made a point of informing Jim that the incident took place during a visit by his new friend Bridget and her children, but it came across as a feeble attempt to demonstrate he was coping. When asked to explain the smashed cups and saucers, he described the incident as a light-hearted jest.

'I don't see it as funny. In retrospect, do you, David?'

'I've said all I want to say, Jim. I think you should go.' He lifted up the bottle. 'You can take the rest of the wine with you.'

'I must warn you, David. The way you're behaving is going to make things a lot easier for Jane's solicitor.'

'What do you mean?'

'Think about it, David.'

This was the final straw. David stood. 'Time to go, Jim. Maybe I'll keep the wine after all.' He put the bottle out of Jim's reach on the furthest worktop from the table. For the second time that day he resolved to rearrange where things were kept in the kitchen.

Jim stood. 'Have you understood my message, David?'

'Absolutely. I won't set fire to any more of Jane's clothes and I won't smash anything she thinks she can take without asking.' He looked him in the eye. 'You know where the front door is. If you don't mind you can show yourself out.'

'Very well.' Jim turned and left the kitchen. Seconds later the front door shut with a little more force than was needed.

David considered this meeting with Jim a milestone. At last he was released from something. Perhaps from Jane.

Chapter Fourteen

Bridget laughed. ‘Why didn’t you tell me her clothes were in the shed?’

‘I suppose I was worried you’d think I was a complete and utter idiot.’

‘No, I don’t think that. The fire was an accident, you didn’t mean to burn them.’

‘That’s true enough but Jane intends to make me suffer for it. Within a couple of days I’d got a letter from her solicitor listing alleged loss to the tune of £5,000.’

‘For clothes! Are you going to challenge that?’

‘Yes. I’ve decided it’s time to get my own solicitor. We had our first meeting yesterday and I’ve passed everything on to him. In the end I reckoned I had to get help, it was too complicated handling the separation myself. I want the financial split resolved quickly.’

‘Ah yes, it’s one of the things on your famous list, isn’t it?’

David reddened, something he did rather often in front of her. ‘Look, Bridget. The list …’

‘Yes, David?’

‘Nothing.’ He paused before an outpouring. ‘Actually I must explain. I was just messing around when I wrote it. I had a few minutes to spare so I jotted down some daft things. I was all set to throw it away because Rachel had already seen my short term objectives and had teased me.’

‘So everything you wrote was daft, was it?’

‘Well, not …’

David was about to outpour further when he detected the impish grin. Bridget was following in Rachel’s footsteps with the teasing. He was torn between a final serious statement and self-mockery. Bridget eliminated the need for either. 'Actually, I'm quite forgetful. Maybe I should write lists, too.'

They were chatting away in a restaurant and all was going well. Though he didn't obsess about the ill-fated list, APMLTO4 (action plan medium/long term objective number 4) had moved a step closer.

Bridget had telephoned him soon after the fireworks debacle to check everything was OK, and once she'd ascertained that he wasn't bothered about the shed, to thank him for such entertainment. Their conversation had naturally moved on to the cups and saucers incident.

'Bloody hell, you didn't.'

'I did. I was so irritated the way she was taking things without asking.'

'So you decided to smash them!'

'It wasn't planned, it just happened.'

Towards the end of their telephone conversation Bridget had suggested a meal out, insisting she would pay, having got a big bonus for her October sales. Objections would not be tolerated.

'I was wondering where to go, but now there's only one choice. It'll have to be Greek,' she had declared.

'Why?'

'So you can practice your crockery smashing technique.'

'Ha ha.'

'Actually they don't go in for that sort of thing where I'm thinking of, but the food's great.'

Here they were, sitting at a cosy table in the lively Bouzoukia Restaurant in Muswell Hill. There was a giant poster of the Acropolis on the uneven white brick wall to their side. Conversation was flowing easily, interspersed with much laughter, no doubt influenced by the bottle of retsina they had emptied at great speed.

They had shared a starter platter of hummus, goat's cheese, pitta bread, olives, tzatziki, and dolmades – the very food David had intended to buy for the Guy Fawkes meal. Now they were on their main courses. David cut the last piece of lamb off his kebab. Bridget was eating vegetable moussaka.

'Good to see you eating lamb again,' she noted.

'Yes, I think I'm much more at ease about what's happened now.'

She took hold of his hand and gave it a gentle squeeze. 'I think you are, too.'

'Thanks, Bridget. Shall I get some more wine?'

'Blimey, no, I'm already halfway under the table. I'll order some for you though, if you'd like.'

'No. I'm fine, too.'

There was a lull in the conversation. David plucked up the courage to ask. 'We're always talking about me, but I'd like to know a bit about you.'

'Sure. What?'

'Maybe this is an odd request, but you said your husband died in an accident. I'm wondering what happened.'

'I have no problem talking about it if that's your choice. Let's get some coffees, maybe ouzo too.'

She called the waiter over and placed the order.

'I think I've already told you about me ending up in the art gallery that exhibited his works. Things went well for a while, but then they got difficult. Roland's sculptures weren't selling, he was feeling rejected, and stopped working. He was depressed, began drinking a lot and taking a fair old cocktail of drugs. He'd adopted the "no one understands me" syndrome that people involved in arts think they have the sole right to. I was trying to be supportive, but he took his frustration out on me. He became abusive. Cruel.'

She continued at a tangent, speaking about her parents

with great affection. They had died a couple of years ago within two months of each other, and she missed them so much. Unfortunately they played an indirect but important role in the death of her husband. They sensed the tension between Bridget and Roland even though she hadn't mentioned anything specific, and suggested the pair took a break to see if they could sort things out. They volunteered to pay for a holiday and look after the kids.

Bridget researched the web and found what she thought would be the ideal place to inspire Roland to rediscover his creativity and perhaps improve their relationship. They travelled by plane to Inverness, then hired a car and drove to a remote rented cottage at Fanagmore in the far north-west of Scotland. It was a beautiful place right by the sea with stunning cliff formations. There wasn't a shop for miles around, the nearest was a general store that made a Tesco Metro seem like a hypermarket.

'Every day we'd go for a long walk, the first couple of days setting off on foot from the cottage, then later on getting into the car and driving along tiny lanes to deserted coves and cliffs. The scenery was spectacular, as was the weather; one minute blazing sun and the next, dark storm clouds throwing down a torrent of rain.

'One day, at the start of our second week, it was my turn to drive. I had no idea where we were heading, but we ended up at an amazing lunar-like landscape of bare rock. I'd never seen anything like it, jagged outcrops stretching out a huge distance towards a fierce sea. I can still visualise the scene. I often do.'

The waiter arrived with two tiny cups of coffee and the glasses of ouzo. Bridget knocked hers back in one gulp then took a sip of the thick, black espresso.

She described their walk that day, heading out towards the wild sea, gingerly treading over the slippery rocks laden with barnacles and seaweed, stepping into small clear pools. She and Roland were getting on a little better – perhaps their relationship had a chance after all. At some stage she stopped to remove a shell lodged between her toes. Sitting on a large boulder, she took off her trainer and looked back towards the red sandstone cliff. As she turned sunbeams struck parts of it, producing a view of such beauty that she had to stop and admire its grandeur. She was just about to call out for Roland to look back when she was interrupted by his shout.

'I turned to face the sea. He was smiling, a rare event over recent times. 'Look what I've found,' he yelled. He was perched on a high outcrop of rock holding a large crab. 'Here, catch it.' And he pretended to throw it across to me but as he did so, he stumbled backwards.

'It looked really funny, him losing his balance and hovering like in a Buster Keaton movie. He swayed backwards and forwards, the crab still in his hand. The expression on his face, the puzzled look of "should I be letting go of this crab now?" Then he tumbled sideways and went crashing down.

'I stopped laughing when I saw him close up. There was a large gash on his forehead and he was out cold. The crab had escaped his grip and was edging away into the pool of reddening water. Loads of tiny crabs were scuttling away. I forgot, what do you call a collection of crabs?'

'A cast, I think.'

'Another ouzo, please,' she called out to the passing waiter. 'Do you want one, David?'

'No, thanks.'

'We never took our mobiles on the walks, we decided nothing should disturb us. God, it was all my fault. Getting as far away as possible from civilisation had been my suggestion. There I was with an unconscious husband and no way of contacting anyone quickly. It was an hour or more's walk, then a drive, to reach help.'

She described how she lifted him out the pool then made her way back as quickly as the difficult surface would allow.

She knocked back her second ouzo.

'An hour and a half later, a rescue team was with me. I told them the location as accurately as I could, and they looked at me with such pity. What an idiot I was. The tide, the fucking tide. I should have realised. They found him two days later, his body washed up a couple of miles down the coast in a sandy cove. I'd left him to drown.'

She had been looking down while speaking, but now raised her head to meet David's gaze and there was intense sadness in her eyes.

He took hold of her hands. 'There was nothing more you could have done, Bridget.'

'Surely something. I should have dragged him up to higher ground or yanked him step by step all the way back. God knows what injuries that might have caused, maybe to me as well as him, but at least I would have saved him. Or died in the attempt,' she added solemnly.

'Sir, madam. We are closing soon. Can I make up your bill?' David looked past the waiter to the otherwise deserted restaurant. Bridget nodded.

'Well, that's the story. My parents felt guilty, it had been their suggestion we went away. Dad came up for the inquest and Mum stayed with the kids. I couldn't have coped without them.'

The waiter had returned. Bridget lifted her credit card out of a lilac and pink striped purse crammed full of cards and receipts. 'Remember, I'm paying,' she said as she entered her pin number. The waiter thanked her and walked off.

They stood and Bridget smiled as David helped her on with her jacket.

'I can't think of anything to say to console you, Bridget. I'm very sorry you had to go through such an awful experience. I realise it's quite a time ago, but if I can do anything to help …'

‘Thanks, David. And I know you’re genuine about that. Hey, how did you get here?’

‘I drove.’

‘Well you can’t drive back in your alcoholic state. There’s a room at mine if you’d like.’

‘I wouldn’t want to trouble you.’

‘No trouble. Come on, let’s go.’ She took hold of his hand and they departed.

Chapter Fifteen

Who would have thought holding hands walking past youngsters noisily hanging around outside bars and late night food stalls in Muswell Hill Broadway could be so wonderful? Even seeing a girl dressed as if she was a midsummer evening fairy staggering about before vomiting right in front of them was bliss. And hearing a short stocky boy with a knife in his hand yelling 'I'm gonna get them cunts' was a delight.

'It's getting worse and worse on Saturday nights,' Bridget apologised. 'I'm struggling like mad to keep my two away from this. Andy's happy enough to stay in, he's quite a loner, but I don't think there'll be any stopping Kay in a couple of years. She's one for adventure and dares.'

'Where are they tonight?' David asked, feigning casual chat but with a strong hope they would be staying over at friends.

'At home.'

'Oh.'

'What about your two?'

'Both with friends.'

'Just as well you're staying with us then, otherwise you'd be a home alone.'

They left the main road and walked down a tidy street of Victorian terraces. He followed Bridget along a small tiled path and entered her house through a flaking, navy blue door with a large brass knocker. They stepped into an emerald green narrow corridor. The lighting was subdued. It was like walking through a canopy of rainforest trees.

The interior style of her home could not be more different to his, which suddenly seemed rather dull and austere. His walls were 'spot the difference' shades of white. Following Jane's instructions he had bought paint with names like almond white, orchid white, jasmine white, barley white, nutmeg white, vanilla white, blah, blah, blah. Here, there were violent explosions of dark, rich colours – scarlet, turquoise, orange, violet. Bare polished floorboards were partly covered by oriental rugs; tops of lacquered Chinese cabinets and carved Indian cupboards were heaped with books and magazines. There were sculptures, too, smooth stone abstract shapes, skeletal metal torsos. David assumed they were Roland's works.

His neat kitchen was fitted from floor to ceiling with units that hid everything except for the precisely placed toaster, kettle, microwave, and exhibition piece retro coffee maker. The kitchen where he now stood had irregularly shaped dressers and two untidy tables stacked full of cans, crockery, bottles, and spice jars. A haphazard row of saucepans ran a considerable length along one of the walls.

'Sorry it's a bit messy,' Bridget apologised, noticing David's inspection. She poured hot water into the cafetiere. 'Leave the kids alone for one evening and this is what you get.'

No two children, not even teenagers, would be able to create this anarchy in one evening. But he accepted Bridget's ironic explanation, warmly drawn by this contrast to his own clinical existence. Bridget pushed away some recipe books to make room for their mugs.

Andy and Kay came in. Andy was carrying an empty crisp packet and a bottle of Red Bull. He put them in the dustbin. Kay put her unfinished Coke in the fridge before turning to Bridget and David.

'Hi Mum, hello fire man. Have you had a good time?'

David smiled. 'Hello, Kay. Yes we have, thank you.'

'You should be in bed, Kay,' Bridget ordered.

'Yeah, I know. I'm going.' She turned to David. 'I was

hoping to see you again, I've got a request.'

'And what's that?'

'Could you burn down my school?'

'Don't forget to say please,' Andy added.

'Tell me where it is and I'll give it a go.'

'Enough requesting for one night,' Bridget intervened. 'Bed now, please.'

'OK, night, Mum.' Kay kissed her mother then turned to leave.

'Manners, Kay. Say goodnight to David.'

'Goodnight to David.' She kissed him on the cheek.

'You'll see him at breakfast,' Bridget continued, 'he's staying over.'

Andy stayed put, hovering awkwardly.

'What have you been up to tonight?' Bridget asked.

'Bit of TV, some computing. Nothing much. I'm going to read for a while, night Mum.' Bridget got a reluctant kiss, then as an afterthought, Andy added, 'Goodnight David.'

They sat drinking coffee and chatting for a while, touching upon David's frustration at work. He was about to talk about his café idea when she stood.

'I'm shattered. Bed time.'

She led him upstairs to the spare room. He'd never seen a black ceiling before and there were tiny specks of silver, too. Bridget noticed his inspection. 'It was Roland's idea. Apparently the dots are the patterns of the star constellations but I've never been able to see the resemblance. There are some planets, too,' she added, pointing out a slightly bigger splodge inside a circle that was meant to be Saturn. 'Let me get you some stuff.'

He continued to gaze at the ceiling, looking for other planets. He was still searching when Bridget returned with a toothbrush, towel, and an oversized t-shirt which she held up. 'I don't stock pyjamas, do you want this?'

'No, I'll be OK thanks.' The embarrassing morning

after the reunion came to mind. 'Actually, maybe I will.'

'We're lazy on Sundays, breakfast is around ten. But of course you're welcome to come down whenever.' There was a dramatic pause. 'Best to wear trousers as well as this when you do though.' She was grinning broadly as she handed it over. 'The bathroom's second on the left – there's a dress code there too, I'm afraid.'

'OK. I get the hint.'

'I've enjoyed this evening, David. Thanks.'

'Well I need to thank you, for the meal.'

'A pleasure.' She approached, put her arms round his neck and kissed him. A gentle kiss, lip to lip. It was she who pulled away; he would have remained locked in that embrace for approaching eternity. 'Goodnight, David.'

'Goodnight, Bridget. Bridget?'

'Yes?'

'About my list. I don't think I explained myself well earlier. The things I wrote down aren't in themselves daft, it's more the way I expressed them that is.'

'Well at least they're to the point, there's no room for misinterpretation.'

'I suppose you're right,' David said, again missing the tease until he looked up to the sardonic smile.

'See you in the morning, David.'

It was impossible to sleep with Bridget close by; the same difficulty as the night after the reunion. He strained to hear any sound from her bedroom and caught the click of her light switch as he lay in semi darkness, a nearby street lamp casting subdued shadows across the room.

Logical thought was impossible when there was such an intense longing to be in someone else's bed a short distance away. The problems at work dealing with Mary surfaced and then his attention drifted to failed marriage and the struggle for an amicable divorce. He must have dozed for a short while, waking with a start from a dream of the four of them, Jim and Jane, Bridget, and David, on holiday together and having a huge row by the hotel swimming pool.

He pressed the button to activate his phone light. It was 1.29 a.m. Back to Bridget – work and Jane issues were insignificant in comparison. Surely the kiss was an indication that she was interested in a relationship. But she had drunk rather a lot, perhaps hers wasn't much different to the random snogs between the youngsters they had observed on Muswell Hill Broadway. No, Bridget wasn't a teenage reveller, she was a mature, cultured woman. It must have meant something. But, another but, how much was she still mourning the tragic loss of her husband? How much unwarranted guilt remained for her part in the accident?

1.59 a.m. He would stare at his phone until the new hour arrived then put it down. 2.00 am. If her children hadn't been home perhaps he would be in bed with her this very minute. To stifle his arousal he thought about last month's painful visit to the dentist. Somehow the dentist's drill had located a nerve not reached by the injections even though his mouth, chin, tongue, and left ear had remained numb for hours after the root treatment. The focus on pain did the trick.

He picked up his phone again. 2.21 a.m. What next with Bridget, another meal? He would insist on paying this time. Or maybe something cultural like theatre or an art exhibition. Careful planning was needed to ensure no kids were present wherever they ended up sleeping, though the assumption that she would want to be alone with him at one of their houses was a big one. That took him back into the loop. Was there any evidence that she was interested in a relationship?

He was more comfortable in this house than in his own. He needed colour on his walls. Which room would he do first? Probably the bedroom though maybe the lounge.

2.58 a.m. This is silly, drop it until the morning. Stop

thinking. But wait a minute, there could be a pathway based on the action plan. Assume all points listed were steps to the ultimate goal of having sex with Bridget. Three short term objectives were accomplished – telling his mother about the separation, tea at Harrods with Jabulani, and the first meeting with Bridget. That left one incomplete action – finalising the divorce from Jane. Getting that done would have a positive impact on the Bridget situation. Why wait for Jane to take the lead? What was constituted as fair in dividing their assets? Does fairness come into it bearing in mind she walked out? She was out to get what she could, fair or not, as indicated by the bill for the clothes lost in the shed fire. He began to construct two lists, one of assets for him, one for her.

It was a bit like counting sheep. Finally, he slept.

Chapter Sixteen

Rachel was standing by the lounge door. 'Where's the telly, Dad?'

'Morning, Rachel. It's under the dust sheet, I don't want to get any paint on it.' David was in the hall on his way to the lounge, carrying a large pot of emulsion, a tray, and a roller. Rachel allowed him to pass then followed him. The furniture had been stacked and covered in the centre of the room. Plastic sheeting protected the floor and a ladder rested where the television once stood. David opened the lid and poured paint into the tray. He placed it on the ladder platform then climbed up two rungs, roller in hand and paintbrush upturned in the back pocket of his jeans that had seen better days and were dotted with an assortment of off-white splodges. He dipped the roller into the tray and ran an untidy line across the wall close to the ceiling.

'Are you mad?' Rachel exclaimed. 'It's orange.'

'Burnt umber actually.'

'Well it's orange as far as I'm concerned.'

'Read the label on the tin. It's burnt umber.'

'Sam,' Rachel called out. 'Quick, come here.' They heard a scamper downstairs then Sam entered. 'What colour is this?'

Sam frowned, confused by the simplicity of the question. He looked over to David, anxious not to give an incorrect answer.

'Orange,' he declared meekly.

'Not according to Dad. He reckons it's burnt something or other. Which of course is hardly the point. Our living room is being turned into, I don't know, a headache-inducing hippie hideout. Dad, will you stop painting and listen?'

David paused, roller at the ready. It was surprisingly quick to do, but would need a second coat. The big decision was whether to do one wall in this colour or all four. He looked down at his two children. 'I'm listening.'

'Why are you doing this?'

'I feel like a change.'

'But why not one of the colours we usually have?'

'Rachel, I didn't realise how conservative you are. I want to be bold, to try something completely different. Why not make some tea?' He applied another line of burnt umber. The previously applied paint was already drying – it was darker.

'No I fuc – no I won't. I'm going to have to watch telly on the computer.' She left the room and marched upstairs.

'I'll make tea, Dad.'

'Thanks, Sam. Maybe some toast, too.'

David continued painting, humming favourite songs as he worked. He'd do all four walls to recapture the spirit of Bridget's house with its dominant dark colours and moody, shadowy spaces. He'd barely started the second one when Sam came in with tea and toast.

'I'm not sure about this colour, Dad.'

'Nor am I to be truthful, but never mind.'

He set the roller down on the near empty tray and sat on the floor with his son to eat and drink. 'I suppose we'll get used to it,' the diplomatic youngster suggested.

David finished his tea and sprang up. 'Thanks, Sam. I'd better get going before the roller dries out.' He added paint to the tray, shifted the ladder round, and resumed painting. He was all set to start the fourth wall when there was a ring at the doorbell.

Rachel called out. 'I'll go, it'll be Daisy for me.'

It was Jane. David heard her announce that she'd forgotten her key. There was no response from Rachel; he heard his daughter head back upstairs.

Jane was standing by the lounge door. 'What are you doing, have you gone quite mad?'

'Hello, Jane. No I haven't gone mad, but thanks for your concern.'

'It's ghastly, you're ruining our lounge.'

'It's not "ours". You don't live here, remember?'

'But I do own part of it. If we need to sell who's going to buy a house with an orange lounge?'

'Someone I know would,' David said, the hint not picked up. 'Anyway, it's not orange, it's burnt umber.'

'Well it looks orange to me.' She watched him spread colour on the previously Almond White wall. 'We need to talk, David.'

'I'm rather busy.'

'It's important.'

David didn't want the roller to dry out or the remaining paint in the tray to harden. But he had yet to escape the habit of doing what Jane wanted when she wanted. He got off the ladder and wiped his hands across his jeans, creating two uneven burnt umber stripes.

'Ridiculous,' Jane fumed as she led him into the kitchen and switched on the cappuccino machine. 'Coffee?'

'No thanks, I've just had tea.' Once again he resolved to move things around as he watched her glide from cupboard to cupboard collecting the necessaries. He would reduce the clinical neatness in the kitchen too.

They sat at the table. Jane took a deep breath then began. 'I'm here to talk about one thing, but before I begin I must comment on Rachel's appalling behaviour. She's still refusing to speak to me. I think you're at least in part responsible, David.'

'Me? I don't quite see how.'

'You could talk to her, she listens to you.'

'Jane, she's your daughter as well as mine. It's you

she's angry with so it's up to you to sort it out. I'm not getting involved.'

Jane frowned. She wasn't used to resistance from her soon to be ex-husband. 'Well that isn't why I've come over. Jim and I are planning a holiday and we'd like to tie going away with getting married. We need to push ahead sorting out finances and then the divorce.'

'Fine by me. I want to get moving too,' he said, based on what he'd decided when lying in bed at Bridget's house. That was over two weeks ago. They had spoken several times since, but had yet to meet up again.

'Good,' Jane said with a degree of suspicion. 'I've made a list of what I think are our assets and my solicitor suggests we have a fifty-fifty split.'

She handed him word-processed sheets and David glanced at what was written. There were appropriate sub-headings. Some of the items on the list indicated an input from Jim or her solicitor because Jane had never shown enough interest in financial matters to identify things like Cash ISAs, fixed and variable rate savings accounts, government and corporate bonds, shares and premium bonds. Jane's contribution clearly kicked in with possessions in the home. These were catalogued in intricate detail with estimates of values added in a second column.

At the bottom of the sheet the house was dealt with. '*To be retained by David until children reach school leaving age and then either sold and the price less any remaining mortgage split or David hands over a sum equivalent to 50% of the value of the house as agreed by two independent estate agents.'*

David looked up. Jane spoke before he could comment. 'Jim thinks everything is covered but says you must add anything else we own. It's your responsibility to be honest about this.'

'I'm not quite sure what Jim has to do with it.'

‘He’s my partner – we share things.’

David paused to contain rising anger and succeeded in remaining detached. ‘There are a couple of things that come to mind. Who pays the mortgage while I’m living here with the children? And do you intend to contribute towards the children’s upbringing?’

‘Not for Rachel the way she’s behaving.’

‘Let’s assume that’s a short-term issue.’

‘I’ll need to speak to my solicitor about it. And Jim, too.’

‘Yes, you do that. Actually this list isn’t very far removed from the one I’ve been putting together with my solicitor. I’m surprised you haven’t received it yet because I authorised him to send it a few days ago.’

‘You have a solicitor?’

‘Yes.’

‘I thought we could do this amicably, David.’

‘But you have a solicitor so I need one too. It’s only fair.’ The expression on Jane’s face didn’t suggest fairness was high on her list of considerations. ‘I’m sure you’ll get the letter soon, I want this sorted as much as you do. Look, I must get going before the roller dries out. I hope to get started on the bedroom today, too. Put the mug in the dishwasher on your way out, please.’

‘The bedroom? Why, we only did it last year?’

‘I think it needs a warmer colour than Apple White. I’ve chosen Redcurrant Glory.’

‘Red!’

‘It’s more purple than red.’

With a shake of the head and a sigh Jane left.

David hadn’t decided on the bedroom colour and had no intention of starting to decorate it that day. It just seemed like good fun to wind Jane up. However, he painted with less enthusiasm now; the conversation with Jane had depressed him. Although he’d tackled the financial separation with gusto, the thought of the next step, divorce, filled him with trepidation.

Having applied the second coat he was left with a room that was dark and perhaps overwhelming. Why had he done it? To be like Bridget? To make him more attractive based on wall colour?

His confidence waned. The telephone conversations with Bridget over the past two weeks had been friendly enough, but she'd declined his suggestions for meeting, claiming children and work prevented any socialising.

Later that afternoon, while checking his emails, he clicked on a lastminute.com message that advertised secret theatre seat deals. He took the risk and booked two tickets for the following Thursday. *Chicago* came up. Next he called Bridget and asked if she'd like to come along to the show. She agreed.

'It's not high culture,' he apologised.

'I'm OK with low culture,' she replied.

'But what about no culture?'

Chapter Seventeen

'Thanks for that, David. It was fun. And I love these old theatres.'

They made their way towards the exit from the third row in the stalls, their super seat at the Garrick Theatre.

'I enjoyed it too. I needed a bit of escapism; it's cheered me up no end. Fancy a drink before we head back?'

'Not tonight, I don't like getting home late when the kids are alone. I've got a busy day at work tomorrow, too. I'm setting up an exhibition for a new artist at the gallery.'

Bridget had an impressive knowledge of the geography of Central London. With authoritative strides she led David through tiny lanes and alleyways as they made their way to the Underground. Kitts Yard gave David the impression that they were in a time warp. It was a long passageway devoid of cars, each side housing two-storey brick warehouses that had seen better days. Old-fashioned street lights provided a hazy, yellowish glow. Remarkable such a place existed just a stone's throw away from the affluence and bustle of the West End.

They walked in silence, comfortable with each other's company and content to soak up the atmosphere.

'You two. Stop!' growled a voice. They turned to see a shape in the shadows, leaning against a dustbin that was overflowing and surrounded by loose rubbish piled high. His hoodie dispelled the Victorian ambiance.

Without the need for consultation, Bridget and David took the sensible decision to continue walking with a quickened step, but the tall, stocky man stepped out in front of them.

He stood close to David, blocking his path. 'You 'eard me. I said stop,' he yelled, presenting David with an unpleasant combination of stale beer and body odour. 'I want your stuff.'

David was affronted that their peaceful walk had been disturbed. Commendably, he had absolutely no fear of danger.

'What stuff?' he jibed.

'What d'you mean 'what stuff'? All your stuff – yer money, yer phone, yer cards,' the assailant screamed into David's face. He turned to Bridget with a slightly softer tone as if in deference to her femininity. 'And yours.'

'I've got a watch, would you like that, too? It's good quality. Sekonda,' David teased as he lifted up his wrist to exhibit a silver timepiece with a black leather strap. He glanced at Bridget, who was looking at him with incredulity.

'Don't mess with me. Hand yer valuables over. Now!' His voice had somehow increased in volume from the previous scream.

'There's no need to shout.' David was enjoying this fearless flippancy.

'What?' he shrieked as he grabbed David by the lapels.

'I said there's no need to shout.'

David's attitude was not welcomed by Bridget. 'Let him have what he wants and let's go,' she suggested.

'I'm only advising him not to shout, Bridget.' David turned to face the man, their noses touching. 'It's not good for your health.'

The attacker was somewhat taken aback by his victim's concern and their noses disengaged. David continued. 'If you act like this it'll give you high blood pressure. Do you get heart palpitations?'

'Do I what?'

'Does your heart thump when you're robbing people? You know you could have a stroke if you're not careful.

And that's not to mention the potential damage to your vocal cords …'

The last thing David heard before he hit the floor was 'Don't you take the piss with me.' He was vaguely aware of his jacket being opened and things taken out, then being rolled onto his stomach and his wallet lifted from the back pocket of his trousers. As he regained a sense of the now, he saw Bridget surrender her handbag to the man. They both looked down at David.

'Scumbag,' the man spat, before giving David a light-hearted farewell kick to the ribs and heading off.

Bridget was left kneeling down by his side. David was all set to tell her what a cheek it was being called a scumbag by a man who was one hell of a scumbag himself. He wanted to make light of the whole incident, to jump up and head off to the Underground in the hope the thief hadn't taken their tickets. It was a disappointment to discover he was unable to sit, let alone jump up, and he couldn't speak.

Two observations flashed through his mind ahead of passing out.

This was the second occasion in their relatively short time together that Bridget had seen him punched and floored.

And this punch was substantially more forceful than the one Ben Carpenter had dispensed at the reunion.

David regained consciousness as the ambulance was pulling up at the hospital. He was lying on a bed and the left side of his face was excruciatingly painful, a dull thud running from his temple through his ear and down to his chin. He lifted his hand to his face and traced a bandage wrapped up and around his head. It was fastened with a bow. Realisation of how ridiculous he must have looked brought back the memory of what had happened. He lifted his head to see if Bridget was still with him.

'Best to keep your head still, sir.' He glanced sideways to the blur of a powder blue uniform. 'We're all set to get you out.'

'Gigget?' he enquired, now concerned for her well-being. His flippancy had put her in danger too.

'Yes, I'm here, David. Everything's OK.'

'Garldy, I gug look rigigulus.'

'No, you look fine.'

David was impressed with Bridget's language skills. However he wasn't sure whether he was glad she was with him or not. It wasn't going to do much for his I-am-a-cool-man-who-you-want-to-have-a-relationship-with image.

By now the door was open and he was being stretchered off the vehicle. He looked up to a modern, attractive high rise with lots of glass and very little concrete visible.

'Gare ar gee?'

'Pardon, sir?' the paramedic asked.

'University College Hospital, David.' Bridget's interpretation skills again impressed him, but aware that he sounded absurd, he decided not to test them further.

The A&E reception was immaculately designed and maintained. The staff were impeccably dressed, polite and efficient. What a pity about the patients. Being late evening in Central London, the place was heaving with patients who were either drunk or on drugs or both. Judging by appearances, they had overdone it to the extent of inflicting self-harm or subjecting others to their uncontrolled aggression. Two policemen were on guard, twice having to intervene to break up fights in the short period before David was seen.

A nurse assessed the severity of the damage and commissioned an X-ray.

'Good news,' she said when she returned a short while later. She held the X-ray aloft. 'The doctor says it's a dislocation, not a fracture.'

'Guy is gat getter?'

'Exactly,' answered the uncomprehending nurse. 'The doctor will be in to see you soon.'

The next half hour was not pleasant. He was given two injections to numb the pain and then had to sit up while a doctor juggled with his face, using his thumbs to push David's cheeks this way and that. He was told that this was to get his face back to the right shape. Then on went another bandage with the bow on top.

At this point Bridget was called in for the discussion about next steps. A prescription was issued to provide anti-inflammatories and muscle relaxants. He was then presented with an eating and drinking regime of liquids and blended soft foods for the next two weeks. Even yawning and sneezing were covered. The doctor, a stout bearded fellow with a Scottish accent, simulated a yawn to demonstrate how David would need to support his jaw with his hands to prevent over stretching. And there was Bridget witnessing all this demeaning dialogue. Are they going to cover pooing and farting next, David wondered.

But that was it. The doctor stood. 'Well, I'm finished. I'd better tackle some of the lovelies waiting out there.'

'Gank oo. Go I neeg to cun gack?'

'Pardon?'

'He's asking if he needs to come back.'

'No, we'll write to his GP and a visit there will suffice.'

By now David had become aware of a further embarrassment – he was drooling. Saliva was gushing out his mouth and down his chin, to be soaked up by the bottom of the bandage.

Standing by the door to the cubicle, the doctor turned to look at David. 'You're a lucky man,' he said. 'With a good woman like this to look after you, you'll be fine.'

The good woman took him home in a taxi and spent time explaining to Rachel and Sam what care would be needed. She then ordered a second taxi to take her home.

'I'll call you tomorrow, David. Look after yourself.'

'Gank oo, Gigget. Solly agout togite.'

Chapter Eighteen

The next day Rachel took time off school to care for David.

By the time he woke she had Googled 'diet for dislocated jaw' and David entered a kitchen that resembled a food factory. She had been to the supermarket. Orange juice, soda water, yoghurt, bouillon cubes, and a large container of straws were lined up on one of the counters. The liquidiser stood on another work surface. Fortunately this was not one of the items Jane had decided to commandeer because it was to prove very useful over the following week or so. Next to it were potatoes, vegetables, cottage cheese, apple puree, two pots of organic baby food, bananas, and a large cube of tofu.

'Wow, ganks, Gachel.'

'That's OK, Dad. I'll be an expert before long.' She lifted up the tofu. 'I wouldn't dream of touching this muck normally, but I read that you need lots of protein and this is good because it's soft. We can invite Bridget and her children round to share it, it's bound to be one of their favourites.'

'Very gunny.'

'Seriously though, everything needs to be blended. I thought for breakfast you could have tea and a fruit smoothie, then maybe vegetable soup for lunch and mashed spaghetti for dinner.'

She made the tea and smoothie and handed him two straws.

After breakfast David sat in the lounge feeling sorry for himself. The burnt umber ambience didn't go well with a thumping headache and a sore jaw; the painkillers might be helping but not enough.

Mid-morning there was a knock on the front door.

Rachel came into the lounge followed by a policeman and woman. The hospital had informed the Mill Hill constabulary about the attack and the two officers had been sent to interview David ahead of writing a report and opening a crime investigation. The recording process was slow since unlike Bridget, these two were unable to understand what he was saying. He had to write down answers to their questions and the policewoman then copied them onto an electronic notepad. David was of the opinion that it didn't matter what was written as the chance of anyone being caught was nil. He was given a crime number which at least would be useful in making an insurance claim.

Over the next few days the large pack of straws was used up in the consumption of mushy concoctions. Gradually Rachel thickened the consistency of the meals and within a week he was able to eat using a teaspoon. During that time he had visits from Bridget (twice), Jane with Jim (once), and Jabulani (once).

He was ready to go back to work the following Monday, ten days after the attack. Rachel provided precise instructions about what he was allowed to consume. She had been a tremendous help even though he had to put up with a large dose of teasing.

He'd forgotten this Monday was the date for his annual staff review. He found an email reminder prefixed by a High Importance exclamation mark. At 9.55 a.m. he made his way down the corridor to Mary's office. Today she was French Sophisticate with a navy and beige hooped jumper, chocolate brown pencil skirt, and hair in a ponytail.

Her office said quite a bit about Mary. At an exact forty-five degree angle on the corner of the large desk was a framed photo of herself in ski gear. No children, boyfriend, or husband in sight. Her plant of choice was cactus, a line of five were evenly placed across her windowsill. A good plant for her, he reckoned – sharp, aggressive, arid. Art work on her walls comprised of two certificates, her first class degree diploma and a Price Waterhouse Coopers Employee of the Month award. Books and files were stacked immaculately on shelves. As he sat down, David had the urge to disturb the tidy column of A4 sheets in front of him.

She droned on about the purpose of the staff review, how it gave both parties the opportunity to step back from everyday activity to reflect on the past year's achievements and to consider objectives for the following year. *Yes, Mary*, David thought, *I do know all this. I have conducted staff appraisals for over twenty years.*

'Nice cacti,' he remarked when she'd stopped.

'Oh, thank you. But let's get started. I forgot to mention something, David. This is very much a two-way process and you're welcome to provide feedback about my performance. And everything said is just between us.'

In assessing his effectiveness at work including his level of enthusiasm and motivation, Mary revealed her two main concerns. She was unsure whether he was managing his team well and she feared family issues were impacting on performance. Although furious that his family was up for discussion, this being totally out of order, David declined to raise an objection.

His answers were monosyllabic.

Did he think he could improve his team's awareness of budget restraints?

'Yes.'

Might it be possible for family affairs to be kept out of the workplace?

'Yes.'

For instance, were his children able to travel home from school alone?

This line of questioning was unacceptable for a

manager to ask – he could report her to Human Resources. But what the hell. He plodded on, responding with indifference.

'Yes.'

And so it went on.

She set his objectives for the following year to include taking part in a course on interpersonal skills for financial managers and an in-house training session entitled Dealing With Awkward Customers.

Isn't it more a case of dealing with awkward line managers? David would have liked to ask.

'Mary, I'm OK with customers, they're never awkward when I speak to them.'

'You're wrong there, David. Some have insisted on speaking directly to me because they want access to the head of department. When I confirm they aren't going to get the funding they expected they become very awkward indeed.'

'That's because we keep changing, or should I say reducing, what they're entitled to.'

'That's beside the point. Irrespective of the reason, they *are* awkward.'

And so it went on, Mary not accepting any counter arguments.

After a pointless forty-five minutes she concluded. 'So I *am* putting down this training session as an action. I want you to do it.' She was taking notes as she spoke; she didn't look up to gauge his reaction. 'Well, I think that's about it, David. Thank you.' There was an obvious candidate in the room for a course on interpersonal skills for financial managers and it wasn't him.

Her handwriting was neat, tiny and jet black, in sharp contrast to the turquoise swirls and loops on the get well card that Bridget had sent him. It had a picture of a person swathed in bandages; only the left foot was exposed. Even the face was covered bar tiny gaps for mouth, eyes, and the base of the nose. A doctor stood by the side of the bed, speaking to a nurse as they gazed down at the foot. 'Good to see so much improvement in only a week.' Bridget had written *To David, my hero – but perhaps best not to take on a mugger next time! Love Bridget.*

Mary was talking. 'David, are you listening? I said I nearly forgot to ask. Is there anything you'd like to discuss about my performance?' She glanced at her watch before turning to her computer screen.

'Yes there is, Mary. To be truthful, it's awful. You treat me like an idiot and are more patronising than I would ever dream of being to my own children. I know you've been on lots of management courses because you're forever telling me. I'm just surprised that with all your training you don't recognise that you can get more from your staff by motivating rather than trying to terrorise them.'

Mary was pleasantly speechless. David continued. 'I'd like my comment recorded in your notes, please.'

'Yes, I will. And thank you for your frankness, David – I'll reflect on what you've said. If I appear forceful it's only because there's so much needing to be done here.'

To David that comment confirmed her failure to listen – her attitude was ingrained. He stood up and extended his hand. 'I've enjoyed the discussion, thank you for your time, Mary.' He grabbed the hand coming up to meet his own and deliberately shook it with considerable force.

He went straight into the small kitchen to make a cup of coffee. Once there, he took a plastic bag out of his jacket pocket and extracted a digestive biscuit. Rachel had allowed him to bring these on condition that he dunked them to make them softer. He used to keep his biscuits in one of the cupboards in the room, but they got pinched at an alarming rate so now he stored his regular supply in a desk drawer in his own office.

Jabulani entered and strode towards him, grabbing hold of both of David's hands. For a man who always had a broad smile, this one was gargantuan. 'My news is wonderful. I've been waiting for you to come out of your meeting, I can't sit still.'

'What is it?'

'My brother is alive! We received a call yesterday evening from France.'

'Fantastic. What happened?'

'It was all solved with money. The prison guards were bribed by some of my brother's colleagues at hospital. I'm so very glad, but for others it was terrible. The police had to produce a body to fool their officers so someone else was brought into custody and murdered with the pretence that it was Farai.'

'My God! Great news for you, but unbelievable that things like that can happen.'

'I'm ashamed that that is what goes on there now.'

'What will your brother do?'

'He'll soon be in England with his family. He worked with an English doctor in Zimbabwe and the man has told him he can organise a work permit for the hospital where he's based. It's in London, Stepney, so we'll be neighbours.'

'Stepney to Queensbury isn't quite neighbours.'

'No, but it is more neighbour than Zimbabwe to England or heaven to earth.'

Jabulani talked about his love for his elder brother, reminiscing about their childhood in happier times, how they both sang and played guitar, and now they would be able to make music together again.

As David reached his desk his mobile rang. It was Bridget. There was a showing of the reworked *Brief Encounter* at the Phoenix in East Finchley and would he like to go on Saturday. Both of them had identified it as one of their favourites when they'd talked about films at the Greek restaurant. They agreed to meet outside the cinema then chatted on. David had mentioned Jabulani and the trip to Harrods and now he was able to give her the good news about his brother.

'And wasn't it your staff review today?' she continued.

'Yes, 'fraid so.'

'Didn't it go well then?'

'I decided to tell her what I thought, I reckoned what the hell. I'm restless here, Bridget, and if I'm forced to leave then so be it. I'm going to investigate this idea I have about opening a café.'

'They can't kick you out because of what you say in a staff review. Must go, a customer's come in. We can talk about it on Saturday.'

Chapter Nineteen

David wiped away the silent tears with the back of his hand as the credits rolled for *Brief Encounter*. He looked across at Bridget, who was dabbing her eyes with a tissue.

She gave him a watery smile. 'Daft, aren't we?'

'It's powerful stuff.'

They left the cinema, crossed the road, and stepped into The Five Bells. It was noisy and young so they did an about turn and walked on. They reached The Alexandra which was also crowded but quieter with an older clientele. Bridget grabbed a table by the window that was in the process of being vacated while David got the drinks.

Bridget was the first to speak. 'My two are out tonight. A rare invite to a party for Andy and an even rarer acceptance, and one of Kay's friends has got a sleepover.'

'Mine are out, too.'

'Then you could invite me round to see the new colour on your walls.'

David considered whether his principal long term objective, two if the flippant repeat one was included, was about to be achieved. Excitement and nervousness surged.

'With pleasure, I'd love to.'

They had a second drink then walked to East Finchley Underground. They'd chosen public transport to get to the cinema having decided to go for a drink after the film. The journey to Mill Hill East was just a few stops on the Northern Line. Bridget took hold of David's hand as they sat on the platform waiting for a train.

The carriage they entered was near empty; it was too early for the young pub goers to be heading home. Almost opposite them sat a shabbily dressed old lady. She had a large, paisley handbag on her lap and they watched with curiosity as she rummaged through the plentiful contents. She took out a buff-coloured envelope and extracted a letter written on matching paper. She began to read it. David glanced at the neat, old-fashioned script. There were three sheets which she no more than skim read before folding them carefully inside the envelope and placing it back in her bag. Then she pulled the letter out again and re-read it, this time more slowly. As she did so she sighed then began to cry.

Bridget stood, walked across the passageway and sat by her side. 'Can I help you?'

The woman looked up startled. 'No dear, it's something I've got to deal with all by myself.'

With great compassion Bridget eked out her story. Of a beloved husband who had died having completed this, his final letter, while wasting away in a hospital bed. He had passed away on the very day of their sixty-seventh wedding anniversary. That morning the lady had made a carrot cake, his favourite, to celebrate the occasion. But by the time she arrived the curtains had been drawn around his bed and a nurse greeted her with the news. Bridget consoled her with talk of the importance of memories. She spoke of her love for her own father and the pain of the loss.

'Is that your husband?' the old lady asked, looking across at David.

'No,' Bridget replied, 'but he's a very good friend.'

The woman refolded the buff sheets, fitted them back inside the envelope, and then placed it in her bag. Bridget supported her as she struggled to stand up. 'Well, home I go to start my new life,' she said, able to produce a watery smile. 'Thank you, dear, you're very kind.'

She looked across at David. 'And you're a lucky young man to have this woman.'

'I know.'

The train stopped and the fellow passenger left. Bridget sat down next to David in the now deserted carriage.

'Not much point sitting, Bridget. We're at High Barnet, it's the end of the line.'

'I thought Mill Hill was the last station.'

'We were meant to switch trains to the branch line a while back, but we missed the stop.'

'Oh, God, I am sorry. I got carried away chatting to the poor soul.'

'Nothing to be sorry about. As she said, you were so very kind.'

They stood up and exited the train.

Bridget continued to chat as they walked. 'Well I don't know about being kind, I didn't like seeing her upset. Shall I tell you something? The Underground drives me up the wall. Whatever's happening, passengers ignore each other. If you speak to someone they look at you as if you're mad. A few days ago the woman next to me was reading *Fingersmith* which I'd just finished. I told her I'd loved it and she turned her back on me. It's not as if I look threatening, is it?'

'No, you don't look threatening.' David put a hand on her shoulder, pulled her closer, and kissed her. It made his jaw ache but was worth the pain. They stood close together for a while.

'Come on, let's cross platforms and head back to your place.'

As they walked, a rush of intense affection hit David. Bridget's physical beauty was matched by a personality he had grown to love in such a short time. Her brief conversation with the old lady and the passing comments about the Underground typified her good nature. The kindness and compassion. The strong views about what was right and what was wrong with the world.

Half an hour later they were in David's house and Bridget was complimenting his choice of paint in the lounge.

'Orange is my favourite colour,' she exclaimed.

'I've started the bedroom too,' he said. 'I've only done one wall so far. I'm considering whether to do the others the same colour or whether that would be too much.'

'Well, we'd better have a look then, hadn't we?'

Up the stairs they went, David's heart pounding. He'd painted the wall behind the bed Redcurrant Glory and Bridget indicated approval before turning to face him. Now it was she who began the kissing, having placed her arms around his waist.

'I love you, Bridget,' he whispered.

Bridget took off her cardigan and dropped it to the floor. 'Let's get undressed.'

David began to unbutton his shirt. 'Here, let me help,' Bridget said. She flicked her tongue over his chest as she undid each one.

'My turn to assist, ma'am.' Now David took off Bridget's blouse, mimicking the licking before planting a delicate kiss on the erect nipple visible through her bra.

As he was undoing his belt there was a strong vibration inside his trousers. It was his phone which he'd set on silent before the film had started. His inclination was to ignore it, but weekend calls were from his children and he felt duty-bound to look at the screen.

Bridget was down to her underwear, her knickers matching the pretty, lacy bra. As David lifted the phone out his pocket she was in the process of unhooking her bra.

'Hello, Sam,' he said as her bra fell to the floor to reveal a miraculous development for the woman who had once been known as 'Titless'. The sight of her breasts inevitably caused an erection, though having Sam on the other end of the telephone presented an interesting counterbalance. If a penis could ever have a mind of its own and be confused then this was it. At that instant the force in favour of erection was winning, but as the conversation developed shrinkage took over.

Sam had had a massive bust up with Adrian and they had come to blows.

'Can't you make up, Sam, at least stay on until the morning … the problem is I can't drive because I've been drinking … that's kind of Adrian's mother … you've already left … in Cranbrook Drive, OK see you in about five minutes … bye, Sam.'

Bridget had caught the gist of the conversation and was getting dressed.

David must have had a look of distraught dismay on his face because Bridget burst out laughing. 'Poor you, but it's not a disaster, there'll be another opportunity. Actually I quite enjoy doing a striptease when the audience is on the phone to one of his children. Is there a bed for me? You'd better show me where it is before Sam gets back.'

As David was taking Bridget into Rachel's room the front door opened. 'I'm up here, Sam,' David called out. 'Bridget's upstairs too, she's staying tonight. We'll come down.'

As they walked downstairs, Bridget put a hand on David's shoulder. 'Persevere and you'll get me,' she whispered.

In the kitchen Bridget watched as David cleaned up Sam's cut lip. She remained in the room as an irate David threatened to call Adrian's parents there and then. Sam reassured him that he gave as good as he got and that things like that happened between friends. Finally David relented and the three of them went upstairs together.

Alone in his bed, David considered getting Bridget into his bedroom when Sam was asleep. But he decided against it and slept happily, knowing it was merely a case of having to wait a little while longer.

He woke refreshed and went downstairs to prepare breakfast. To his surprise he heard the front door open. It was only nine, far too early for Rachel's return. Jane entered the kitchen.

She was carrying a brown A4 envelope and came straight to the point. 'Thanks for sending me those documents, David. I agree with everything you've suggested. To speed things up my solicitor thought I should come round to get you to sign the papers rather than doing it via your solicitor.'

'Leave them on the table in the hall and I'll have a look at them later.'

'I was hoping you'd sign them now then I can take them back with me.'

'Sorry, no time.'

'Why are you being obstructive? You haven't changed your mind about the settlement, have you?'

'No. I've told you, I just haven't got time now.'

'What's so important to stop you getting this sorted?'

Bridget was standing by the kitchen door. She was wearing the Simpsons T-shirt David had lent her. The family were in a line smiling, Homer was holding baby Maggie who was looking up in admiration at her frazzled father.

'Probably me.' She stepped into the room. 'You must be Jane, I've heard so much about you.'

'Who are you? This is my house, you're in my house.'

David laughed. 'I think you're being silly, Jane, bearing in mind the circumstances.'

'Are the children here?'

'Sam is.'

'Well then I think this is different to my situation. Having a woman stay here isn't fair on the children.'

'I'll be the judge of that. They've met Bridget before and they like her. Perhaps it's best if you leave now.'

'How you've changed, David. And I don't like what I see.'

'Well you didn't like the old me either, so what's new.'

Bridget stepped forward. ‘I’m starving, any chance of breakfast?’ She took hold of David’s hand.

Jane stood her ground for a few seconds, looking from David to Bridget then back to David again. ‘OK, I get the message, I’m going.’

‘I’ll look at your papers later. Would you leave them on the hall table?’

Jane turned and left the room. They heard a thud as the thick envelope was dropped on the table, followed soon afterwards by her customary slamming of the front door.

Chapter Twenty

Bridget was keen to get home before her children so immediately after breakfast David drove her back. Their conversation was subdued as they chatted about what was not to be the night before and their morning meeting with Jane. Bridget was stoic and saw the funny side, David wasn't and didn't.

'Thanks David, I enjoyed yesterday,' Bridget said when the car had pulled up outside her house. 'Take care, I'll see you soon.'

David moved towards her in an attempt to kiss her. Bridget backed away. 'Not a great idea if you don't mind. I've got some very nosy neighbours.' She opened the door and got out. He watched as she walked up the driveway. She turned and waved before closing her front door.

David's thoughts were all over the place as he drove home. There was a sense of joy that a relationship with Bridget was imminent despite last night's frustration. When Jane informed Bridget that it was her house and she had no right to be there he'd been furious. But now he found himself facing up to mixed emotions as he reminisced about the time when he and Jane had been so close.

They'd rented a flat together about a year after meeting and had worked hard to make their first home attractive with furniture from Habitat and wallpaper from Laura Ashley. It was here that Rachel was conceived, the pregnancy coming quicker than planned. They'd talked about buying a bigger home before having children and would have liked more opportunity to save for the deposit needed, but the delight of a forthcoming child far exceeded financial concerns.

He couldn't deny that Jane had been an ideal partner. David still remembered the wonderful words that Jane had uttered on their way home after the doctor had confirmed her pregnancy. 'A child with you is my greatest dream come true.' She was a light-hearted counter to his rather serious self. Somehow that part of her personality had withered away over the years.

During the pregnancy the topic of moving house frequently cropped up; they wanted more space and a garden for their child. Jane scanned the local paper and made appointments to view houses. One Saturday morning, less than eleven weeks before Rachel was due, they saw their dream home. They sensed it as soon as they walked inside the 1930s semi with original art-deco features, much concealed by appalling renovation. David did the financial calculations for buying the property while Jane worked out what would be needed to update it and at what cost.

'£20,000 would more than do for the deposit and refurbishment,' David announced.

'What's the gap?'

'We've only got about £11,000 saved.'

'Let's ask the parents for a loan.'

One evening the following week Jane's parents and David's mother were brought together for a lasagne followed by cherry sponge with ice cream, washed down with two expensive bottles of Chardonnay. The trio hadn't sat comfortably together at previous meetings. David's dour mother didn't respond well to the frivolity of the couple. On this occasion it was worsened by the obvious tension between Jane's parents. Her father's cutting sarcasm was matched by her mother's snide remarks. They announced their separation soon afterwards.

Jane brushed aside the friction and addressed the issue as soon as her father had complimented her on the cherry sponge.

'David and I have been thinking things through, what with the baby on its way. We're keen to buy a house so we can have a garden. Trouble is, we haven't got enough for a deposit and we were wondering if you could help. Just a loan, though we don't know when we'll be able to repay you.' David appreciated that Jane was far better at getting straight to the point than he and was happy to let her do the talking.

And she did get her way on this, easily and quickly.

'See what's around and how much you need then we'll see what we can do to help,' her father had suggested.

'We know what we want, we've seen our dream house. But we need to act now in case someone else snaps it up. We're £9,000 short.'

The parents agreed to split the burden equally, with an unwritten commitment to be paid back as and when. David had been unsure whether his mother would be able to afford anything, but she was happy to contribute her share.

The house was vacant, the current owner having separated from her husband and moved closer to her sister in Surrey. As a result, contracts could be exchanged quickly. That gave David and Jane a month to reshape the house before the birth and, to her credit, Jane contributed with astounding energy considering her state.

Yes, she'd been right to say it was her house. There was much evidence of her influence in it. He could understand her discomfort and resentment in seeing another woman there. But surely he shouldn't be feeling in any way sorry for her, bearing in mind it had been her decision to leave.

He had reached home. He parked in the drive and switched off the engine, but remained in the car as he struggled to figure out when there had been the first indication that all was not right with their relationship. There were many milestones to draw upon as evidence of closeness. The first meeting at a university disco and then together pretty well every day and many nights towards the end of his final year at university. Visits every weekend during the year when David had started working and Jane was still studying. Naturally still close when they married. Rachel and Sam's births. Coping with the helter-skelter of joyous and scary events during the early childhood years. The same wavelength until ... until when? David had thought things were still fine during their holiday in Brittany. Clearly that was not the case.

And how quickly things were shifting for David, because he now felt completely detached from his wife.

When Jabulani had popped into his office the previous week he'd talked about how he'd always been close to his brother. But during the time when he thought he was dead that closeness had strengthened and the loss had felt unbearably painful. He referred to the wisdom of the saying 'absence makes the heart grow fonder'.

By contrast, although David had been equally close to his wife, only months after she walked out he didn't miss her.

'You know, there's another saying suggesting the complete opposite. 'Out of sight out of mind'. I'll tell you what, Jabulani, at times in the not too distant past it was like we were telepathic, our relationship was that strong. Now when I see her she's like a stranger. The detachment hasn't developed gradually, it's been as sudden as a cliff edge. I feel that I have nothing in common with her. How on earth can that be the case?'

There was a pause for thought before Jabulani replied. 'I think people are like onions. We have a multitude of layers, in our case layers of personality. You think you know someone inside out, then they strip off a layer or two and you don't know the new person at all.'

'An interesting idea,' David replied. 'I'll tell you something, I think that applies to me. At my age I'd expect my behaviour to be set, but in a new situation with a new person I'm behaving completely differently.'

'There are lots of layers, David. You might carry on shedding them until the day you die. You can put them back too as problems are resolved.'

'That would be great.'

'I assume you're thinking of your new woman.'

'Not quite my new woman yet, but very close to it I hope.'

'I hope so, too. You deserve happiness.'

David looked at his watch; he'd been sitting in the stationary car for over half an hour. He got out and went indoors.

How would the onion analogy pan out with Bridget? His passion for her seemed stronger than what he had ever felt for Jane, though this might be a trick of memory. Surely the current lust had been there for Jane in the early days even if he couldn't recall it now. And if it had been there for Jane and it was now forgotten, what long term hope was there for the survival of any new relationship? Would Bridget become the current Jane – distant, stale, and forgotten as further layers of his onion were discarded?

Chapter Twenty-one

He had failed by a whisker to achieve APMLTO4 and maybe even APMLTO5 the previous night, but he was confident that success was imminent. At least he would be able to get number one out of the way today. Hardly compensation, but better than nothing.

Medium/Long term objectives

1. Take a cookery course (APMLTO1)

Sam was watching television, a repeat of one of the Attenborough nature programmes. David came in and sat down next to him. They gazed in awe as male penguins huddled together in the freezing Antarctic, delicately balancing eggs on their webbed feet in anticipation of the return of their mates as soon as the weather improved.

'Oh, Rachel phoned,' Sam announced as a female polar bear was introducing her two cubs to the harshness of the Arctic. 'She'll be back some time this afternoon.'

When the programme was over Sam switched off the television and headed off to do homework. David started to prepare food and within ten minutes was calling out. 'Sam, lunch is ready.'

His son came into the kitchen. 'That's quick, what are we having?'

'Welsh rarebits.'

Sam didn't look enthusiastic. 'Shouldn't it be a roast, it's Sunday.'

'No time, because guess what I'm off to do this afternoon? A cookery class.'

'That's a good idea.'

'Except I thought Rachel would be back by now. Will you be OK at home by yourself?'

‘I’m not a baby.’

The phone rang and Sam got to it first. The conversation was brief. ‘That was Rachel. She’s staying over at Hannah’s again tonight, it’s one of their friend’s birthdays.’

‘Oh, maybe I should cancel then. I don’t want to leave you alone for hours.’

‘Don’t be silly, I’m thirteen, I’ll be fine. I’ve got loads of homework to do.’

Satisfied that Sam would cope, David headed off to the local further education college to take part in the half-day *Learn to Cook – Anyone Can Do* It course. The promotional information made the claim that the course would provide instant confidence in buying the right ingredients; perfect preparation; high-quality cooking including the making of sauces; tips on how to serve up in style; and if time, an insight into dessert making. Presumably without the pun intended, it was described as a ‘taster’ course, with discounts offered for follow-ups: *Great Grilling and Roasting*, *Simple Italian*, *Cup Cake Champion*, and *Fantastic Fish*.

David thought the promise of what would be delivered during a single afternoon session was well over the top, but having surfed the internet for ages he had selected this course because it was the nearest to home.

The roads were Sunday-clear and in less than fifteen minutes he was walking through near deserted corridors on his way to the kitchen classroom. The room itself was a fabulous facility with no expense spared. In fact the whole college was an impressively designed new build opened a little over two years earlier at a cost of sixteen million pounds. There had been a lot of money to spend ahead of the stringent government cuts.

He was the first to arrive. Before long there were eight of them, four men and four women, standing around waiting for their tutor to appear. Conversation progressed from name introductions to 'what made you come to this?' He discovered two men were in a similar position to him, newly separated or divorced. Stephen was keen to develop the quality of what he could offer his children when it was their turn. Luke's children were aged three and six and they stayed with him every other weekend. He claimed their mother brought them up on a diet of pizza, beans, and chips and he wanted to improve on that. The fourth man was Nathan. He had a burly physique and tattoos covering his arms. He was a car mechanic who wanted a career change to chef.

The four women varied in age from late teens to old age pensioner. The teen, a confident girl called Tanya, talked about how much she enjoyed cooking but claimed that what they were told to prepare in school was dead boring. The oldest lady, Mildred, was looking for something of interest now she had stopped work as a librarian; once she got talking it was hard to get her to stop. The two other women, both called Janet, were fed up providing the same old stuff over and over again for their families.

Robert, the professional chef engaged as the course tutor, was an instant hit. He started with funny stories about how he had been a hopeless cook at first. 'So if you feel culinarily challenged, join the club. There are millions out there like you, but the difference is that you're prepared to do something about it. Today I'm going to rock your socks off, or tights for the ladies. You're going to go home and shock your dinner companions, whether it's a would-be lover you want to impress or a rowdy gang of kids or,' he looked across to Brenda the pensioner, her grey hair permed with a hint of lilac rinse, 'to prove you're never too old to try something new.'

He announced the menu for today, seasonal vegetable soup with cheese croutons followed by pan-roasted free range chicken with tarragon and crème fraiche sauce. If time, there would be blueberry tart to follow.

Robert ended up with a round of applause and the participants with an impressive meal to take home. Before leaving, David booked into the Simple Italian course. This would be a six-week evening class led by Robert that started in January. Five of the other participants would be joining him.

By the time David got back to his car there was a light dusting of snow settling; perhaps it would be a White Christmas. Sam greeted him at the front door and followed him into the kitchen.

With a degree of pride David laid out his offering on the kitchen table.

'*Voila mon enfant, le diner.*'

'*Merci, Papa, c'est delicieux.*'

It was delicious, and Sam volunteered to try anything his father brought back from a cookery class.

David cleared away the dinner things. He was feeling high-spirited, the course had been an enjoyable success and there were more cookery lessons to come. The relationship with Bridget was burgeoning. And not to forget, every one of his short term objectives had been achieved. The feeling of absurdity in having put any action points down on paper had diminished – the process had given him direction. That being the case, now was the time to consider the feasibility of the two long term objectives yet to be confronted.

Medium/Long term objectives

2. Quit my job and pack in accountancy
3. Open an arts café

David thought he should get some advice. He knew all about business plans and with his accountancy background had sound financial knowledge. However this didn't make him an entrepreneur, not if the way some of his friends operated was anything to go by. Top of that list was Ross, who moved from project to project, indifferent to the threat of failure. He'd met Ross at university and they'd kept in irregular touch ever since, meeting every six months or so. Ross always had a new venture on the horizon. 'If this doesn't work I'll dump it and try something else' he would explain when David confronted him with all the what-ifs. He was a millionaire despite twice being declared bankrupt. The last time they'd spoken Ross was about to set up in online pet food sales, having already suffered one e-commerce woe when the dot com bubble burst and his online theatre ticket agency went under.

'Why would anyone want to buy their pet food online, Ross?'

'It'll be cheaper.'

'But what about delivery costs.'

'Well they won't see those until check out and people rarely cancel once they've got that far.'

David could never work out whether he liked or despised his ex-university friend. Ross could be ruthless, aggressive, and insensitive, but it was fun to spend an evening with him and at times he could be extremely kind-hearted. Like when he managed to get sought-after concert tickets for Rachel during her short period of obsession with Girls Aloud.

Jane knew Ross from their university days and joined in when they met up. She liked to bitch about the variety of women that Ross brought to their gatherings. There had been a lot of recent ammunition. About a year ago, with Wife Number Three present, the atmosphere had been deadly, a battle for which of the two of them could be the nastiest. David didn't know at the time, but Ross had been caught having an affair with a work colleague. It was this colleague who came along to the next get-together, an embarrassing evening with the couple entwined and eager to depart. When Ross phoned a few weeks later he told David that the work colleague had chosen her husband over him. But never mind because he was madly in love with a new woman. 'Woman' was a misleading descriptor – 'girl' would have been more appropriate. Ross had met Hazel at a drum and bass gig. It was Hazel who had accompanied him at their most recent meal out and David had expressed his shock to Jane on the way home. *Look*, she'd replied, *he's got money, she's got looks. Maybe it'll be fine.*

Nothing was fine when he called Ross to get his advice on the coffee bar.

David began by informing Ross that Jane had left him. Ross stated that it was all for the best since he'd always thought that she was stuck-up and frumpy. 'Let's face it,' he'd said, 'older men attract younger women. It's a man's market out there, David. See this as a great opportunity. And it never works the other way – older women are hung out to dry.' He treated women like his money-making ventures. You win some and you lose some and if you fail you move on.

David outlined his idea for a coffee bar and Ross laughed. 'You're hardly going to make your millions with that.'

'That's not the point.'

'Then what is the point? Setting up a new business is a big ask even if it's only a piddly little café. If that's what you want and you're serious about it, I am prepared to pop over and talk it through with you. But I can tell you now, it's a waste of time.'

David thought he would take up Ross's offer despite his dismissive tone. But beforehand he needed to work on the plan himself.

There he was with a blank pad and an unused pen in front of him and he was unclear where to start. He had no knowledge of anything to do with opening a café. His reasoning for this massive career change, at the outset clear, was now vague. He liked cafes but so what? That wasn't going to help. He also liked films but that didn't mean he was able to be an actor, director, or owner of a chain of cinemas.

He decided to begin by assessing need. Most cafes closed soon after the shops. For a while the town centres were near deserted and then the young descended to take possession of the high streets, moving between near-identical pubs with music blasting and bouncers at the door. The old were unwelcome in the vicinity, 'old' meaning anything over thirty let alone mid-forties like him. Some pubs might not be populated by the young, but these were often run down and uninviting. Wouldn't it be good to have a coffee bar open throughout the evening, a place to visit after cinema or theatre, a venue for events like concerts, poetry readings, book clubs, and art exhibitions?

David decided to run the idea past Bridget ahead of any consideration of things like location and costs. She would have an opinion about its viability. He doodled *Bridget, am I mad?* at the top of the page and was all set to put down his justifications when there was a ring at the doorbell.

Chapter Twenty-two

It was approaching eleven and the ring took him by surprise. Rachel had a key and no one else was expected at that hour of the day.

During the short walk from lounge to front door he'd deduced that it would be Jane and he was plotting how to keep any conversation brief. But it wasn't her, it was a policeman and policewoman, the pair who had interviewed him after his mugging. In between them was Rachel, propped up by her escorts.

'Good evening, Mr Willoughby. We've brought your daughter home,' the young woman said as she edged into the house, the snow on her jacket and hat melting and dripping onto the floor as she stepped inside.

'This way,' a shocked David gestured. Sam was out his room and on the landing peering through the wooden slats of the banister.

They led Rachel into the lounge where she slumped down onto the couch.

'Did you just push me? Don't you dare throw me down, I'm fragile,' Rachel growled.

She noticed David. 'Hi there, Dad.'

She looked round the room. 'Oh good, I'm home. But fuck these bloody orange walls, they'll make me be sick again.'

David turned to the two police officers who were standing there dripping. 'What happened?'

'Your daughter was staggering along the High Street with her friend, barely able to stand and exhibiting the sort of lewd behaviour that we don't tolerate,' the policeman said.

His companion continued. 'She was very close to being arrested, bearing in mind how aggressive she was when we started to ask questions. It's fortunate for her that her boyfriend was more cooperative. He told us their names after your daughter had refused to, then he let us know what the pair of them had had to drink. This young lady –'

Rachel butted in. 'I wasn't doing anything wrong. There can't be a law against having fun.'

'Be quiet, Rachel,' David ordered, but curiosity got the better of him. 'Who's this boyfriend of yours?'

'I'm not a kid, I can have a boyfriend. And if these stupid idiots had left me alone then –'

'Quiet,' he snapped.

'There's something I have to ask them. Mr and Mrs Police, what colour are these walls?'

'Don't be silly, Rachel.'

'It's a reasonable question.'

'Rachel!'

The policewoman removed her hat. Her jet black hair was in a tight bun. She used a handkerchief to wipe water off her brow before continuing. 'That's good advice, Mr Willoughby, because if she carries on like this we still have the option of pressing charges.'

Despite her comatose state Rachel sensed the potential seriousness of the situation and at last fell silent.

The policeman, a middle aged I've-seen-it-all-before type resigned to wasting his time with such incidents, indicated to his colleague that they should head on. He spoke as they edged towards the door. 'It's a great pity we're distracted from more important duties by this sort of behaviour. As my colleague has indicated, there will be no charges on this occasion but,' now he looked down at Rachel, 'if we catch Rachel in this state again she'll be in trouble.'

The policewoman looked across to David. He wondered whether they had a standard script as she took over. 'We have identified that she's a minor so you should be aware that the responsibility to look after her rests with you, Mr Willoughby.'

'I can only offer my apologies. She told me she was staying with her friend.' He looked down at Rachel who was staring ahead of her with no sign of remorse. 'Clearly that wasn't the case.'

'Clearly not,' the policewoman responded with an accusing tone.

As soon as the door closed he returned to Rachel. 'What's been going on?' he asked.

'Not talking now,' she said as she tried to stand. She failed first time round and dropped back onto the couch. She was more successful at the second attempt and was commencing an unbalanced struggle towards the door where Sam was standing.

'I'll help her up, Dad,' he offered.

David watched his two children struggling up the stairs, wishing Bridget or even Jane was there to support him with advice about how to deal with this. As he sat there thinking things through, the sound of Rachel vomiting in the bathroom was audible.

He decided to call Bridget. The phone rang for quite a while before she answered. 'Hello?'

'Hello, Bridget, it's me.'

'Hi, what do you want?' she mumbled.

'Just a chat.'

'A chat? Do you know what time it is?'

He looked at his watch, it was a little after midnight. 'I didn't realise it was that late. I'll call back tomorrow.'

'No, it's OK, I'm awake now. I'm all ears.'

'I've been on a cookery course.' He began to describe his afternoon in meticulous detail.

Bridget interrupted when he'd reached the preparation of the main course. 'For God's sake, David, this is interesting but perhaps you could tell me the rest when we meet up.'

'Yes, but there's something else, Bridget.'

'Yes?'

'Rachel got brought home by the police this evening.' He presented her with the list of things Rachel had done wrong. Lying about who she was staying with. Not telling him about a boyfriend. Getting blind drunk. Resisting police questioning. General aggression.

'So what have you done?'

'Nothing yet. She isn't in a fit state to speak, which is for the best because I need to think through what to say. The problem is, I haven't got a clue. Any ideas?'

'I don't think I have. For a start, I don't know Rachel well enough to suggest what might work. Be open and tell her that at the very least you expect honesty. Have you considered asking Jane to help?'

'No, maybe I should.'

'Think about it. I'll call tomorrow evening to see how you got on.'

'Oh, one more thing.'

'David, it is a bit late, I've got a busy day tomorrow.'

'I know. We don't have to now, but I'd like to talk to you about my café idea.'

'That list of yours keeps cropping up, doesn't it?'

'You've got a good memory.'

'Hard to forget. Yes, I'm happy to talk about it. And I haven't forgotten the other things you wrote. To be truthful having you in bed with me right now is a nice thought.'

'Sequentially it fits in after the café, but I think I could cope with changing the order!'

'Well, let's both have sweet dreams about the bed part. Mmmm, mine is starting now. Night-night, David.'

Chapter Twenty-three

David checked on his daughter after he ended the call. She was sprawled diagonally across the bed, fully dressed and snoring, her head close to a bucket. A rancid streak of yellow-brown on the carpet around it indicated that she had partially missed her target. He straightened her so her head rested on the pillow and then covered her with the quilt like a dad tucking in a little child. Only this child was now a young adult with actions and thoughts that she kept to herself. He emptied the bucket down the toilet and washed it in the sink before replacing it in Rachel's bedroom just in case.

The next morning he left her to sleep off her hangover, having written her a note.

Rachel,

Have to go to work early. I'm very disappointed by your behaviour and I expect a full and truthful explanation tonight. Text me if you want picking up after Fiddler. I'm assuming you are going to school at some stage later.

Dad

He was glad to get out the house. He needed to plan what to say to his daughter and whether to involve Jane. However busy he was at work he'd make time to think things through.

As he drove to the local authority offices he was deep in thought, the lack of concentration culminating in the scraping of his bumper on a concrete column in the car park. He inspected the damage – now there were identical striations on each side of his vehicle. In anger he lifted his leg and gave one of the front tyres a kick. The resulting bounce back of his foot was enough to set off the alarm on the neighbouring vehicle which he recognised as Mary's BMW. He fled.

There was a Post-it from Mary on the corner of his computer screen. *Please come to my office as soon as you can.* Things with Mary had got better following his staff review; the tone of her emails was not as accusatory as in the past and there was less questioning of his competence. He had responded by showing a little more enthusiasm to her suggestions for departmental improvements despite a belief that much of what she wanted was unworkable.

He entered her office in anticipation of criticism and was surprised to be greeted by what was remarkably similar to a smile. He considered the possibility that he was misinterpreting a sneer, scowl or snarl but she held the facial posture and it continued to resemble a smile. This was a first in all his contact with Mary and it made her look quite different. Almost pleasant.

'Are you alright, Mary?' he enquired.

'Yes. Why do you ask?'

'Nothing in particular.' But there was a lot in particular to note, a wide range of modifications to go with the smile. For a start, Mary had transformed her hair. The soft curls had gone, replaced by a severe asymmetrical cut, the hair on the left side brushing her shoulder while on the right side it barely reached the bottom of an ear adorned by a dangling silver earring. The previous uninteresting hair colour, a sort of mud brown, had been enhanced by blonde highlights. She would have used make-up in the past, but nothing as noticeable as today's deep red lipstick and black eyelashes. She stood to greet him and David stepped back in amazement. She was wearing the same maroon and lime green skirt and beige cardigan that Bridget had worn at the cinema the previous Saturday. Was this a remarkable coincidence or was she stalking him with a weird follow-up as a punishment for his harsh words at the staff review?

He abandoned his usual pastime of guessing what name colleagues had invented to describe her appearance. She looked good, very good. He was so taken aback by her transformation that he had remained rooted on the spot by the door.

Still smiling, she walked across to a low cupboard. 'You don't have to wait for my permission to sit down. Would you like a coffee?'

Could it be possible that her voice had changed too? Softer, slower, seductive. 'Yes please,' he squeaked. If she had walked past him outside of the work environment he would not have recognised her.

He sat and watched in silence as she prepared the drinks with her back to him. David noted a very attractive shape. He'd never thought of her in terms of her femininity before, she'd just been his unpleasant boss. Mary set down two mugs, a milk jug, a cafetiere, and a plate of chocolate biscuits on the desk between them.

'I hope you like the real stuff,' she said as she poured. 'I'm a bit of a coffee snob.'

'Me too.'

'Well at least that's one thing we have in common then.' She looked at him solemnly. 'Look, I owe you an apology. I've been obsessed with proving something since I started this job. I wanted everyone to know I was in charge and intended to turn things around. Working for the council is different to my experience of the private sector, but that doesn't make it worse here. My behaviour's been poor and I'm sorry.'

She picked up a biscuit, broke it in half, and took a bite. David noted the chocolate smear on her upper lip and the lipstick smear on the uneaten section of the biscuit – this meeting was inducing sexual thoughts mixed with a sense of disloyalty to Bridget. Surely Mary couldn't be aware of his state of mind, but she had noticed something in his demeanour and was smiling with intent as he nibbled his own biscuit.

'Good biscuits, aren't they,' she teased. 'But back to work as I know you've got loads to do. I hope you're prepared to forget what's happened in the past and we can move on as a unified team.'

'Yes, I am,' David uttered as he struggled to eliminate confused thoughts of both Mary and Bridget.

Back in his office he struggled to focus on work. Finally accountancy replaced fantasy as he addressed the challenge of establishing procedures to prevent future budget difficulties. Accountant's habits die hard and before long he was engrossed as he waded through spreadsheets. This focus came to a sudden halt when he remembered that an altercation with Rachel loomed. He had to plan how to deal with it. He must have been frowning when Jabulani appeared and placed a small flyer on his desk.

'Oh dear, not a happy face. Another bad meeting, I assume.'

'What?'

'With Mary.'

'No, she was fine. I don't know what's got into her,' or who, he contemplated, 'but she's completely different.'

'Long may it last. Then why such a gloomy face?'

'Oh, something to do with my daughter. She was brought home drunk by the police last night.'

'I'm sorry to hear that.'

'I'm sure I'll be able to sort it,' David replied, more in hope than expectation.

'She's sixteen, isn't she?'

David nodded.

'Well at least I've got a few more years before I have those sorts of worries with my children.'

David had lifted up the flyer. As he read the sheet Jabulani announced: 'You are to be an honoured guest at our first gig in England.' He and his brother, both their wives, and three other Zimbabweans had formed a band. They were called Kanjani and were performing at The Duchess of Devonshire the night before New Year's Eve.

'I'd love to come.'

'And will you be bringing your new woman?'

'She still isn't quite my new woman, but we are getting on well.'

'You must bring her, then she'll be an even closer friend.'

David smiled. 'I certainly will.'

'Excellent. And how are you progressing with onion layers? Have you stripped them all off yet?' Jabulani joked.

'Actually I think some layers are back on, I'm much happier now. Tell me, what gave you the idea of using onions to explain personality? It's neat.'

'I made it up though I'm sure I'm not the first to use it. I could just as easily have said carrot or sweet potato; onion happened to be what came out.'

'Carrots and sweet potatoes don't have layers.'

'No, quite true. What a wise man you are, David. Well I'd better get back to work, see you later.'

There was a concert to look forward to. David called Bridget to get her to put the date in her diary. They'd already talked about spending time together over the Christmas holiday period and this would be the first they'd planned.

Bridget had bad news. On Christmas Eve she would be heading off to Ireland with her children to visit her aunt. 'My cousin phoned this morning. Her mother's very poorly and if I want to see her again I've got to do it quickly.'

After offering sympathy he asked the big question. 'When will you be back?'

'I'm going for about week. I'll be home on the second or third.'

‘So you’ll miss the gig?’

‘I’m afraid so.’

Bridget sensed his disappointment and made light of it. ‘I know you want to chat about your café and then there’s that other matter. Both straight after I get back, I promise. What about Rachel, have you decided what to do?’

He hadn’t even begun to think about it yet. How on earth would he be able to be open about the risks of, well risks of what? STDs, contraception, alcohol abuse, drug taking? Past conversations covering homework, menus, and even smoking were trivial in comparison.

‘I’m going to ask Jane to join me for this,’ he announced, as much to himself as to Bridget.

‘I think that’s the right decision. I hope it goes well.’

Chapter Twenty-four

The decision to involve Jane was high risk since there had been no dialogue between Rachel and her mother since Jane had left. But Jane had been at the heart of all child crises for sixteen years and he needed her now.

Sitting in his car in the driveway, which was emerging as the favoured venue for thinking things through, he called her and explained what had happened. She agreed to come over to take part in the evening's meeting.

Rachel hadn't gone to school that day. By the time David got home she'd showered, cleaned up her bedroom floor, gone to the supermarket, and cooked dinner. She greeted David with a smile, but there was no apology. They made small talk at the dinner table. When Sam had left the room, David could begin.

'Rachel, we need to discuss last night. It's a serious matter and your mother's joining us.'

'We don't need her.'

'I do, I'm not sure I can do it alone.'

'What do you mean by 'it'?'

'Well, all sorts of things.'

As if on cue they heard the front door open and Jane joined them in the kitchen.

'Hello, Rachel.'

Rachel gave her a cursory nod as she sat down.

David began. 'We're all aware that there are family issues, but I hope we can put those aside for a while to find out from Rachel what's going on. Both agreed?' Neither Jane nor Rachel replied so he moved on.

'Firstly, you told me a lie, Rachel. You said you'd be staying at Hannah's.'

Rachel admitted that she'd been at her boyfriend Joe's house. It was news to David that she had a boyfriend and he expressed deep concern that she'd spent the night with him.

'Actually his parents were in. I slept in the spare room.'

David was relieved to hear this but less so when Rachel continued. 'I'm not a child, Dad. If his parents had been out I would have been in his bed.'

Jane spoke. 'You are a child, Rachel. You should not be *in bed*, as you put it, with a boy at your age.'

'I'm sixteen, it's legal.'

'That's not the point. We don't even know him. Who is he?'

'Someone at school.'

'Don't you think it's important we meet him?' Jane persisted. 'That we at least have the address of where you're staying?'

'I can't see what meeting him has got to do with it. He hasn't got to be approved by you.'

'You're wrong. Meeting is important and if I was still here I wouldn't allow you to go out with him until we'd met.'

'Well you're not here. And your obsession with meeting is absurd. I *have* met Jim, is that supposed to make it easier to know you're fucking him?'

David sat back with resignation as a furious Jane let fly.

'There's a lot for you to think about, Rachel. For a start, some respect. Questioning my behaviour coming from you is a bit rich, I've heard all about David getting summoned to school to be told what you've done wrong. After what happened last night if I was your father I wouldn't trust you to go out.'

'Thankfully you're not my father because it's nice to have one parent who cares about me.'

'Just you remember everything I've done for you, whatever you've asked for you've had. That's true isn't it,

David … No, Rachel, don't answer back because I haven't finished … where do you think you're going? I haven't finished, come back here this instant, Rachel!'

Jane and David were left alone.

'I was hoping to resolve things a bit more amicably,' David said.

Jane got up and walked towards the cupboard above the worktop to the left of the sink. 'I need a coffee, would you like one?'

'Yes, why not.'

She opened the unit. It was full of tins of food and jars of spices. 'The mugs have gone,' she declared.

'They haven't gone, they've been moved.'

'Why?'

'I felt like a change. They're in that cupboard,' he said pointing, 'but the milk's still in the fridge.'

He hadn't removed the holiday snap attached to the door; everyone in it was still smiling. He sat in silence as Jane manufactured two perfect cappuccinos. She put the milk back in the fridge, pausing to examine the photograph. 'That was a fun holiday, wasn't it? Do you think we'll get over the unpleasantness, perhaps do some things as a family?'

He didn't reply.

'Thanks for asking me over, even though it was a bit of a disaster. I just wish I hadn't lost my temper.'

David realised he wasn't bitter about what had happened anymore. They sat chatting for a while, in agreement that their lawyers had earned enough money and it was time to sign the financial agreement.

As soon as Jane left Rachel came downstairs to apologise to David for walking out. His daughter was changing. In the past, engulfed in a whirlwind of emotion, she would explode with rage and tears then show huge remorse when it had subsided. Now, though the apology seemed genuine enough, she was calm, detached, and hardened. She dismissed his attempt to question her further beyond an acknowledgement that the drinking and rudeness to the police would not be repeated.

David called Bridget and relayed the evening's events. He was keen to see her ahead of the trip to Ireland, but it wasn't going to be possible – she had too much to organise.

The last days at work before a break that would stretch Bridgetless from Christmas Eve to beyond the New Year were quietly festive. Colleagues put up streamers and displayed their Christmas cards on their desks and window sills. David's office remained bare, but at Jabulani's insistence he did join in with mince pie eating and the trip to the pub for lunch on the last day. The new Mary was at the heart of the festivities. Laughing away, drinking rather a lot, and declaring to cheers that there was no need to return to work for the rest of the day.

On Christmas morning Sam got his model racing car and Rachel got a compact camera. David was given a shirt and tie. They then set off to visit his mother, regarded as an undesirable but necessary duty by all three of them. She gave the children £20 each and in return received three handkerchiefs with embroidered flowers on the corners, a bottle of sweet sherry, a box of chocolates, and six luxury mince pies. David went without a gift from his mother.

'He's too old to get presents,' his mother claimed when Rachel questioned her.

'What about you then? You've got presents and you're even older.'

'That's different,' was the explanation offered. 'Sit in the lounge and I'll make tea.'

They stayed overnight and on Boxing Day morning Charlotte and her family popped in on their way to her husband Donald's parents. By the end of her visit David was convinced that the saying 'blood is thicker than water' was false. His sister had little interest let alone sympathy regarding his separation from Jane. Rachel and Sam fared little better with their two cousins despite being almost identical ages. Donald sat in sullen silence.

After two cups of tea Charlotte announced that they had to get going to reach Donald's parents in time for lunch.

'Great to see you all,' she lied.

'Yes, we must catch up again soon,' David lied in response.

Lunch consisted of dried-out turkey, boiled to near death Brussels sprouts, and rock hard roast potatoes. Sam later identified the only decent thing to be the jar of cranberry sauce. He was usually compliant, but on this visit he displayed a trait previously unseen by David – sarcasm. 'I can't wait for Her Majesty's speech.' '*The Sound of Music*, my all-time favourite.' 'Morecombe and Wise, has there ever been anything funnier?' This sarcasm passed over his grandmother's head. Instead she took great delight in their shared interests.

Despite the drudgery of the visit they stayed on for a second night, trapped by the guilt induced by David's mother. It was dull for all three of them, but without Bridget there was little urgency for David to return home. Rachel nagged to leave, but David was adamant they remain, happy for her to miss opportunities the festive season might provide for getting into trouble.

On the day after Boxing Day they watched lousy repeat television programmes, played countless games of cribbage, and once again ate traditional Christmas fare of leftover turkey (as dry as the day before, but now brown as opposed to white meat); fat-saturated sausages (a depressing new addition); boiled to near death Brussels sprouts (again); and rock hard roast potatoes (again).

Rachel volunteered to clear up after a lunch. When she failed to return to the lounge for over an hour, David checked to see if there was a problem. She was sitting at the Formica kitchen table, her chin resting on her elbows.

'What are you doing?'

'I'm watching the second hand go round,' she said, pointing to the clock on the wall above the birthday calendar. 'It's the most exciting thing on offer.'

'Can I join you?' At least he'd made Rachel smile.

When David's mother was in the kitchen preparing afternoon tea, he suggested to his children that they should stay on for a further day.

'If you do, I'm getting the train back,' Rachel declared.

'And I'll reveal my true thoughts about Morecombe and Wise,' Sam added.

His mother came into the lounge and set the tray down on the top of a nest of tables. 'As soon as we've had this I'll start to get dinner ready.'

'Sorry Grandma, we've got to get back tonight. If I don't start my coursework I'll be kicked out of school.'

David relented – he'd had more than enough. 'Yes, tea then I'm afraid we're off. It's been a great couple of days though.'

'I'm sure you've all got more important things to do than stay with me.'

'Yes, we have,' said Rachel, mimicking Jane's method of tackling the guilt trip.

Chapter Twenty-five

'Dad, everyone knows it's a drug den.'

'Well, everybody except me, Rachel. I went to hear the music.'

'Do you realise you're a marked man now, with a police record? Soon you'll get the sack and no one else will employ you.'

'Very funny. Actually the police were extremely apologetic about keeping us there for so long, but they wouldn't let anyone out before a search. The owners were arrested for dealing.'

'Dealing. You're even using the right term. I bet you know all the slang names for the drugs, too. I'm not sure I'd have let you off if I was the police.'

'Ha-ha.'

'Seriously though, next time you score skunk I'd love some Black Russian or White Widow.'

Rachel and David were sitting in the lounge drinking tea; Sam was in bed. David had called her from the pub a little before midnight to explain the situation. He told her not to wait up, but not surprisingly curiosity got the better of her and anyway there was a run of *Buffy The Vampire Slayer* episodes on TV to keep her occupied.

'Enough, Rachel, go to bed now will you,' David implored. 'I'm exhausted.'

Jabulani's gig had been at the Duchess of Devonshire, a pub he'd walked by many times. It was a double-fronted mock Tudor building, shabby and run down. On the night of the concert its hanging baskets contained dead flowers ravaged by frost. A sign promoted the night's specials –

sausage with mash and cottage pie. Next to that stood a display board informing potential customers that all Sky Sports Premier League matches were shown and that while football was on there was a three for the price of two pints offer. A hand-written note was pinned to the door. *Tonight: Kanjarny from Zimbarbwe. Entrance £3.*

As he stopped to read it, he was tapped on the shoulder. 'Hello there.'

'Mary! I didn't know you were coming.'

They stood by the notice. David pointed out that the proper name of the band was Kanjani. 'It means "hi there", Jabulani says.'

'They're not too hot on the spelling of the country either,' Mary added.

They laughed as they entered.

Inside the pub there was no evidence of a band. The two giant TVs were showing a darts match which none of the few customers was watching. Four boys of questionable drinking age were playing pool while vying for the attention of the two girls sitting on a bare wooden bench next to the table. David heard an eczema-faced, greasy-haired youth exclaim 'me ball's tight against the hole again', followed by an explosion of laughter from the girls pretending it was a joke of stupendous magnitude.

The only other customers were a middle-aged man and woman sitting at a table with half empty pints of Guinness in front of them, she gesticulating wildly, he oozing disinterest. As David and Mary were passing, the woman leapt up.

'You ain't listening, are you?'

'That's 'cos I've heard it all before.'

'If you supported me I wouldn't keep goin' on about it, would I?'

'I do bloody support you!'

'I'm goin' home!'

'Suit yerself, I'm finishin' this.'

She stormed out and the man tipped the remains of the one glass into the other.

'We can't be at the right place,' Mary said as they approached the bar.

'What can I get you?' asked the landlady, buxom and middle-aged, dark roots exposed at the base of her bleach-blonde hair.

'We're here to see Kanjani – the band,' David answered, self-conscious of his posh voice.

The barmaid nodded towards a door at the far end of the room. 'There.'

'Do you think they're filming *Eastenders* here tonight?' Mary joked.

They were joined by four others from the local authority. Charlie, Mitch, Dee, and Freddie worked on David's floor – they were the ones who made up the nicknames for Mary. And seeing him with her now, despite being coincidental, would no doubt provide scope for malicious office gossip.

The six of them entered a very different world to the room they had come from. Here there was subdued lighting and the dark walls were covered with retro rock concert posters. There was a small lit stage in the corner. They dropped their entrance money into an open tin and walked in – it was already crowded.

Jabulani approached with another man by his side. 'You've made it, wonderful. This is my brother, Farai.' There were handshakes all round. 'Take your coats off, the cloakroom's over there. We're playing soon.'

'Come on, let's get away from this lot,' Mary whispered, looking across at the four who had arrived with them. 'They drive me up the wall with their immaturity.'

David recognised a few other local authority employees. Judging by choice of clothes and hairstyles, the rest of the audience could best be described as ageing hippie.

On reaching the cloakroom, rather a grand name for a small table with a rail of hangers behind it, Mary took off her North Face Polar Protection coat. He struggled to avoid a gasp as guiltily he embraced the pastime of selecting a name based on her attire. Tonight she was Rock Chick and if he had to be truthful, Divine Rock Chick.

Mary was wearing open-toed, high heeled sandals with each toe painted a different vibrant colour; a pair of tight fitting jeans with rips across the knees; an equally tight fitting black T-shirt with a jazz musician playing a trumpet, his head pointing upwards; and a multi-coloured large bead necklace. He had to have a second take.

Of course all this happened in a split second, but when he looked back up to Mary's face he sensed that she was well aware of his inspection.

'I think you deserve a drink on me,' she said, utilising her newly acquired slow, sensuous voice.

Taking hold of his arm she led him to the bar and ordered a bottle of wine. As she was filling their glasses the band came on stage. There were seven of them, three women and four men, dressed in matching kaftan tops and baggy white trousers. The shirts were white with a purple animal with horns as a motif.

The music started, acoustic guitar and two instruments Jabulani had told David about – the *mbira* and the *hosho*. It was highly rhythmic with hand clapping, harmony vocals, and dancing. The appreciative audience swayed along. Farai did lots of talking between numbers, explaining the origin of the instruments and the inspiration for their songs. Briefly he referred to the political situation in Zimbabwe, too.

'Tatenda, thank you.' he called out after one song. 'Now we'll put our instruments down and sing 'Steam Train'. These trains were running in my country long after they had stopped here, so we as children were brought up with the shushing and the clattering. We would race along the side of the track waving to the passengers.'

As the hissing harmonies began the audience started to dance. Mary, having downed her second glass of wine, took hold of David's hand and dragged him towards the dance floor with a determination reminiscent of Bridget at the school reunion. They remained on the dance floor for another song, this one slow and melodic. Mary put her hands on David's shoulders and he responded by laying his hands on her waist. She applied pressure to pull them closer. He enjoyed the physical contact and offered no more than a minute degree of unnoticed resistance in deference of loyalty towards Bridget.

'God, I need another drink,' she said, leading him back to their table. She knocked back her third glass. 'We're getting low, shall I grab another bottle?'

'Well I've had enough, in fact I feel quite light-headed.'

'It's the dope.'

'What do you mean?'

'There's so much cannabis around you don't have to smoke it to get stoned, just breathe.' She moved closer to him. 'You're quite an innocent, aren't you, David.' She moved closer and their lips met. For an instant, actually for quite a bit more than an instant, he enjoyed the soft warmth of the kiss before drawing back.

'No, Mary, we can't.'

'Why not, David? I know you've separated from your wife, I thought maybe we …'

'Oh it's complicated, Mary. You see …'

Their conversation was terminated by a group of six policemen and women bursting through the door and ordering the band to stop playing. The policeman in charge, the very same man who had visited David after his mugging and then again when he brought Rachel home drunk, announced that everybody was to be searched for drugs.

It was an efficient operation with the audience divided into five lines to be interviewed by a designated policeman. The sixth officer, the policewoman he also knew from the two previous incidents, acknowledged him with a nod. She had been allocated the task of assembling those passed on by the interview officers. David assumed they were the ones to be arrested for the possession and perhaps sale of drugs. Amidst moans and groans, the audience were told no one could leave until all had been seen. However, once their name had been recorded and they had been searched they would be allowed to use their phones. This is when David contacted Rachel.

Finally at 1.30 a.m., departures were permitted except for the dozen or so who were led into two police vans. Mary followed David out. He'd hoped to exit alone to avoid any conversation about their pre-raid dance and kiss. She took hold of his hand. 'Sorry if I've been pushy or misunderstood your situation. Hey, it was a fun night though, wasn't it?'

'No need to apologise, Mary. It certainly was an interesting evening. I enjoyed it.'

'We've done rather a lot of apologising recently, haven't we?' she continued as she took hold of his other hand. 'My taxi's here, I'd better head on. I hope you have a good New Year – I'll see you back at work.' She drew him towards her and once again planted her lips on his. David was drawn in by the arousing contact. This time the duration of the kiss was considerably longer; he wrapped his arms substantially more firmly around her waist until their bodies were clamped together; and he provided more than a hint of a noteworthy response as their tongues met.

He watched Mary as she got in the taxi. Turning, he saw that Charlie, Mitch, Dee, and Freddie were also watching.

Chapter Twenty-six

Bridget called David to wish him a Happy New Year on the dot of midnight as Jools Holland finished the countdown. Sam and Rachel were still up watching the show; David left them in the lounge and took the phone into the kitchen.

There would be no mention of the concert and no need to say anything about Mary. After all, it wasn't as if he'd done anything wrong – all the chasing had come from her. 'I've missed you,' he said.

'Missed you, too.'

Although responding to the first kiss was just to be polite, he had been a tiny bit aroused. But that was no more than a man's normal physiological reaction. 'When do you get back?'

'Late tomorrow evening.'

Yes, Mary had looked great. But there was nothing wrong in appreciating another woman's attractiveness. 'When can we meet up?'

'Sunday. Come over at tea time. There's something I need to tell you.'

That was good news; he would be seeing Bridget before having to deal with Mary back at work. He wasn't sure what to expect from Mary, but he knew how he would act. Polite. Professional. Friendly. Detached.

The second kiss had been very enjoyable; in fact if he were truthful the whole evening with Mary had been enjoyable. 'Great, see you then.'

'Bye.'

'Bye, Bridget.' But not nearly as enjoyable as being with Bridget.

They sat on a sofa in Bridget's lounge drinking peppermint tea. A Sade CD was playing. He edged closer and kissed her. Her response was a little clipped; he sensed tension which matched his own because he was considering owning up about Mary.

Bridget pulled away just as a track he loved was playing.

'Will you be my friend until the end of time?' David asked, repeating Sade's words.

'There's something I need to tell you, David.'

'But will you?'

'Listen, please.'

'I am listening,' he said as he stretched across to kiss her again. A New Year, a new, more assertive approach to cementing their partnership was his tactic.

'This is important, please stop,' Bridget ordered with a raised voice.

A surprised David edged away, switching his gaze to her anxious face. 'I am listening,' he repeated solemnly.

'There's something you have to know. Roland didn't die in an accident, I killed him. You're in the same room as a murderer.'

David expected a smile but she remained serious. She had a great sense of humour, dark and cynical. The punch line to a joke was about to follow. He allowed the pause to build up, but nothing ensued. He broke the silence.

'Don't be silly, Bridget.'

'I'm not. It's true. I killed him and I was lucky not to get caught. I can thank my dad for that.'

'You're telling me you murdered Roland and your father helped you do it? I don't believe you.'

'Well my father wasn't there when I did it, but he made sure I got off scot-free. Let me tell you what happened.'

David nodded, still half anticipating an amusing twist.

'You already know a bit about what Roland was like; not all the nasty details because there's no need. Dad and

Mum were aware of how unpleasant Roland had become, they saw it every time I visited. They'd never liked him in the first place and warned me off marrying him, but who listens to their parents about things like that?

'One day when I went to see them they could tell I'd been crying, not much detective work needed for that. The night before Roland hadn't come home and when I'd asked what was going on, he told me he'd been with one of his students. He did some part-time teaching at the art college and seducing students was his favourite pastime. I'd had enough – I told him that was it between us and he let fly. My mum eked out the sordid details of our relationship and I admitted that our marriage was a complete joke. They were worried that a separation would be awful for their grandchildren.

'What I told you the first time round about what she and Dad suggested is true. They volunteered to look after Andy and Kay and to pay for a holiday to see if there was any chance of sorting things out.

'I had no enthusiasm to go along with their idea because to my mind we were finished, but they urged me to try one last time and I relented. I searched the web and came across a lovely cottage in the Scottish Highlands by the sea. I booked the flights and the car. By then our social lives were pretty well apart, but it didn't need much persuading to get Roland to come along. He was always ready to grab something given to him for free.

'I decided I might as well be positive, to make an effort to rekindle something. But it was hopeless from the outset. Starting with the train journey to the airport, he was as unfriendly and deriding as ever, and I knew being stuck together in a relative wilderness for ten days would be a nightmare. True to form the first week was hell and I counted down the days to get back to London. Roland was probably doing the same. There were four days left.'

‘My turn to drive, Roland. Let’s head north, the guide book says there are stunning views a few miles away.’

‘I don’t want another fucking walk. Can’t we find somewhere with shops or a cinema or even a bowling alley?’

‘Tell you what, let’s make this the last one then head back to Inverness tomorrow and spend some time there.’

‘I don’t fancy this, I’m knackered.’

Bridget grabbed his hand in an act of friendship, but he pulled away.

‘Come on,’ she urged. ‘The last walk. Tomorrow we’ll book the fanciest hotel in Inverness, one with a spa. Then we can lie around relaxing for a few days.’

In silence they collected their boots, rainwear, and the packed lunches Bridget had prepared. Their phones remained where they had put them on the first day, on the kitchen table. Since there was no reception there was no point taking them.

Bridget drove while Roland cursorily flicked through the guide book. He looked thoroughly miserable. ‘Where the hell are we heading?’ he asked after they had been travelling for a little under half an hour.

‘I’ve got a rough idea though it hardly matters, it’s all so beautiful.’ And it was – the scenery was stunning. A blue sky illuminated the patches of snow that remained in the dips below the rugged peaks; they were dazzlingly bright. Waterfalls tumbled then crashed against the rock faces. Lower down, the bare grey-brown rocks gave way to meadows of purple and yellow flowers.

It was still well outside the mainstream tourist season and even the major roads were traffic free. When they turned onto smaller roads the scenery was theirs alone to savour. Finally they went along little more than a track and reached an irregular rocky pavement facing out towards the distant sea. They got out.

‘Ready?’ Bridget asked, her smile and light tone

attempting to illicit less resistance from Roland.

'If we must,' he uttered, avoiding eye contact.

Roland strode off, head down, lost in his own dark thoughts. Bridget trailed behind, crossing the uneven ground with care. Her husband kept going, not once turning back to check on her wellbeing. No attempt to wait for her, no conversation, no interest.

'It's over,' Bridget muttered, 'it really is over.'

She stopped to investigate the discomfort on her left foot. Sitting on an unusually smooth block of stone she took off her boot and sock to see the damage. There was a painful blister on the protruding joint of her big toe. She looked back towards their starting point, admiring the rugged beauty behind her. Then she heard Roland call out and she turned back towards the sea.

'Look at this,' was all she could make out against the roar of the water. The tide was coming in, she noticed. He was smiling as he came running towards her.

'Careful, Roland, it's slippery.'

He kept going and she saw what he was holding up in his right hand, a giant crab. His malicious smile was well known to her.

'Catch this,' he called out when he was still some distance away. He leant back, swung his arm, and hurled the crab towards Bridget. It landed with a crunch on a rock a few paces in front of her, its shell crushed to pieces, its pincers twisted. The noise of the crab's landing was followed by a much heavier thud as Roland slipped from the rock he had been perched on, dropping head first onto the jagged terrain.

Bridget remained seated for a few seconds, her wish for calm silence disturbed by the breaking of waves and the shrieking of gulls.

'Roland? Are you OK?' Bridget called out as she replaced her sock and boot. With little urgency she walked towards her husband and saw him lying quite still on the edge of a rock pool. He was out cold and blood was running from a gash at the side of his head, turning the water pink and sending a group of tiny crabs scurrying for safety. The left side of his face was resting in the water.

Bridget considered the options as she gently shook Roland, trying to rouse him. 'Wake up, will you.' And one option was so easy she couldn't resist it. She turned his head a fraction so that his face was angled downwards. Next she moved him sideways just a tiny bit until his nose and mouth were fully immersed under water. She watched as the pool reddened further and air bubbles escaped, marking Roland's last breath.

Bridget took out a cheese sandwich from her backpack. She looked up. The tide was advancing quickly so she'd have to get a bit of a move on or else the sea might trap her. She removed the cling film from the sandwich and took her first bite as she headed back to seek the help that she knew was already too late.

'Much of the rest of what happened is what I told you first time round, except for what was going on in my head. Instead of any panic that I had to find help, there was relief that I didn't need to. I strolled back to the car, though not too slowly in case someone saw me. Then I drove towards the small cluster of cottages that we'd passed on the way there. In all it took about an hour and a half before I was banging on the door of one that had smoke coming out its chimney. An old lady greeted me. 'My husband's out there,' I said, pointing behind me. 'He fell over, he's injured and out cold.' She phoned the emergency services then made me a strong cup of tea with loads of sugar and a tot of whisky. I acted as if I was panic stricken, which wasn't such an act because I was getting paranoid about the chance of being found out. All those TV dramas I'd watched about the police uncovering what the perpetrators had thought was the perfect crime.

‘Eventually two policemen arrived. The older one, he must have been very close to retirement, was very kind. He explained that the tide had advanced well beyond the point where I’d left Roland, by now it would have reached the cliff edge. I knew that would be the case, but I had a good go at gasping in shock. He then told me that a rescue team had already set off by boat. I carried on with my show of grief, sobbing, ‘I’ve killed my husband.’ As soon as I said it I wished I hadn’t because while the one policemen was consoling me with, ‘There’s a good chance the boat will have got to him’ the other one kept quiet and frowned with what looked like recognition of over-acting and as a result, suspicion.’

Bridget went on to describe calling her parents. Her father travelled up to Scotland to support her while her mother consoled the children. He arrived at the cottage two days after the incident, on the same day Roland’s body was washed ashore. Bridget was in the middle of telling him what happened when there was a knock on the door and the policeman who had appeared suspicious came in to break the news. Throughout her whole time there Bridget only saw the two who had first arrived on the scene; it was that small a place.

‘Can I have a word with you alone please, officer?’ Bridget’s father requested and the two men went into the kitchen, closing the door behind them. Bridget heard murmurings. When they came back into the sitting room her father announced he would be the one to identify the body. She questioned why and he came straight to the point. ‘Because I’m afraid it’s nothing more than the remains of a body, it’s best if you keep away.’

Bridget burst out crying, an unexpectedly genuine feeling of sadness for Roland’s death. Later her father explained he had deliberately elicited grief to allay any distrust the policeman might have ahead of the regulatory autopsy.

Her father was a forensic scientist and knew what was needed to prevent the coroner's suspicion. He made a point of befriending him ahead of the session, reminiscing about past gruesome cases and the substantial differences between working in Oxford and rural Scotland. Bridget was briefed on how to act during the post-mortem, in particular to describe everything as accurately as possible until the point when she had moved Roland's head into the water and held him down. If asked about their relationship she was to avoid indicating all was fine, even admit to difficulties if pushed, in case a decision was made to call outside witnesses.

Accidental death by drowning was recorded and a relieved Bridget followed her father back to Inverness where they deposited their hire cars and flew back to London together.

'What do you think of all that, David?' Bridget asked. 'I'm a murderer.'

'Hardly. Even if you'd done nothing more than leave him there, he would still have drowned. It's not as if you would have been able to carry him to safety.'

'Maybe not, but I made sure, didn't I? The whole thing still hangs over me.'

David moved closer and put an arm around her. 'I can understand that, but in case you're worried, it doesn't affect how I feel towards you.'

Bridget smiled her first smile of the New Year.

Chapter Twenty-seven

Four women were central to his life and problems with each of them were piling on the pressure. To cap it all, there was the possibility of a massive transformation to consider – quitting his job and opening the café.

How things had changed from the pleasant simplicity of only a few weeks ago. The unfulfilled night with Bridget, but with the certainty that it was only a matter of time before they were in a relationship. A tyrannical boss making the case for leaving the local authority clear cut. His increased confidence in being able to cope to all intents and purposes as a single parent.

Bridget topped the pressure list. She had asked him to leave as soon as she had recounted the events around the death of Roland. 'Death' was his choice of word, she continued to use 'murder'. She was adamant he should have time to think about the impact of knowing this. He declared there was no need – that her involvement in Roland's death didn't influence his feelings towards her. She wouldn't have it so he relented and agreed to call her the next evening. On the drive home he switched on the radio to dismiss his emerging feeling that perhaps there *was* an issue after all.

There was a discussion about deceit and infidelity on Radio 4 which allowed him to switch his thoughts to Mary. While there had been no infidelity in his case, maybe not telling Bridget about Mary's involvement during the evening of the concert could be defined as deceitful. He had no idea what to expect tomorrow, the first day back at work after the Christmas break. On arrival he'd go straight to Jabulani. He was undecided whether to raise the topic of Mary, but he'd certainly find out more about the drugs raid. At least then he'd have a topic of conversation with Mary to distract her from talking about the 'other thing'. He wasn't convinced that all the flirting had come from her, perhaps he had contributed. It was all down to their tongues meeting during that last kiss. If her tongue had journeyed into his mouth then she was solely to blame and there would be nothing to tell Bridget. If he had extended his to meet hers half way then it was a shared responsibility. He still wouldn't tell Bridget, but he would be being deceitful.

Tomorrow was also the start of the new school term for the children, Rachel's return following her drunken escapade. After the visit to his mother she had spent the rest of the holiday revising for forthcoming exams, refusing to answer any questions about her personal life. David heard earnest whispered conversations when he passed her bedroom. He assumed they were with her boyfriend. With school starting they would be together again and there was nothing David could do to stop it. Though why should he? Sixteen-year-olds date. But what was this boyfriend like and how well did he treat his Rachel?

And then there was Jane. It was the week when they had agreed to sign the financial settlement papers ahead of completing their divorce. This thought generated a bizarre cocktail of relief, remorse, regret, joy, and failure for David.

Unable to sleep, he sat in the lounge drinking wine. Putting the women issues aside he focused on the café. For a man usually risk-averse, quickly he made a bold decision. The way he saw it, the choice was between sitting at a desk surrounded by spreadsheets for the rest of his working life or setting up a coffee bar offering music, films, and poetry. It had to be the coffee bar. Even if the end result was to be remembered as the man at the council who helped citizens to get funding to care for elderly relatives at a time of economic austerity, or the man who set up a coffee bar with great vision but insufficient customers for it to be a success – he'd still opt for the café. He wanted to make something of his life and this was the opportunity. With the decision made the detailed planning needed to begin.

He finished his third generous glass of Merlot and got ready for bed, hoping the wine would ease him into a restful sleep. But as soon as he lay down he thought of Bridget. This was a common pastime in bed for David, but tonight's line of thought was somewhat different to usual. From their first meeting at the reunion onwards he'd been enchanted by a woman who seemed to possess unlimited serenity and kindness. This perception had been challenged by Bridget owning up to murder. Mind you, it was only slightly a murder – Roland would have died anyway. But the concept of 'slight murder' didn't make any sense and it certainly wouldn't to the police, a lawyer, judge or jury.

David moved on to contemplating the meaning of 'Justice'. Surely Roland deserved what he got? But despite an internal struggle to make the case, he couldn't accept that cruelty merited death.

David then considered 'Truth', or perhaps more to the point, lying. Bridget had lied to him when she'd first told him the story of Roland's death. The way she'd described it second time round could be equally untrue. Perhaps she had a compulsion to lie and a third version would be forthcoming. He dismissed this as unlikely – anyone would be reluctant to tell a virtual stranger she had murdered her husband.

There was no reason not to start a relationship. Or was there? Was 'Morality' at stake? Did he have a moral duty to turn her in? And what about 'Fear'? Should he be concerned that she might murder again? Even murder him?

Justice. Truth. Morality. Fear. Concepts philosophers dedicated their lives to considering. He'd done so when half-asleep in a matter of minutes and had reached a conclusion. He'd call Bridget tomorrow after work to put her mind at rest and arrange to meet. Just the two of them, no children around.

With decisions about Bridget and the café sorted and with the signing of the papers with Jane a formality, that only left Mary and Rachel to deal with. Enough for one night – he could sleep peacefully.

The next morning, a cold and grey January day, a weary David journeyed to work. He barely had time to sit at his desk when his phone rang and the name flashed up on the display. 'Good morning, Mary.'

'Hi, David, can you pop in for a minute?'

'Sure, I'll come now,' he replied, disappointed he wouldn't be able to chat with Jabulani first.

'Great. I'll make some coffee.'

He strode in, having planned a professional, detached dialogue. Mary greeted him with a watery smile as she stood by the window pouring the coffee. He smiled back as he sat down. Part of his brain wasn't sticking to the plan. He couldn't help but notice how attractive she was. He resisted the temptation to cast his eyes down from her striking face to her striking body. She was looking at him looking at her; he was in danger of giving the wrong signal.

'Quite an evening wasn't it,' she began.

'It was.'

'Did you get home OK?'

'Yes, I enjoyed the walk; it calmed me down a bit.'

'Look I'm sorry …'

'I hope you don't think …'

Their statements collided, to be followed by a few seconds of silence in anticipation of the other person taking the lead. Then they laughed together.

David was first to speak again. He explained that her understanding that he had separated from his wife was correct, but he had met someone else since then, a woman he was very fond of … No, not yet, but they were on the verge of starting a relationship.

The atmosphere became more relaxed as they chatted. David let it be known that despite the police intrusion he had enjoyed the evening with her.

'Maybe the raid contributed towards the fun,' Mary suggested. 'How come you knew some of the police there?'

'It's a long story, but nothing important.'

'Good. I wouldn't like to think we were employing a criminal!'

There was another pause ahead of David spurting out an unplanned statement. 'I hope you don't mind me saying this, Mary, but I think you're an extremely attractive woman. Quite beautiful.'

'That's nice of you to say that.'

'It's the truth.'

'I always miss out on the good guys, that's my life story.' She went on to chat about past partners who resented what she admitted was her over-assertiveness. During these relationships disagreement and argument was the norm. Recently she had gone for men who were compliant, but their submissiveness drove her up the wall and she abandoned them as dull lost causes.

'Which category would I fit in?' David asked.

'I think neither. I respected you when you answered me back the other week, I deserved it. And I thought your nicknames about my dress sense were quite funny …'

'They weren't mine! How did you find out about them?'

'I have ears, idle chat in the kitchen spreads you know. But David, there's a sensitive side to you, I like the combination.'

'Thanks,' David said with sincerity combined with a guilt-ridden sense of a wasted possibility.

Mary stood, walked around her desk, and faced him. 'There are a lot of things about how I behave to deal with. I think I'm all the better for meeting you.'

She extended her arm and placed it on his shoulder. She moved closer still and planted a kiss on his right cheek. 'I hope you don't mind that.'

'Not at all.' The feeling of her lips on his cheek lingered as he walked back to his room. It took quite a while to get Mary and all her stories about partners off his mind. He wondered how many there had been. Certainly more than his clumsy fumble with a girl during his first year at university followed by over twenty years with Jane.

There was a lot of work to catch up on having been out the office for two weeks. He switched on his computer and then commenced to work through the spreadsheets that he hoped to abandon in the not too distant future.

He was in the kitchen at lunch washing up his sandwich container and mug when Jabulani came in.

'Back in your boss's office again this morning I see, David. You are a dark horse indeed.'

'Shh, Jabulani, not in here.'

'There's more of an onion in you than meets the eye.'

'Please not here, the walls are incredibly thin. Come into my office.'

Despite being in the confines of his room with the door closed and speaking in a whisper, David had no inclination to talk about Mary. But Jabulani had noticed the slow dance and the first kiss. And having observed the second kiss, Charlie, Mitch, Dee, and Freddie were ensuring that gossip went endemic across the finance department.

'Typical of that lot. Still, they work in School Bus Transport so I suppose they need something to spice up their lives,' David complained.

‘True enough, but I’d like to know what’s going on.’

‘She’s a bit fragile and vulnerable at the moment,’ David said, in an attempt to lay all responsibility with Mary.

‘It’s more than that, she likes you, man, I can see it. And you seem pretty keen on her, too.’

‘Bridget is the one for me, Jabulani,’ David asserted, declining to tell him the woman he loved had confessed to murder. And that indeed he was attracted to Mary.

They talked about the gig. David was full of praise about the performance – the singing, the dancing, the musicianship, and the way the band had engaged the audience. Jabulani and Farai had been kept behind by the police after everyone else had been allowed to leave, questioned about what they knew of the pub owners. There was little to contribute. Jabulani’s brother had visited several venues in an attempt to get bookings and this was the first to sign them up. They would have received £150, barely enough to cover costs, but at least a start. What with the arrests they didn’t even get paid.

‘We didn’t know we were performing in a place that sold drugs. Anyway, we’ve got some other gigs now; I hope you’ll come along to one.’

‘I’d love to.’

‘Of course I’ll make sure Mary’s invited too.’

‘Get lost, Jabulani!’

Early afternoon David picked up a text from Rachel asking him to collect her after a *Fiddler on the Roof* rehearsal. He set off a little before six and met her on the wall in front of the school gates as usual. A boy was sitting next to her; they were holding hands. As he approached they stood and walked towards the car. Rachel opened the front passenger door. The boy was tall and lean with straight blond hair down to his shoulders.

‘Hi, Dad, this is Joe, alias Lazar Wolf.’

‘Hello, Mr Willoughby.’ Joe had a welcoming face.

‘He’s my boyfriend and a star in this musical of ours. Lazar Wolf’s the second most important male in the show.’

David was glad to meet her boyfriend though wondered what the couple’s agenda was. Joe made it clear. ‘I’m here to apologise for my behaviour the other week. I don’t make a habit of getting drunk and nor does Rachel. It was the end of term and we’d been to someone’s birthday party and things got out of hand. It won’t happen again, I promise you.’

‘Well I appreciate you talking to me, Joe. Thanks.’

Rachel shifted to get into the car but Joe took hold of her arm to stop her. ‘One thing though, Mr Willoughby. I love Rachel – I’ll do whatever I can to make her happy.’

How does a father respond to that? Bridget, Mary, Jane, Jim, there was no reason why two sixteen-year-olds should be excluded from the mess called love.

‘I’m glad to hear that. Well, we’d best be heading off now, I’ve had a really busy day. Nice to meet you.’

David could do nothing other than watch as Joe pressed Rachel against his car where they entwined for a protracted kiss.

‘He’s nice isn’t he, Dad,’ Rachel said as they departed.

Well, at least he’s not a murderer, David thought. He’d call Bridget as soon as he got home.

Chapter Twenty-eight

David was an accountant and accountants plan meticulously. They research to get the facts exactly right. They take notes and rehearse what to say. They are guarded against making false claims.

He would have liked to have spoken to Bridget from the heart, not the head, but years of doing things a certain way couldn't be swept aside overnight. Maybe down the line, when he was running the coffee bar, he'd grow a ponytail, have his ears pierced, get a tattoo, and be spontaneous. But for now he was David the Accountant so he worked out a precise script for the forthcoming conversation. He decided on a light touch, using humour to make her feel at ease.

With the handwritten prompts by his side he dialled her number. He was nervous, a lot was at stake. 'Hello, Andy, is Bridget around?'

'No, she's setting up an exhibition at work. She said you might call and told me to let you know she'll ring back tomorrow evening.'

'Alright, but please make sure you remember to tell her.'

'Of course I will,' Andy replied in an 'I'm not stupid' voice. 'Must go. Bye.'

The impasse continued the following day. David was about to call Bridget mid-afternoon when he received a text.

Hi. Setting up this event a nightmare, back v.late tonight, will def. speak tomorrow. Sorry. B xx

Possibly the most important conversation in his life again put on hold.

On his return home after work he opened the thick A4 envelope sent by his solicitor. He was informed that the terms of the financial settlement with Jane had been scrutinised with due care and attention and were correct. All that was needed were signatures and then the redistribution of assets could commence. This was it – the beginning of the end of twenty or more years together with Jane, now referred to as 'the other party.'

David double-checked the content. All correct, though wading through a document that listed everything they had accumulated and seeing one of two names against each item was a soul destroying experience. The final decisions had been made when Jane had visited a couple of weeks beforehand. They'd stood in each room taking it in turns to select. This part of the separation had been the hardest, for Jane as well as him, as they examined the things they had once shared.

'I think I'll have the sideboard.'

'In that case I'll take the sofa.'

'Which one?'

'That one.'

'OK, I'll have this.'

It had been far less traumatic dealing with money despite being of higher value. Bank accounts, shares, and ISAs were just bits of paper – they were distributed with a fifty-fifty split. The house would remain under joint ownership with Jane contributing a third of the mortgage repayments until Sam reached the age of eighteen, when they would sell and split the net income after repaying the balance still owed. Finally, as long as Jane remained employed, she was required to contribute towards child maintenance.

Along with the documents was an invoice from his solicitor for work to date. David wrote out a cheque for £2,326.58 and enclosed it with the signed papers and a covering letter. As an act of great generosity the buff envelope had been provided free of charge, but the cost of the postage was itemised in the bill. He baulked at having been charged twenty pence per sheet for photocopying and fifty pounds for each telephone call, however brief.

With that out of the way David countered the wretchedness of the task by looking forward.

The café.

He'd already done some research. Just before the Christmas break he'd surveyed work colleagues to test whether a market existed. When he collated the returns of a questionnaire he'd prepared, there was universal agreement that those not drawn to the bars frequented by the very young would stay out after a meal or a film if only there was somewhere decent to go.

David had also investigated how to attract daytime customers bearing in mind every shopping centre was already full of coffee bars, virtually all of them part of a franchised chain. The same colleagues had been given a second questionnaire the next day, David deflecting curiosity by explaining that it was for his son's Geography project.

Would you like to see more independent coffee bars on the high street?

Do you currently shop at the coffee bar chains?

If an independent coffee shop opened would you switch?

Every response was 'yes', 'yes', and 'probably'. Not much help.

Although his market research could in no way be regarded as analytical or conclusive, it was clear that to have a chance his café would have to be different – a venue and not merely a coffee bar. A venue with music, films, poetry readings, and art exhibitions. A place where at lunchtime you could get interesting homemade sandwiches; in the afternoon upmarket cakes and pastries; and in the evening a glass of good quality wine sitting at the same table as someone ordering a coffee.

He Googled 'how to set up a café' and was confronted with scope to access a staggering 192 million websites. He browsed through the eleven on the first page after having made a mental note that there could be 17,454,545 pages on the topic.

He wanted to find out how people had gone about setting up coffee bars and which commercial organisations supplied them. Lists seemed to work for him so he constructed a new one.

1. Should he buy or lease a property?
2. What size of premises was needed?
3. Where should he locate?
4. What was the process for obtaining alcohol and entertainment licenses?
5. Who were the best suppliers of furniture, coffee machines, food and drink?

He browsed and took comprehensive notes until approaching three in the morning. He was pleased with the night's work but now sleep was needed. He'd love to have Bridget with him. He could show her his new list.

Chapter Twenty-nine

Work the following day began in Mary's office as they set about preparing budgets for the next year. He could feel the warmth of her body and smell the subtle fragrance of her perfume as they sat side by side. He struggled to focus on Bridget. Yes, he wanted Bridget (despite the murder), though Mary was a worthy reserve.

At home he waited for Bridget to call. Rachel and Sam were in good spirits; their school examinations had kicked off successfully. The three of them were eating raspberries and yoghurt when the phone rang.

'It'll be for me,' David declared, taking hold of the receiver and dashing out the room. He took his prompt sheet out his trousers pocket as he walked. 'Hello, Bridget, I'm just going upstairs.' He went into his bedroom and closed the door behind him.

'Hi, David. Sorry I've been out of contact for a couple of days. We're launching a new artist and he's obsessive about how his work's displayed. He keeps changing his mind.'

David had thought long and hard about his first statement. He'd revised it several times before coming up with something light and humorous, but also filled with passion. It was perfect.

'You know how fond of you I am, Bridget. I don't care how many men you've murdered – I still want you!'

There was a pause without laughter from the other end of the line.

David broke the silence. 'Bridget? Are you there?'

'I expected a little more sensitivity, David. It wasn't easy plucking up the courage to tell you.'

'It was a joke.'

'Not a very funny one.'

'Oh.'

'I spend a lot of time thinking about what I've done and the last thing I need is that sort of comment. Apart from my father you're the only person I've ever told, I hope you appreciate that.'

'Yes, I do.' David was frantically scanning his prompt notes in search of something to improve the atmosphere. He reached a line that would do the trick.

'I've done a lot of research about the café. It's really exciting.'

'Don't change the subject. Do you get what I'm saying? I can't have you joking about what happened. Not now, not ever.'

'You're right, I'm sorry.' This statement was off script. In fact the piece of paper with his notes had dropped to the floor and might as well stay there. Probably for ever because this was shaping up to be a final conversation.

There was an awkward silence, David speechless. Bridget introduced a glimmer of hope. 'Look, let's meet up to talk things through, it'll be easier than a telephone conversation.'

David was barely listening. The unstoppable march towards a relationship had come to an abrupt end and he would be informed of this when they met. He tried to sound upbeat. 'Good idea, I'd like that. When?'

'Sometime this weekend. You're going to have to come here though because I can't leave Kay. She's gone down with a temperature. Something's going round at school and if that's what she's caught it'll take a week to clear.'

'Poor thing,' David said, in the hope that Bridget might appreciate the concern for her daughter. 'Do send her my love. When's a good time to come over?'

'What about Saturday evening?'

'Great, I'll see you then.' He was squeaking, not

speaking. While wondering what to say next, Bridget ended the dialogue with a curt 'bye' and put the phone down. He listened to the ringing tone for a while.

It would be a mammoth under-exaggeration to state that the conversation hadn't gone particularly well. Even the word 'disaster' wasn't strong enough. He'd completely misjudged the capacity for humour and as a result had in all likelihood antagonised Bridget beyond redemption.

Drinking two thirds of a bottle of Soave helped him sleep.

He woke up convinced that his immature one-liner had ruined everything with Bridget. A second thought was laden with disloyalty and deceit – he needed to foster the relationship with his first reserve just in case. He was becoming a rake, a cad. He'd reached an appalling layer of Jabulani's onion.

Ashamed of this thought, nevertheless he was particularly nice to Mary that week. He complimented her on her dress sense, made her coffee, brought in a packet of Waitrose's luxury Belgian chocolate biscuits, and worked hard to get all the budget sums right. Mary responded with plenty of smiles and some platonic physical contact that seemed anything but platonic. It's amazing what message a hand placed on an arm can give, especially when the hand lingers and caresses.

Following the confused week of mixed messages that flowed between him and Mary, David was relieved when Saturday evening arrived and he could set off to see Bridget. He was torn between whether to plan what to say or be spontaneous. Since his usual approach of planning had failed so miserably during the telephone conversation, he opted for playing it by ear though starting with an apology. He'd follow this by being friendly, but not too close until he could assess Bridget's mood. And in the unlikely event of her being forgiving, he'd discuss the café.

Bridget greeted him at her front door with a warm smile followed by a kiss, a quick one but still worth savouring. Then she took hold of his hand and led him into the lounge. He sat. She remained standing, looking down at him.

'A big apology, David, I was dreadfully curt the other night. I've been working twelve hour days with my boss and the sodding artist driving me mad. I was exhausted and then I got home and discovered Kay was ill. I had to be at work the next day and had no idea who'd be able to look after her. In the end Andy skipped school to assist.'

'Don't even dream of apologising, that has to come from me. I was an absolute idiot saying what I did and I'm desperately sorry.'

'Thank you, I appreciate that. So we're both sorry then.'

'I don't want to lose you.'

She sat next to him. 'Well, you haven't got me yet, have you?' She leaned across and they kissed, a longer exchange than the one at the door. She poured out two glasses of wine then sat back, a little apart from David.

'We shouldn't be doing this kissing, should we?'

'Why not?'

'Because you need to tell me what you think about Roland's murder.'

'Bridget, I've thought a lot about that. Were you right to do it, were you wrong?'

She interrupted. 'That's easy to answer. Murder is wrong.'

'Yes, I agree. I started thinking of different grades of murder, but came to the conclusion that was ridiculous. I don't know the details of how badly Roland treated you, but what's done is done and I want to help you move on.'

Bridget smiled. 'And then you'll be able to tick off the objectives on your bloody list.'

'Yes, you've sussed me out, that's the only reason.

Actually, I've made another list.'

'Shut up!'

David started talking about the café as he handed her a piece of paper.

'You really have got another list. I thought you were joking.'

'This one will help, it's the key decisions I'll need to make.'

Bridget came up with practical questions related to money. How would he get the finance to set up?

'I might offer the house as collateral,' he suggested.

'Are you able to do that if Jane is a co-owner?'

'I'm not sure, I'll need to discuss that at the bank.'

Bridget poured herself another glass of wine. 'More?'

'I'm not staying tonight, am I?'

'No, best not with Kay at home and unwell.'

'Then I'd better abstain.'

For a short while they sat in silence, nestled together on the sofa. Having her lying against him was such a relief bearing in mind his earlier anxiety. But she was so still that David wondered whether she'd fallen asleep. Then she sprang up. 'This café idea. Might you want a partner?'

'Why do you ask?'

'I'm fed up with my job and wonder whether you'd be interested in taking me on. I think I could help.'

'Well, of course yes, I'd love that. But what's up at work? I thought you enjoyed the gallery.'

Chapter Thirty

Bridget had been thinking of a career change for quite a while though with no idea of what to do instead. Work in the art gallery had become less and less satisfying. She had no interest in what she was selling and she despised a significant number of her customers.

Friday's experience had placed another nail in the coffin. 'This isn't art,' she'd declared as she looked at the new exhibits.

'Don't be a dinosaur, Bridget,' her boss Bradley had proclaimed as they regarded the frame housing an opened condom stretching towards a scrappy ink sketch of a vagina. 'It evokes the degenerate pursuit of short-term self-gratification in the twenty-first century.'

'You don't really think that, you can't.'

'Actually I read it, it's how Sean Holloway describes the piece.'

Bridget had first met Sean when they were setting up the exhibition and he was a pretentious ignoramus. 'The condom work has to go next to the crushed plastic bottles' he'd declared. 'The two materials are in harmony. Surely even you can appreciate that.'

Sean Holloway was flavour of the month, an artist of working class origin who hadn't lifted a pencil or paint brush for his first twenty-five years. Then he was arrested for graffiti offences in Sidcup and the art critic in the *Sunday Times* claimed there was an intense energy in his art. For some reason a minor art college offered him a place based on the newspaper article, perhaps attracted by the lure of publicity. They kicked him out after less than a month, hinting that he was a talentless no-hoper. Despite that rejection he started to sell and the bandwagon rolled.

'He can't draw, he's useless,' Bridget persisted. 'Abstract artists must go through the discipline of drawing. You know that, Bradley.'

'It doesn't matter what we think, we're a business. I got these works for a great price and I bet we sell them before the end of the month.'

Bradley was wrong thinking they would sell within a month if the first day was anything to go by. At that rate they'd be gone within a week. And good riddance!

At just after 1 p.m. on Friday, the opening day of the sale, a young couple had come in. He was dressed in a pinstripe suit with powder blue shirt and silver tie. She had on the casual clothes of the young and rich, a pseudo-destitute look with skimpy, scruffy jeans and frayed leather jacket. The designer labels gave the game away.

'I've heard you've got some Holloways in. Let me see them,' the man asked with something approaching a Cockney accent. Bridget took an instant dislike to him and had a strong urge to tell him off for not adding 'please'. She led them to the ten or so exhibits on display. His first sighting was the condom artwork and he roared raucously.

'Bugger me; come 'ere doll. Look at this!'

Bridget, who was not a snob, cringed at the *'ere.* Was it the remnant of a past at odds with his new-found City wealth or the attempt of a posho to be seen as one of the lads? 'Doll' was manicuring her nails. She looked across. 'Blimey.'

'Fuck me, and this one,' City boy exclaimed, looking at a diaphragm surrounded by speckles of red and to its right, a poorly drawn cartoon of an erect black penis. 'These are great,' he exclaimed. 'Aren't they?' he ordered rather than asked his girlfriend.

The young woman glanced up again, irritated by the disturbance. 'If you like them,' she muttered as she lifted a lipstick out her handbag, 'get them.'

‘How much are these things?’ he asked Bridget. The prices were listed along with the titles and artist’s name underneath the works. Perhaps he was illiterate; she couldn’t bear the man. She pointed at the labels before summoning enough false enthusiasm to speak. ‘Have you seen this sculpture, sir?’ She had directed him to the bottles. ‘If you decide on the condom you must get this – the two materials are in perfect harmony.’

‘Yeah, I see what you mean, they are kind of similar. Bit pricey though,’ he added, having taken the trouble to read the large print labels. They were £24,000 each. ‘Would you do a deal if I bought both?’

‘This is an art gallery, not a supermarket. We don’t do deals.’

Bradley was by her side. ‘Apologies, sir, Bridget is having a tough day. We can take 10% off if you purchase both.’

The deal was done with Bridget loitering in the background and Bradley casting dark looks. She adjourned to the small kitchenette and had her Marks & Spencer avocado and pine nut sandwich, tropical fruit cocktail, and cranberry juice. Bradley ignored her when he came in for his own lunch.

As soon as she stepped back into the gallery another customer came in, an older man with a thick mane of salt and pepper hair. Bridget thought his smile was a leer and kept a physical distance.

He was another of the pinstripe suit brigade, though not as style-conscious as the previous customer. His polka dot tie clashed with the navy and white striped shirt. Why bother purchasing art if you’re devoid of aesthetic taste, she would have liked to have asked him.

‘Rumour has it you’ve acquired some Holloways in this treasure trove.’ He had a booming, pompous voice. ‘Oh, there they are.’

He brushed past her and walked across to the Holloway

area, now with red stickers on the corners of the sold works. ‘Two already gone, eh?’

‘Yes, though in my opinion nowhere near the best,’ she said, resigned to drumming up sales to boost her commission. They approached an appalling attempt to draw a table on which rested a syringe and a flattened can of Red Bull.

He examined the information below the work – this one was priced at £31,000. Since it was no more skilfully painted than the others, Bridget could only assume price was set based on size. It was working out at about £50 per square inch – maybe she should point that out to customers to demonstrate value for money!

‘I think they’re awful but they are shooting up in value, eh,’ the polka dot man said. He took out a Filofax and turned to a page with jottings. Bridget glanced across and noted dates and prices. March £12,000. July £21,000. December £26,000.

‘I’ll take it,’ he said. ‘It’ll be up to over forty by the end of summer, eh.’

And that was that. He took out his cheque book and Parker pen while Bridget contemplated the point of the ‘eh’ when upper class men spoke. Were they taught to use it at school?

‘Jolly good value, eh,’ she jibed as he was writing. She caught Bradley giving her a filthy look. She didn’t care. Three pieces of absolute crap sold in an hour for over £70,000, and a furious boss.

‘I feel terrible, do you mind if I leave early?’ she asked.

‘Good idea if you do,’ Bradley replied.

She put on her coat and walked out without casting an eye on the artistic offerings displayed. The Holloways were at the bottom of the talent list, but there were some close calls for the runner up.

The Northern Line was down again due to signal failure so she resorted to edging through central London in an overcrowded bus. She was tired, tired of the daily commute, tired of what the West End had to offer, tired of selling poor quality, high-priced so-called art to buyers only interested in the shock of the new or the investment potential. Perhaps she was being arrogant to categorise art into good or bad with such authority. Over a hundred years ago many had laughed at the Impressionists and it was left to pioneers to buy their works, quite likely for the same two reasons as her customers. At school she had loved Impressionism but at college she'd been weaned off it by lecturers who considered the movement too mainstream and no longer challenging.

Today Bridget had to have a shot of Impressionism. She jumped off the bus as it reached Trafalgar Square and spent an hour wandering around the late nineteenth-century rooms in the National Gallery. The colour, the movement, the sheer emotion of the works relegated the modern stuff to pretentious insignificance.

The visit had lifted her spirits, but sitting on a less crowded bus as she continued the journey home, she considered whether she should quit what until now had been her single career. By the time she alighted the decision was final. She needed to find other work, though quickly, what with two children to provide for. But she had no idea what she should do.

The reaching of a crisis point was perfect timing as far as David was concerned. With trepidation he double-checked her suggestion. 'Do you really think your new work could be running a café with me?'

'Well, I've given a tentative yes. It is possible, but I need a lot more detail about how you think it could work. Actually I sound far too cautious – I'm really excited.'

Kay calling out brought an abrupt end to their discussion. Bridget went up to see what she wanted. Back downstairs she suggested David should leave so she could change bed linen and pyjamas and make a hot drink for her feverish daughter.

'Let's meet up to talk things through as soon as Kay's better,' he suggested as he stood by the door.

'Absolutely yes,' she replied from half way up the stairs.

Chapter Thirty-one

David's list of objectives was hidden in his office filing cabinet, tucked away in the middle of an uninviting document called 'Procedures against care homes following their failure to report the death of a resident'. It was safe there – the cabinet was kept locked and since he was the only one responsible for dealing with such occurrences, no one else would ever need access.

Although he knew the list by heart, he took it out for a cursory glance.

Medium/Long term objectives

1. Take a cookery course
2. Quit my job and pack in accountancy
3. Open an arts café
4. Have sex with Bridget by 20 February
5. Have more sex with Bridget by the end of the first week of March

Only one thing achieved so far, progress could perhaps be classed as 'satisfactory' for the rest. He replaced the sheet inside the document between page twenty-six, his house number, and twenty-seven.

Rachel and Sam were hovering in the hall as David returned from work on Monday evening.

'Dad, we've got something to tell you. Well, to ask.' Rachel looked concerned and David feared another school incident.

'Mum's got tickets for *Billy Elliot* on Saturday evening and she's asked if we can stay over – at Jim's. We don't know whether to say yes or no. Part of me thinks what's done is done and we might as well move on. But I don't want to offend you. Would you mind?'

David zoomed in on the opportunity this might present. 'No, not at all. I think moving on is a sensible idea,' he replied with great generosity.

Having made certain the children were out of earshot he called Bridget to invite her over for dinner that Saturday. She accepted.

The next evening he had a trial run of Saturday's meal. It was still early days on his Simple Italian Cooking class. The 'simple' was proving to be a misnomer and he wasn't confident he could deliver a Tuscan or Sicilian delight. He decided to revisit what he'd produced on the *Learn to Cook – Anyone Can Do It* course.

He began with seasonal vegetable soup and cheese croutons. Theoretically this should have been followed by pan-roasted free range chicken with tarragon and crème fraiche sauce, but in preparation for Bridget he replaced the chicken with Quorn. The children were suspicious of this soggy new ingredient and stabbed at it with their forks. David gave it a try before rejecting it as unappetising. After work the next day he scoured the supermarket shelves for a substitute before serving up a near-identical meal for his bemused children, but with marinated tofu replacing Quorn. The children moaned but he thought it was better. As a reward for resilience he cooked them unadorned chicken on the Thursday.

Saturday at last.

He drove Rachel and Sam to Jim's house, an attractive semi-detached building on the border between Finchley and Mill Hill. He'd visited many times and it was disconcerting to return now that it was Jane's home. Out of curiosity rather than need he escorted the children up the path to the front door. Sam rang the bell and Jane answered.

'Hello, everyone.' She looked at David intently.

‘Thanks for letting them stay here, I appreciate it. Would you like to come in for a coffee?’

David noticed the small table and above it the painting of a man and woman at the seaside, stretched out on striped canvas deckchairs, munching ice cream cones. He and Jane had bought the painting in Brighton way back, before the children were born. Until a few days ago both table and painting had been in what was now his house.

‘Thanks, but I need to head on. I’ve got rather a lot to do today.’

‘Anything nice?’

He didn’t answer.

Jane continued. ‘We’re thinking of going ice skating at Somerset House tomorrow afternoon. We’ll bring them back after that.’

‘That’s fine,’ David said. He looked across at his children and gave them a reassuring smile. ‘Have a good time,’ he added as he headed off.

Once home and full of nervous energy, he embarked on worthless garden maintenance, considering the bleakness of the early January day. He then took a shower and began to prepare the food.

Bridget arrived soon after 7.30. As he greeted then took hold of her, David was hit by a powerful physical force like an electric charge. The effect of that first contact, just a touch against the fabric of her soft purple jumper, was so intense he pulled away.

Bridget stepped back. ‘Objective number four tonight, isn’t it?’

‘Maybe we should postpone that and work on my coffee bar plans instead,’ he joked as he put his arms around her shoulders. Then they were back in an embrace, kissing passionately.

Dinner was a success with Bridget complimenting him. He wanted her to think that the meal was one of a range of menu options at his disposal. But he’d forgotten cookery was included in the list of objectives she'd seen.

'Have you started your cookery course yet?' she inquired.

'Sort of, just half a day so far. But now I've signed up for Simple Italian Cooking.'

'So is this from that first course?'

'I've refined it quite a bit. Have some more wine,' he added, keen to change the subject.

They'd already finished a bottle of Vouvray and were on their second. Bridget took a couple of sips from her newly filled glass then stood and walked round to David's side of the table.

'Now, where were we up to last time I was here?' she teased as she began undoing his shirt buttons. 'This too, I seem to remember,' she added as she leaned forward to kiss his chest as she opened each button.

He removed her cardigan and bra. 'We got this far I believe. Upstairs?' he suggested.

'Yes, good idea. I know it worked in *Lady Chatterley's Lover* and *The Postman Always Rings Twice*, but having sex on a kitchen table's never appealed to me. Come on, up we go.'

David laughed as he followed Bridget up the stairs. The wine had made him rather light-headed. He leaned forward in an attempt to caress her naked back but misjudged her stepping speed, stumbled, and ended up on his knees stroking a stair.

Bridget turned and gave him a puzzled look. 'You OK?'

'Yes, fine. I thought I saw a tack poking through the carpet but I was wrong.'

'Shall we keep going then?'

In the bedroom he hastily undid his belt and pulled down his trousers. He struggled to take them off, but they tangled with his shoes and he toppled down onto the bed.

Bridget was smiling at him; he was acting like a first-timer.

'Here, let me help,' she offered as she bent down to untie his laces and remove his shoes. She then yanked off his trousers and took off her own skirt. 'You need some space around here too by the looks of things,' she added, looking at his erection. She slid off his boxers, running her hand against his penis as she did so. With David motionless she took off her own knickers. He stood, took hold of her and dropped them both onto the bed.

'Finally. Alone together,' he exclaimed looking into light blue eyes exuding far more confidence about what was to happen than he felt.

He adjusted his position until their bodies pressed together. He was all set. At last. He caressed the small of her back and moved his hand downwards.

'Err, just one thing, David.'

'Mm?'

'I hope you don't mind me asking.'

'No, what?'

'Socks.'

'Yes?'

'Your socks are still on. I've got a bit of a thing about having sex with a man wearing socks.'

David sat up with a start, his head colliding with Bridget's. After the initial shock and shot of dizzying pain they both laughed. He took off his socks, noting with horror that his right foot big toe had been poking through a hole. He looked down at his shrivelling penis and then with intense embarrassment, up to Bridget. Her smile was wonderful, but was it to share or directed at him?

'Come here, you,' she said as she pulled him close. His erection was restored and they were engaging in blissful foreplay. As he was about to enter her he had one more practical thought and considered it his moral duty to raise it.

‘Bridget’

‘Yes?’

‘No condom.’

‘What?’

‘I haven’t put on a condom. They’re in the drawer.’

‘No problem, don’t need it, I’m protected. That is, for contraception, not STDs. But somehow I don’t think you’re a risk.’

At last conversation ceased, replaced by heavy breathing and gasps of joy.

He woke with a dull ache where Bridget’s head was resting on his upper arm. He looked across at the clock, could see it was 3.17. The light was still on in the landing so he could see her face, a face that had enchanted him from the instant they’d met at the reunion. The quilt was pulled up high to her neck. He was hungry to see more of her so edged it down to expose her breasts. She giggled in her sleep as he stretched down to kiss a nipple. Turned on, he moved his hand down to her stomach, onwards through her tight curls of hair, to between her legs. She responded, still half asleep, stroking him. This soporific foreplay continued for quite some time until, with Bridget wet and David hard, he entered her with far greater conviction and self-confidence than the first time and they made serene and rhythmic love.

When they woke late morning Bridget was the first to speak. ‘That was lovely, David, wonderful.’

‘You’re amazing.’

‘You’re not bad yourself. I suppose congratulations are due.’

‘What for?’

‘You’ve accomplished objective number four and five, the latter well ahead of schedule. It’s only the café left, isn’t it?’

‘Yes, but I’ve given myself permission to repeat numbers four and five as much as you want!’

Chapter Thirty-two

‘I love it!’

David and Bridget were chatting about the café while brunching in his kitchen. She’d produced two perfect cappuccinos using the espresso machine that until then only Jane had mastered. When they’d divided possessions he’d queried her omission of this prize asset, but Jane didn’t need it because Jim had purchased a top of the range machine as a moving-in present.

David waited for the next round of bread to pop out. Jane had taken the previous toaster. As a counter to her ‘top of the range’ jibe, he’d bought the most expensive replacement he could find, an Art Deco black and silver steel model.

Focusing on the café wasn’t easy. Bridget was wearing the same *Simpsons* T-shirt that David had provided during her first visit, the family in a line smiling. She was naked underneath and he could see the outline of her nipples through the material. To make matters worse, or better depending on how you looked at it, the garment had ridden up to the top of her thighs.

Bridget was blissfully unaware of his thoughts and was chatting away about the cost of opening and running the café. ‘The arts focus is exciting and I accept what you say about needing a unique selling point, but we must sort out the money side before getting carried away with anything else.’

David agreed but insisted that more research and outside advice would be needed to make any dialogue about costs meaningful. Bridget relented and suggested a consideration of name. Something that stood out. David came up with a title straight away and Bridget declared, 'I love it!'

A Street Café Named Desire.

'I've got to be honest, Bridget, it's a name I've heard before.'

'How come? Do you just mean the play?'

'No, more than that. My uncle was thinking of opening an arts café and he came up with it; well, to be exact his business partner did. They were all set to open near Kew Gardens when his friend announced he was off to Russia to meet a woman he'd found on the internet. That's a story in itself. This guy was a French teacher at my uncle's school. He'd never been married and according to my uncle had never even been in a relationship. He was in his late fifties and there he was deciding to travel across Europe to meet up with a twenty-something woman. You can bet what she was after. I've got no idea what happened, but I can't imagine it ending in anything other than disaster. Anyway, the café idea had to be scrapped.'

'But would your uncle mind us pinching the name?'

'No. I've asked him, he's fine with it.'

'Great. OK, back to planning then.'

'There's a bit more to my uncle's story. He was desperate to get out of teaching and decided to have a go at writing a novel. You'd expect highbrow literary fiction from an English teacher at a girls' independent school, but he wrote an erotic fantasy. *And you thought I was a boring teacher*, it's called. You might have heard of it, there was quite a bit of publicity.'

'What's his name?'

'Henry Derbyshire.'

'That does ring a bell. I think I saw him interviewed on television.

David dropped two perfectly bronzed slices of toast

into the bread basket and sat down.

Bridget had a pad of paper in front of her, so far with nothing more than the café name written down.

'What about location?' She wrote 'location'. David's infatuation extended to being in love with her wild, looping writing.

Wherever they located, with the possible exception of the Outer Hebrides, there would be competition. Our café they decided, (already they were using 'our'), would charge premium prices so needed to be in an affluent area, preferably where there was interest in the arts. Bridget reckoned another factor might be to locate where the predominant politics was left of centre to cater for customers who had a resentment of the café chains.

'That's Muswell Hill all over,' she suggested. David wasn't convinced, having witnessed the behaviour of local youths on the Saturday night he'd stayed at her house. Nevertheless he agreed that Bridget should investigate vacant premises.

They were chatting about what events the café might offer when they heard the front door open. Rachel and Sam called out then came into the kitchen. Bridget pulled down the Simpsons T-shirt. Rather awkward hellos were said before Sam explained that the Somerset House ice skating session had been cancelled because Jim had a headache. A brief chat about the *Billy Elliot* performance followed before the children, sensing their father's embarrassment, headed off upstairs.

'Bridget,' David asked. 'Is it fair to say we're in a relationship?'

'That's a reasonable assumption,' she mocked.

'Then we should let Rachel and Sam know, also your two. It's not as if there's anything to hide.'

'I'm OK with that.'

'I'll call them down then.' David stood then paused. 'Jane left four months ago, that isn't much of a gap before starting a new relationship is it? Do you think they, particularly Rachel, will resent it?'

'I think they'll be pleased you're happy. What was your relationship like in the months before Jane left?'

'In what way?'

'Were you sleeping with her?'

'No. Not for two or three months, even longer.'

'So that adds up to at least half a year of celibacy, you poor thing.'

'Yes, but the kids wouldn't know that, would they?'

'They're probably more astute than you think.'

'Maybe. I'll get them downstairs.'

Bridget stood. 'I'll get dressed,' she said as she headed out the door.

David followed her upstairs, providing a pleasant reminder of the previous night. She went into his bedroom while he approached Rachel's room. Was choice of music a reflection of the listener's state of mind? He hoped so because the angry blasts of stadium rock that had emanated from her bedroom since Jane had left had been replaced by the mellow chords of Coldplay. He knocked and was told to wait. He heard some scurrying around and when the door was finally opened he was greeted by a blast of cold air. Although the window was open the smell of cigarette smoke hadn't disappeared. He asked her to come to the lounge in five minutes.

When he knocked on Sam's door he got a similar instruction to wait. Sam was sitting at the computer examining the pie charts on screen. A parent's sixth sense gave David the feeling that the current display had not been what Sam was looking at ahead of his father's visit. The request to come to the lounge was acknowledged with a grunt.

David rushed back down, put the kettle on, opened a packet of Jaffa Cakes, and took out the mugs. By the time he brought the tea things into the lounge the other three were in there, chatting away comfortably.

As soon as David sat down Rachel fired a question. 'Bridget, here's a question for you. What colour are these walls?'

Bridget played along with the pretence of thinking deeply as she examined them. 'I reckon they're orange,' she finally announced.

'Nope, you're wrong. Do you want to try again?'

'No, I'm happy for you to give me the correct answer.'

'You tell her, Sam.'

'No, I'm not playing.'

'OK, I'll do it. The answer is burnt umber.'

'Yes, I can see my mistake now. What an idiot for not spotting it.'

Rachel liked her reply and the conversation drifted into a description of the colours in Bridget's house and that led to Bridget talking about her background in art and the work she did at the gallery. They were getting on very well while David and Sam sat in silence, drinking tea and munching Jaffa Cakes.

David brought the fringe meeting to an end. 'There's something I need to tell you both,' he announced, surprised by the tremor in his voice. 'It's about Bridget and me. We've grown very fond of each other and want to spend lots of time together. So she'll be staying here and sleeping in the same bedroom as me. I'm sure you realise what I'm saying in terms of what this means as adults, which of course is what we are.'

David had been looking down. Now he looked up to see three smirking faces.

'We're going out,' Bridget summarised.

'Well that was pretty obvious from this morning,' Rachel said. 'Cool, hopefully it'll make Dad a bit more cheerful.'

They carried on chatting, including brief mention of their idea to open a café. The atmosphere was relaxed and

David suggested going out for a meal that evening to celebrate, all six of them. Bridget agreed and set off home to inform Andy and Kay about the new man in her life.

Chapter Thirty-three

The celebratory meal was a success and the children readily accepted the other grown up 'staying over' as David referred to it, though he did overhear Rachel describing it to her boyfriend as 'an OAP fuck fest'.

Mornings in bed together were often spent with Bridget questioning David about his past – his childhood, life with Jane, work and friendships. She evaded satisfying his curiosity about her until early one Sunday morning. It was still dark outside. He fired questions at her. What was life like after Roland died? She'd mentioned failed relationships, but who before him? How had she coped at school when she was regarded as such an outsider? What made her come along to the all-important reunion?

She was relaxed and for the first time since telling him about Roland, was willing to chat about her past.

Turning up at the reunion was as unlikely a coincidence for her as it had been for David. Like him she'd had virtually no contact with her peers of twenty-five years ago and there were no wonderful reminiscences of school life to entice her to come along. She'd been marginalised by the girls and mocked by the boys with the result that by the time she reached young adulthood, she was spending angst-ridden hours fretting about why this had been the case.

She'd concluded that being a foreigner with an odd accent didn't help matters, even though in her case foreign only meant Scotland. She'd arrived at secondary school late, at age twelve, when her father had got a job as a forensic scientist in Oxfordshire. She was perceived as an outsider, an invader, a threat to the firm friendships already in place. A forceful culture of uniformity existed at the school, embracing dress sense, pop music preferences, and indifference at least in public to academic success. Bridget induced hostility because she was an independent thinker who enjoyed study, coupled with an accent from a remote part of the isle.

Defiantly she played on the others' antagonism by exaggerating her Scottish brogue to the point of caricature. And she refused to be bullied into concealing her interest in learning and, most of all, her passion for art. She received little protection from teachers who accepted the lethargy of her fellow pupils as a worthwhile trade-off against the threat of poor behaviour.

Bridget described occasions when her teachers had joined pupils in taunting her for being so enthusiastic.

'Perhaps it's time to give others the opportunity to answer,' she recalled one of them suggesting, and then being infuriated by Bridget's truthful response that no one else was bothered.

There was a notable exception – Miss Harris. Bridget was fortunate to have the same art teacher for all six years of her time at the school. Josephine, as Bridget was allowed to call her when she reached the sixth form, was by far the fondest memory and greatest inspiration during her time at Henley High.

Josephine Harris had long since retired. Judging by the Facebook group set up to inform about the reunion, she wouldn't have been invited even if still working at the school. Some bright spark had named the group 'Teachers Leave Us Kids Alone'. When new signatories enquired whether teachers were invited they were informed 'no way'. Comments indicated that for some, little growing up had taken place over the past quarter of a century. Ginny, who Bridget remembered with little affection, wrote 'pity no teachers, would like to take the piss out of poncy Clive Rees like we did way back then.'

It had been early September when out of the blue Bridget received an email from Pru White. “Friend” was too strong a description, but Pru had been a girl who Bridget did socialise with all those years ago. They shared a keen interest in art and regularly trekked to galleries on Saturday afternoons and during school holidays. They’d kept in touch through their art college years, Bridget in London and Pru in Manchester. Nothing in particular brought an end to their six-monthly or so meetings, nothing more than the general drift of life. As the meetings waned letters replaced them, with enclosed photographs of ‘my wedding day’, ‘Andy aged three’, ‘holiday in Corfu’. Pru’s life became increasingly stable and fulfilling – ‘everyone over for my birthday’, ‘Sebastian’s christening’, ‘celebrating my promotion’ – while Bridget’s was becoming ever more uncomfortable.

The invention of email was the excuse to shorten communication, though even in her brief exchanges Pru was able to fit in ‘fabulous’, ‘enjoyable’, and ‘wonderful’. Bridget’s stock phrases were ‘career continuing to go nowhere’, ‘still having marriage difficulties’, and ‘children getting more of a handful’. There was a recurring statement at the end of messages from both of them – ‘we *really* must meet up soon.’

But they hadn’t met for over fifteen years and correspondence other than a Christmas card ceased after Bridget had sent a long email describing, admittedly with the necessary protective omission, what had happened to Roland. She got a curt reply. *Sorry to hear that, poor you. We really must meet up soon.*

Then the out of the blue message arrived from Pru, informing her of the reunion. A flurry of communication followed with the plan that they would both go. At the point of signing up Pru announced she had been called to a conference in Prague. She couldn’t get out of it so Bridget was left alone. Her first reaction was to drop the idea of attending even though she'd already made plans for the children to stay with friends and she could think of nothing else to occupy her weekend. Visits to Facebook strengthened her belief that taking part would do no more than revive if not quite a nightmare, hardly ecstatic bliss. However, at the very least it would be an opportunity for a rare visit to her old home town. And it would be interesting to see whether the people she'd once despised had improved.

'So I went along. And a good job too.' She turned and gave David a kiss on his cheek. 'Fancy a coffee? I'll make them and bring them up.' She kept some things at his house now, including a shiny black kimono with little sprigs of pink and yellow blossom. She put it on.

'To be honest,' she said when she got back, 'all the boys at school ignored me except one. His name was David and I was hoping he'd be there.'

'Really? I didn't know. I do remember defending you against my friends who thought you were weird for wearing odd coloured socks and doing ink drawings on the back of your hand.'

'You were the only one who checked if I was OK when you saw me crying in the playground.'

'I didn't like to see you hurt. I thought you were nice, too. I wish I'd been bold enough to act on it, to ask you out. All these years wasted.'

'No, not wasted. For a start, if we'd got together then there wouldn't be Andy, Kay, Rachel, or Sam. And it might have only lasted for a week like most of the other school pairings.'

'I suppose you're right. Here's an odd question. You've talked about relationships after Roland and I'm sort of nosy about who and what they were like.'

'That's a bit weird. I'm not going to allocate a score out of ten for each lover.'

'A pity, I was hoping to produce a list.'

'Until you I've not been great at choosing. I hope you realise I feel very secure with you. And don't worry, you're sexy too.'

'Who were you with before me, before the reunion?'

'Jesus, you really are a creep after all!'

Jan had lasted a little over six months. The relationship ended when Bridget discovered he was married. The day they met she'd taken the morning off work to catch the Rothko exhibition at the Tate Modern. She'd been meaning to go for months but had left it until the final day. To avoid the crowds she made sure she was one of the first in and as a result was able to stand well back from the giant canvases to appreciate the colour and movement in them.

'Magnificent,' exclaimed a deep voice behind her.

'It is rather,' she agreed.

'I've never been able to articulate how an abstract shape can take on such a vibrant form. His colours flow like a river.' The accent was Nordic or Germanic, the grammar and intonation perfect, even over-perfect, the comment surpassing pretentiousness. 'And these blocks of colour have become a breakthrough art form. A hundred years ago people would have laughed at them. Don't you agree?'

'I can't say, I wasn't around then,' Bridget replied with deliberate detachment to waylay corny chat up lines that she had grown accustomed to. She turned to face a tall, thin man with a narrow, attractive face and sharp eyes. His honey-coloured hair was unfashionably long, but it suited him. They trekked round the galleries together. He was a smooth talker, interspersing details of his life with observations on the art before them.

She'd got it wrong, Jan was neither German nor Scandinavian. He was a Dutch businessman who regularly came to London to sell his company's graphic art software. Whenever possible during these trips he took in a gallery. Had she been to Holland? Only to Amsterdam? The Rijksmuseum and the Van Gogh were all well and good but she should visit The Hague to see the Mondrians at the Gemeentemuseum. Surely Rothko was influenced by Mondrian.

His knowledge of art equalled hers and conversation flowed. Having coffee together seemed a natural thing to do. Then at his request they walked over the footbridge to St Pauls, taking lunch at a restaurant near the old Billingsgate Market that one of his work associates had recommended. Jan was polite, unthreatening, not at all pushy and yes, she had to admit it, good-looking.

'You work in an art gallery, how wonderful. I'd love to see what you sell. May I meet you when I'm next in London?'

Bridget agreed to exchange numbers. Two weeks later they were together again. He collected her at the gallery ahead of an evening meal and theatre performance. His impeccable gentlemanly behaviour continued over his next three visits, on each occasion ending with no more than a snappy kiss on each cheek. But the next time round there was an offer of a stay at his hotel and she accepted.

'God, this is sounding like a confession, David. Why the hell am I telling you any of this? I'm not embarrassed to admit I enjoy male company and I was more than ready for a new relationship.'

'We all have pasts, though in terms of relationships mine consist of little beyond Jane. I'm not judgemental, I'm interested in hearing about you. It's what's made you who you are.'

Bridget continued. Four months into the affair Jan invited her for a weekend in Amsterdam. Without embarrassment or remorse he came out with it. His wife and children would be away visiting her parents in Brabant so it would be a perfect opportunity.

'Wife? You didn't tell me you're married.'

'I haven't told you I'm not, you've never asked.'

'I'm just your bit on the side then.'

'Have you enjoyed our time together?'

'Yes.'

'Well, so have I. Isn't that what's important?'

'There is such a thing as morality, Jan.'

'Bridget, this is the twenty-first century, not some time in the distant past when adulterers were stoned or burnt at the stake. I'm at ease with my twenty-first century morality.'

'Well obviously I'm still stuck in the past.'

Bridget ended the relationship there and then, about three months before the reunion.

She informed David that was it for the day, or possibly for ever as far as telling him about her past.

They made late morning love.

Chapter Thirty-four

There had been several get-togethers for the two families – meals, cinema, bowling, and a Rachel performance of *Fiddler on the Roof*. Kay and Sam were getting on well. The relationship between Rachel and Andy was civil but distant, with Rachel categorising Andy as a nerd.

'Ready for our big outing are you, Andy?' she'd asked as they'd got into the car.

Rachel and Andy sat in the back as they made their way to Oxford. The younger children were staying with friends. 'Why *are* we doing this?' Rachel asked with dramatic emphasis on the 'are' as they turned off the M25 and onto the M40. Andy had yet to say a word.

David had already told her and was unwilling to go through the reasoning again.

Bridget showed more resilience. 'Look out there. Not a cloud in the sky, beautiful countryside. And when we get there you'll love the architecture. Your dad and I went to Oxford loads when we were your age.'

'Together?'

'No, we didn't know each other then.'

'I thought you were in the same year at school.'

'Well, yes, but we weren't friends.'

'Actually they hated each other,' Andy joked.

'Andy, you're alive. I was worried. They probably still hate each other deep down.'

'No, we don't,' said Bridget as she stretched across to kiss David on the cheek.

'Anyway, Bridget, you can cut out the crap about this being a tourist trip to discover our roots. We're here to be sold the university.'

‘We can include a look, there’s nothing wrong with that is there?’ Bridget replied.

‘Well, maybe not for Andy, but not much point for a lazy thicko like me.’

‘Lazy yes, thick no.’

‘Thanks a million, Dad. Stick to driving will you.’

There followed some rummaging through her backpack before Rachel’s iPod and headphones were extracted and activated. She looked across at Andy playing a nerdy game on his tablet. She reckoned he’d fit in perfectly with the other eggheads doing computing at Oxford. She turned up the volume to drown out Bridget and her father’s voices. She hated sitting in the back on a long journey, it made her feel sick. Her dad knew, but since Bridget had arrived on the scene there had been an assumption that the front passenger seat was hers.

She looked out the window as they were driving through the steep chalk cutting at Stokenchurch. It was OK seeing some countryside while listening to Elbow, the music in harmony with the sheep dotted around the gentle hills. Cows always stuck together but sheep spread out. Why was that, she wondered. Her point was proved as they passed a herd of cattle squashed together in the corner of a field. Some were sitting, did they expect rain or was that idea as absurd as much else she had picked up from adults over the years?

They took the motorway exit to Oxford. The decision makers in the front had opted for Park and Ride. Rachel couldn’t understand why they didn’t drive into the centre of the city, but she decided not to argue her case. There would be more important things to contest.

It turned out that she should have argued because Park and Ride was inappropriately named. It ended up as: find a space right on the outer rim of the jam packed car park. Walk miles to get to the bus stop. Wait. Wait more. Stand up on the crowded bus. Ride to a place called Headington.

Disembark when the bus breaks down. Wait. Wait more. Wait lots more. Stand squashed like anything on the replacement bus which surely was illegally overcrowded. (Though with the benefit of being able to edge up against a dishy bloke with baggy jeans and a Glastonbury T-shirt). Ride. Stop in traffic jam. Ride. And finally get off at a bus station that looked like any other bus station, namely it was full of buses.

Bridget claimed to know Oxford well and marched them off towards a particular place for lunch. Why they didn't stop off at one of the Prets, Starbucks, Caffé Neros, or Costas they passed en route was beyond Rachel's understanding, and she made her view known as they trundled up and down roads because Bridget couldn't remember exactly where her preference was located. In addition to the university assignment, Bridget and her father were on a blatant mission to discover non-mainstream venues to add to their obsessional coffee bar research.

The food was OK, they all chose a pasta something or other, but her Diet Coke was lukewarm. Bridget's reunion with Nellie's Tea Room went way over the top in terms of the great delight it appeared to generate.

'Do you know what,' she announced, 'I think I might be sitting on the same chair at the same table as when I was last here more than ten years ago.'

A flood of sarcastic options emerged for Rachel to select, but she kept quiet, aware that David was eyeing her with suspicion. She contemplated whether she would end up saying things like that when she was older. Near orgasmic ecstasy over a fucking chair. And Bridget wasn't even old and was relatively cool. What must go on in the heads of even older people like the ones sitting opposite them? 'Look at this teapot, darling. It's identical to the one we got as a wedding gift.' 'Do you think this is Linguine or Vermicelli?' 'I think you're incorrect on both counts, sweetheart, I believe it's Fedelini.' It's just fucking pasta; it all tastes the same so eat it.

Rachel's anger grew to boiling point. It was a complete and utter waste of a day and she'd been pretty well forced to come along because, as her dad had put it, 'Andy is coming and he'd appreciate you joining him'. His tablet had been keeping him company, he'd got up to about level eight million on his game and had hardly spoken.

Now they were walking up The High. Bridget had made a point of telling her that the word Street should be omitted and 'The' added. The sign said High Street, but apparently that was beside the point.

They crossed into Queen Street. 'At last, we've reached The Queen,' Rachel tested.

'Yes, Queen Street.'

'Why add 'street' and knock off 'the'? The High lost its second name, why not this one, too?'

'Because when …' Bridget started before ceasing, with explanation barely started. There was an abrupt end to the Scout-like stride they had been subjected to, followed by some whispering between David and Bridget as they watched two sneering men approach.

'What's the matter? Who are those two fatties?' Rachel asked.

'Ex-school mates,' Bridget said as the men moved in position to block their path.

The shorter man spoke. 'Well, well, well, if it isn't our David again.'

'Hello, Ben. Hello, Bill.'

The taller one, Bill, looked across at Bridget then back to David. 'You've managed to hook up with this tasty bit of skirt, you sneaky bugger.'

'I do have a name, though clearly your brain struggles to access two bits of information in quick succession,' Bridget stated with a fair degree of aggression. 'Still, a big congratulations for remembering it's David.'

David had flashbacks to Bill's potential for violence as well as his encounter with the mugger. He hoped Bridget wasn't making the same mistake. 'Ignore them. Let's head on.' The smell of beer on Bill's breath highlighted the danger of replicating the evening in Kitts Yard.

Bill stepped in front of Bridget. 'You were a mouthy bitch at the reunion. Maybe bits of skirt shouldn't try to be bits of mouth. What d'you reckon, Ben?'

Ben appeared to be in a conciliatory mood. 'Let's go. Come on, Bill,' he suggested, but Bill was still having none of it.

'Go, why? Let's join the romantic couple for a Sunday stroll.'

Rachel and Andy had been ignored like they were a pair of walkers who only stopped because they happened by chance to be behind Bridget and David when they were blocked.

The conversation between Bridget and the one called Bill was getting heated, with Bridget accusing Bill of being brain dead and Bill suggesting she must have had breast implants. David and the one called Ben were making unsuccessful attempts to separate the antagonists.

Andy stepped forward. 'Stop being rude to my mother.'

'Who'a, a knight in shining armour. I'm really scared of you.' Bill said ahead of giving Andy a shove. Andy held firm.

'I'd rather you didn't do that.'

'Oh, would you rather I didn't do that,' Bill sneered as he gave Andy a stronger push.

Ben and David were in the process of suggesting the antagonists move apart when Andy grabbed hold of Bill and with what looked like very little effort, deposited him on the pavement. Ben leapt up, furious, his fists clenched.

'I'm goin' to get you for that, you little bugger.'

The previous group of shoppers who had steered clear of the scene had been replaced by a predominantly younger clientele of onlookers who formed a circle to watch as Andy threw Bill over his shoulder and back to the floor. There was a loud cheer. This action was repeated twice more and Rachel found herself joining in the applause. Bill was game for more humiliation, but Ben intervened. He grabbed hold of his staggering, cursing friend and led him away.

Several people came up to Andy and patted him on the back with a 'well done, mate' before continuing on their quest for consumer gratification.

'Under-16 county judo champion,' Bridget announced as they continued down 'The Queen'.

It is fair to say that Rachel's opinion of Andy was elevated, at the very least to Nerd Plus status. She was a little more tolerant than she might have been as they explored Queen's, Magdalen, and Christ Church, at each college entering through small uninviting gateways and stepping into a world of imposing ancient buildings with immaculately landscaped gardens.

Chapter Thirty-five

Over the following week discussion about the café intensified via a flurry of phone calls and emails. David took his ever-growing list of decisions needed round to Bridget after work on Friday. It was a miserable, late March evening – a cruel dark grey sky was hurling down rain, hail, and sleet.

'This is useful,' Bridget stated, having given the document no more than a cursory glance. 'But is there any point doing anything else until we have an idea how much it's going to cost and where we can get the money from?'

David agreed; he needed to wear his accountant's hat for this venture and hats are worn on heads, not hearts. The discussion about costs had been delayed long enough and it was vital for the business plan to be presented to the bank.

There was an added sense of urgency because Bridget had found what she considered to be ideal premises close to where she lived in Muswell Hill. It was a restaurant that had recently closed, a short walk from the bustling Broadway. They examined it online. The size was perfect, big enough for eighty seated customers. An over-large kitchen could be subdivided with a section converted into an open bar area. The shop front was attractive and in good condition; it required little change beyond new signage. The annual rent was £80,000 for a four-year lease, plus business rates of £18,000.

Having established that these premises were reasonably priced compared to others advertised online, they turned their attention to the money needed to set up. They calculated £70,000 would establish a good-quality facility.

It was possible to do it for less but wanting an upmarket venue necessitated high standards of decoration, furniture, and crockery. Another up-front cost would be training for the baristas to allow them to use a leased espresso machine.

Next they turned their attention to what to sell.

'I never realised how much mark-up there is on a cup of coffee,' David said as he gathered his collection of print outs and handed Bridget one of the spreadsheets. 'Look at this. Coffee costs eight pence, the milk about six, but we can have a selling price of £2.20 to match the competition. Even with VAT to pay that still leaves £1.69 gross profit.'

'Yeah, but don't we need to consider things like staff costs and leasing the machine?'

'I've started with gross profit.' David began to explain how accountants distinguished between gross and net amounts, but Bridget soon lost interest, if not the will to live.

She changed the subject. 'What about food?'

David handed over another spreadsheet. 'I've compared buying and making sandwiches and think we should make them. For a start buying in is more expensive, about £1.60 a sandwich. We'd have to place a standing order so there's no flexibility according to sales and there could be loads of waste. Plus the fact that we wouldn't be providing anything that stands out from other cafes if we bought in.'

'How much will making them ourselves cost?'

'It works out at around 80p, depending on ingredients, though that excludes labour. We'll need a smooth operation to make sure customers don't have to wait too long. Mind you, I'm not convinced we're after the mad rush of the lunchtime trade. We don't want our customers to be in a hurry to leave. Which reminds me, we should set up free Wi-Fi.'

'Maybe, though we don't want people in for hours on the internet without buying much.'

‘There’ll be cakes to tempt them. They’re a different proposition to sandwiches, I think we should buy them in and I‘d like us to have a reputation as the place to get the best cakes going, like a Viennese coffee house.’

David was discovering that when it came to figures Bridget had a short concentration span. She yawned when he handed her the cakes spreadsheet and changed the subject. ‘You were going to investigate selling alcohol. Have you done that yet?’

David outlined the need for a premises licence, compulsory training, and the naming of a Designated Premises Supervisor.

‘That’ll have to be me,’ Bridget joked. ‘I’m the expert on alcohol.’

‘Yes I’ve noticed.’ David lifted up the half-full bottle of Rioja Gran Reserva and topped up their glasses. ‘Alcohol is going to be important for us, there’s a huge mark-up on it.’ He handed over another spreadsheet.

‘I can’t handle another one. But see this,’ Bridget lifted up a floor plan of the building they hoped to rent. ‘I’ve been looking at the layout and if we cut the kitchen size down I think we’ve got room for a small stage as well as the bar. It’s best to have a dedicated space if we’re going to have performances.’

‘I’ve got no idea how much that would cost,’ David said.

‘I’ve spoken to the builder and he thinks £15,000 would do it.’

‘Let’s go for that then. God, there’s so much to think about. One thing we haven’t even started to consider is marketing. We need to work out how people will find out about the place and recommend it to their friends. If we go for the one you’ve found it’s not right in the centre of the shopping area; there aren’t going to be loads of passing-by customers.’

And so it went on, the quality of what they wanted to

provide getting better and better and the cost spiralling to match their idea of perfection.

David came up with the sum of £250,000 set up and first year expenditure, excluding the cost of food and drink. In future years at least £100,000 would be needed to keep the place open.

Bridget's excitement and enthusiasm came crashing down. 'That's massive. How are we ever going to afford it?'

'Well, first year costs can be carried forward and are tax deductible in future years.'

'Assuming there's going to be a second year. How many customers would we need to break even, let alone make a profit? And have you made allowances for our time, what we could be earning if we weren't doing this?'

'No.'

'Bloody hell, it's not going to work. All our effort already and we could have done a back of an envelope calculation to see how impossible it is.'

'I'm not as negative as you, Bridget. We're talking about well under a hundred customers a day to break even and remember we're thinking of three very different shifts, lunch sandwiches, morning and afternoon cakes, and then evening entertainments.'

Bridget didn't look convinced.

David continued. 'I've set up a meeting with my friend Ross I told you about. He'll let us know if it's mad or not. I've also booked in with my bank.'

'My head is utterly mangled. I feel sorry for you having to work with figures every day.'

'This is different, it's for us.'

'Another glass of wine before bed?'

'As long as you're the Designated Premises Supervisor.'

'This supervisor is going to dispense with glasses and drink straight from the bottle. Come on.'

Two walls in Bridget's bedroom were purple and the others were dove grey. There was a line of five candles on the fireplace, creating a rich shadowy hue. An incense stick was burning. She must have popped upstairs to produce this calming atmosphere while David was ploughing through figures. He gave her a kiss of appreciation then watched as she removed her clothes. He would never tire of seeing her naked.

She stood near him and drank from the bottle, an act of either accidental or deliberate erotic provocation. She handed it to him and he took a swig.

'Are you going to get undressed or do you need some help?'

'My hands are full,' he said, clutching the bottle with both hands, 'I definitely need assistance. Maybe start with this. And here next please.'

Soon they were naked and exploring each other's bodies, and all thoughts of the café withered away. However they resurfaced with a vengeance during David's restless night as he fretted about all that needed to be done and how they could possibly finance it.

'God, I was out like a light,' Bridget said the following morning. 'Did you sleep OK?'

'Yeah, great.'

Chapter Thirty-six

A critical twenty-four hours had arrived. They were seeing his entrepreneur friend Ross that evening, followed by the bank the next morning. David had arranged a meeting with Mary later that day to hand in his notice. Friday 1st – fittingly April Fools' Day.

They met Ross in a heaving Hampstead pub close to where he lived. The woman with him was even younger than Hazel, the girlfriend David had seen at their previous meeting. As Ross got older his women got younger and if looks were anything to go by, this new girlfriend was close to the border of legality. You'd definitely want to see ID if she was purchasing alcohol. Fortunately this challenge wasn't imminent because it was Ross who set off to the bar to get the first round.

'Come with me, mate,' he suggested. David got up and walked alongside Ross. 'What do you reckon? She's a beauty, don't you think?'

Candy certainly was pretty. There was no point questioning why Ross was dating a girl thirty years his junior, a previous interrogation on this subject concerning Hazel had created an uncomfortable atmosphere.

'I'll tell you what,' Ross continued, 'I think Birgit is a massive improvement on Jane. Well done, mate.'

'Actually, it's Bridget.'

'Yeah, that's what I said.'

Back at the table Bridget and Candy were chatting away, comfortable in each other's company. Bridget took her white wine and Candy was given a lavender alcopop. To her credit she listened intently as the conversation moved on to a discussion about the café and she asked valid questions about their proposal. Although Ross had forgotten to bring the copy of the draft business plan that David had emailed, his comments indicated he had at least read it. His conclusion was that the venture might be feasible, but questioned why anyone would select a café for a business since there was no potential for high profit.

'We'd be pleased if it was a small-scale success,' Bridget asserted in defence of their idea.

'I'd come along and tell all my friends,' Candy butted in with kindness. 'Especially if you get to show those old films you mentioned. I love the black and whites.'

'What sort of things would you want to see?' Bridget asked.

'The film noirs. *Casablanca*, *Brief Encounter*, anything Hitchcock. And any Dmytryk, he's my all-time favourite.'

Candy's conversation wasn't matching David's bigoted perception of what could be expected from someone wearing snakeskin leggings and polka dot T-shirt, together with tattoos, piercings, and studs. She talked about life as a first year undergraduate on a film studies course. David was relieved – at least his friend was dating a girl beyond the legal threshold.

Ross stressed one thing that David was acutely aware of. The bank would expect water-tight collateral in advance of providing funding. He made it clear that if the purpose of this meeting had been to get him to finance it, he wasn't prepared to do so. 'I'm afraid there's no *Dragon's Den* from me, mate.'

That marked the end of the discussion and they headed out. Candy was a passionate girl. With Ross and Bridget looking on in the car park, she gave David a sustained, affectionate farewell embrace.

'Did you enjoy that?' Bridget asked in the car on their way back to his place and David wasn't sure whether she was referring to the meeting or the kiss.

He hedged his bets. 'Definitely worth it.'

The following morning they got up early to prepare for the meeting at the bank. The first task was to consider amendments to their business plan based on what Ross had suggested. They came to the conclusion that his advice provided little added value, but something Candy had said was a different matter. In the section entitled "Market Research" they stated that they had interviewed a substantial number of young potential customers who'd expressed a strong interest in coming along on the nights when old movies were to be shown.

'It's not 100% true,' Bridget admitted as David was word-processing, 'but she did say she'd bring friends so it's fair to assume they like the idea of old movies too.'

David had readily agreed to put the exaggeration into the document. The financial data was all valid; a little leeway in the account of how they reached their conclusions was permissible.

They got dressed for their visit to the bank. David wore his standard work clothes of suit, shirt, and tie. He'd never seen Bridget dressed conservatively – a chocolate brown two-piece suit, beige blouse with a frilly collar, and shiny black patent shoes with glittery gold bows at the instep.

'What do you reckon?' she asked.

'Fabulous. It's like having a new woman.'

'Shut up. Come on, let's go.'

They drove to the shopping centre in silence, feeling the tension. They'd resolved to change jobs and the café was the sole escape route they had contemplated. 'Well, here goes,' David said as they saw the bank ahead of them.

'We'll be fine,' Bridget replied without conviction.

'Your friendly bank' was written on a large banner covering the full width of the window at the entrance. There were two life-sized cardboard cut-outs by the door, a young man and woman with perfect white teeth providing welcoming smiles. A real person who didn't quite match the friendliness of the cut-outs approached and informed them that they would have to wait because they were early. They joined the expressionless customers seated on the horse-shoe of chairs.

Finally, the member of staff responsible for small business support approached them. He led them to one of the open plan areas that had long since replaced proper rooms where doors could be closed to ensure privacy.

David, a long-standing customer, had expected to see the manager. Instead they got Peter Ridge, a brash young man who gave the impression that customers weren't to be trusted and his job was to get rid of them as quickly as possible. David provided financial information with all the accuracy that could be expected from an accountant and watched with frustration as Ridge paid no more than lip service to what he said. Bridget contributed in an attempt to generate enthusiasm, but the stony-faced young man gave no sign of interest and no hint of what he thought about their vision. After thirty-nine minutes of a meeting scheduled to last for forty, he spent exactly one minute summarising the bank's position. It was as they expected – they needed to be aware that any loan for a business start-up had to be accompanied by at least twenty percent of the clients' own money plus collateral of at least fifty per cent.

As they were led out, Bridget asked if he would be recommending approval of the loan. 'I can't say. You'll hear from us within a week,' Ridge said, his back to them as he set off towards the horse-shoe. 'Mr and Mrs Houghton? This way, please.'

Out on the high street they stopped at a café. It was lunchtime and it was jam-packed. Silently, enviously, they observed queues to select food from the self-service shelves, queues to order coffee, and queues to pay. Every table was taken and they huddled together sharing a bar stool by the window.

David spoke. 'We knew he'd ask for a contribution and collateral, we didn't need Ross to tell us.'

‘I hated the guy. I’d rather have hostility than indifference.’

David agreed. ‘Par for the course these days I’m afraid.’

‘Collateral’s impossible for you with Jane owning half your house. But I could do it. I’m the sole owner of mine, the mortgage is paid, and I inherited a fair amount of money when my parents died.’

‘I couldn’t let you fund it, it’s too risky.’

‘You didn’t think it was risky when you were doing the sums the other night.’

‘I thought it was possible and I still do. You were the one with the strongest doubt.’

‘Well, I’ve changed my mind. Or more to the point, what the fuck! Let’s give it a go. We can’t lose all the money we put in, there’ll be at least some customers. If the absolute worst comes to the worst we can shut down and sublet the premises and I’m sure we’d be able to find jobs back in the worlds of accounting and rip off art.’

‘It’s still a heck of a lot of money we could lose. Easily a hundred thousand, perhaps more.’

‘That would be terrible, but I have got that in savings. I want to do it. Have your meeting with Mary and hand in your notice because that’s what I’m going to do at the gallery this afternoon. Come on, finish your £2.20 cappuccino which only costs about 16p to make while I finish my £3.20 avocado, pine nut, pea shoot and hummus sandwich which by your reckoning cost them £1.60 to buy in.’

David sat in silence.

‘No need to ponder, David. I’m serious, I’ve made up my mind. If you don’t join me, I’ll just have to go it alone.’

David nodded in understanding if not in agreement. Bridget chatted away at high speed as he walked her to the Underground. It was small talk, she was nervous. They said their goodbyes and he made his way to the car park.

On the way to work David was hit by a wave of emotion and shed a few tears as he reflected on the generosity and optimism displayed by Bridget. There was no going back now, they were going to do it. He wouldn't let Bridget put up the whole sum needed or provide all the collateral. He had savings too, recently halved and theoretically put aside for Rachel and Sam's university costs. Nevertheless he would contribute as near to half as possible and then work his socks off to make the café a success.

The meeting with Mary was at half past three. The conversation wasn't going to be easy; they were getting on well and he was about to let her down.

She greeted him with a smile as he sat.

'I know you've called this meeting, but there's something I'd like to tell you first. You know me – always straight to the point. I handed in my notice today. I've been thinking about what to do for quite a while. You've been a catalyst, what with our initial difficulties and how we worked through them. I'm going to take some time out, travel a bit, then when I get back possibly work in the charity sector. I've been self-centred, in fact downright selfish, and now it's time to put something back. And I mean put something back. I remember saying that at my interview for here, but that was a ploy to get the position.'

David took advantage of her reflective pause. 'Mary, there's something you should know, too.'

'Hang on. One more thing before you say anything. There's someone working here who is perfectly suited to my job and deserves it. That's you.' Mary waited for David's response. When it didn't come she continued. 'I've put your name forward and Stuart is supportive, he wants you to apply.'

'Thanks for thinking of me, Mary, but I won't be …'

'There's no need to answer now. You must be surprised

by my news to say the least.'

'It's not that, it's –'

'Go away and reflect, will you. I don't want another word until you've thought about it carefully.'

'But –'

'Not a word.'

'OK, I'll pop back soon.'

Back in his office David accepted that he should be considering the new situation. He began by writing a council versus café list. He could itemise reasons to stay at his current workplace with ease – a likely increase in salary, the pension provision, security, enhanced status. The reasons for setting up a café were shrouded in mist – maybe enjoyable to run (but a massive time commitment); maybe profitable (but the risk of huge losses); maybe recognition as a patron of the arts (but the danger of no one attracted to perform at his café and insufficient customers even if he did manage to get entertainers in).

He left the list on his desk and walked back to Mary's office with a purposeful stride.

'I'm leaving too,' he announced as he entered.

He told Mary about the café plan and to her credit she was encouraging. The council would be looking for two new recruits.

Jabulani was standing outside David's office on his return. He knew David had decided to inform Mary that afternoon and was eager to hear how it had gone.

'I've done it, Jabulani. Can you keep another secret?'

Chapter Thirty-seven

'This looks great, Dad,' Sam said as David set down three plates of Portofino Lamb and Artichoke Risotto, the latest creation to come from his Italian cookery course.

'Tastes good too,' Rachel added having taken her first mouthful.

'Let's see if it's as good as the one my tutor made,' David said as he lifted his fork.

The telephone rang as fork reached mouth.

'Leave it, Dad, it'll be a sales call.'

It drove David up the wall. Although he'd enrolled with the telephone preference service to stop unsolicited sales calls, they kept coming. Often they began with a statement about how pleasant the weather was today in London despite incomprehensible accent and not quite proper use of over-formal grammar suggesting they were calling from a faraway land.

David rested the fork on his plate and stood up. 'I'll get it, it might be Bridget. She said she'd ring tonight,' He looked at the telephone display. 'Private Number' was shown; it couldn't be Bridget as hers was entered in the memory. But since he was there he felt obliged to answer it.

'Is that Mr Willoughby, Mr David Willoughby?' he was asked by a man with a strong Indian accent.

'Yes it is, but I'm eating dinner and I'm not interested in buying anything thank you.'

'This is important,' the man persevered.

Yes I bet, David thought. The need to upgrade your computer virus protection; to consider a conservatory now summer was approaching; to hand over bank account details to verify authenticity ahead of carrying out some scam or other. I'm too polite, David reckoned as the man rabbited on.

'Look, I've already told you I'm not interested.' He replaced the receiver and sat down.

A minute later the phone rang again.

Rachel stood. 'I'll go and he won't call back after I've finished with him.' She lifted the receiver.

'You are a disgrace, can't you take a hint and get lost? Goodbye.'

'Well done for not swearing,' David remarked as Rachel sat down.

The phone rang again. 'I'm not having this,' David uttered as he stood. He lifted the receiver and put it on speakerphone so that the children could witness his assertiveness.

'Now listen will you. I insist on knowing who you represent and what your telephone number is. And then I want to speak to your supervisor.'

'I am truly sorry to disturb you, Mr Willoughby, but we really do need your help here.'

'My help? What are you talking about?'

'It's your mother.'

Mr Gupta, his mother's neighbour, actually no longer his mother's neighbour, went on to describe the circumstances of her death. Mrs Willoughby hadn't put out her dustbins on Tuesday night for early Wednesday morning collection, a very unusual omission. Then the Wednesday milk was left uncollected outside her front door and when another pint sat there all day Thursday he decided to investigate. He was a key holder in case of emergencies – and that is what it turned out to be. He found her dead, stretched out on the floor of her lounge in nightwear and dressing gown. He'd called the police and the body had been removed to the mortuary, but now it was time to hand over to her family. He had tried to contact Charlotte several times, but it went straight to answerphone. He'd then rummaged through drawers in search of David's number and fortunately had found her address book.

This information was relayed to the whole family via speakerphone and when David had ended the conversation with an apology for their initial rudeness, the three of them sat in shocked silence.

There was little time for reflection and no time for conversation because Charlotte called. She had picked up Mr Gupta's five increasingly desperate messages. They arranged to meet at their mother's house the following mid-morning.

David, Rachel, and Sam sat in the lounge talking about the last time they had seen her. There was guilt that they hadn't visited since Christmas and that on that occasion they had been bored, impatient, and sarcastic when they should have been warm and caring. The children wanted to help, but it was agreed that they'd go to school the next day rather than join David in Birmingham. If necessary they could stay over at friends'.

When he met Charlotte the following morning there was a rare show of emotion as he and his sister hugged.

'Mind you, she was a bitch and a half,' Charlotte said in between tears. 'But she was still our mum.'

David nodded. He felt the loss, a disconnect, but not as much grief as he considered worthy.

They wandered from room to room looking at possessions one would expect for an old-fashioned woman in her late sixties who had made little effort to move on since her husband had died. Little had been replaced in the twenty-five years since then; only a flat-screen television and a digital phone hinted of a twenty-first century existence. She possessed no computer, no mobile phone, no DVD or CD player.

'It's all quite sad,' Charlotte remarked as they entered

her bedroom, its tea-stained candlewick bedspread, shag pile carpet, and beige velour curtains all striking in their ugliness. 'There's nothing I'd even want as a keepsake.'

'No, probably not,' David agreed. 'Her life's possessions are going to end up either at the Salvation Army if they'll accept any of it, or in plastic bags on a skip.'

They sat in the kitchen drinking lowest grade instant coffee from cups and saucers used by their mother all those years ago when they were youngsters.

'Do you think our kids will feel the same about us?' Charlotte wondered.

'Who knows? I hope not though I haven't got a stack of iPads, Gameboys, and Wiis for them to inherit. I suppose it's just the money we leave that will count.'

'Yes, I suppose so. Talking of money, this house should fetch a fair old packet. I'm assuming she'll have split things fifty-fifty. Mind you, you always were her favourite so maybe I'll get nothing except the bedspread.'

'Well if she's left that to me I'll be generous and let you have it.'

'Very funny. We'll need to see her solicitor, won't we? I know who he is, I'll give him a call. I vaguely know the local vicar too. I'll speak to him about the funeral.'

'Maybe we should see the will first in case she's given any funeral instructions, a preference for burial or cremation and things like that.'

'OK. She might want particular music or a hymn. Maybe Led Zep's *Stairway to Heaven*, although heaven might be wishful thinking as far as she's concerned.'

'Come on, Charlotte, she wasn't that bad.'

'She wasn't that good either. I don't believe in this heaven and hell stuff but if I did and I was in charge, being merely all right wouldn't qualify you. You'd have to have done something special to get in.'

'There wouldn't be many up there then.'

'Don't worry, you'd make it. You always were the family goody-goody.'

They were smiling as they spoke. The death of their mother had brought them closer; such banter hadn't been evident since their adolescent days.

Mr Spratt, their mother's solicitor, was unable to fit them in so they arranged to see him the following morning. David stayed over in the house.

It was an eerie experience without the presence of the person who had lived there for all forty-four years of his life. He popped out to buy fish and chips at the takeaway he used to visit as a child. Now pizzas and curry were on offer in addition to the traditional meal. Back in his temporary home he sat in the lounge in 'his' armchair, switching from channel to channel. Before bed he wandered round the house again, distant memories roused with each item of furniture or knickknack he saw. His parents had collected junk during their travels – a Swiss cuckoo clock, a plastic Venetian gondola, and worst of all a battery-operated lamp in the shape of the Blackpool Tower. He remembered when they'd bought the tower. He was fourteen and had fallen in love with the daughter of another guest family at the hotel. She was sweet sixteen and had led him along for a while until an older boy came on the scene. David saw them kissing one evening by the swings and felt a wave of despondency that he could feel even now as he touched the plastic casing of the tower. He scrutinised the two slim shelves of books, filled with bland best-sellers. He selected the best he could find and was lulled to sleep by the James Bond adventure.

The next morning Charlotte and David met at a smart Victorian double-fronted villa in the centre of Edgbaston, close to the university. It was across the road from a well maintained park with giant oak trees bursting into leaf, surrounded by the yellow and pink of forsythias and azaleas. A shiny brass plaque to the left of the door displayed the name *Clutterbuck, Sharpe and Spratt.*

‘A bit posh for our mum, isn’t it,’ David remarked.

‘I was thinking that, too. Everyone knows it’s the most expensive law firm in the area.’

No expense was spared in the modern reception area with its huge semi-circular light wood front desk, plush leather armchairs, zany chandeliers, and vivid abstract oil paintings.

By contrast, entering Mr Spratt’s room was like taking a giant stride back into the nineteenth century. His office was a parody of a solicitor’s office and Mr Spratt was a caricature of a solicitor. The furniture was dark oak, the desk and chairs covered with the mottled maroon leather that had once been popular. One wall was lined with bookcases and there were piles of paper and files on the floor. The only sign of modernity was a computer on a separate workstation in the far corner of the large, high-ceilinged room. Mr Spratt was the perfect Scrooge as he peered at them above his half-moon reading glasses. He was dressed in a dark suit, crisp white shirt, and navy bow tie. His salt and pepper hair made it difficult to identify age – anything between forty and sixty was possible.

‘Sit,’ he instructed before shuffling papers on his desk and opening a folder. ‘I’m sorry to hear about your loss, your mother was a fine woman.’

‘Thank you for saying that,’ David responded quickly, fearing a sarcastic put-down from Charlotte, who was fidgeting on the uncomfortable chair. Her bearing improved somewhat as Mr Spratt announced that their mother had instructed that her assets were to be equally divided between her two children, or had either been deceased at time of death, to the appropriate child’s own children.

As he read on Charlotte gasped and grabbed hold of David’s arm.

Their mother was loaded. She had inherited the fortune

acquired by a great-uncle who had died when they were infants. Joseph Kirby had manufactured jewellery. During the 1960s and 1970s he had owned the most successful business in Warstone Street, at the heart of Birmingham's Jewellery Quarter. Mr Spratt outlined how the sum inherited had been managed by the financial consultancy that his firm recommended to their clients. They had successfully played the markets across good and bad times and had even been able to hedge against the current economic downturn.

Charlotte had grown impatient. 'So how much? How much is there now?'

'I haven't got the current year figure to hand, though being well into April, I expect a statement very soon.'

'How much was it worth last year then?' Charlotte persisted.

Mr Spratt lifted a sheet from the collection of papers in front of him. With a deep, austere tone he read. '£1,427,345.86.'

Charlotte let out a scream. Mr Spratt continued. 'This sum refers to Joseph Kirby's portfolio which has been kept apart from everything else. Your mother had additional assets to add to the total – some shares, a substantial savings account, jewellery, and the house of course. Though you must remember that beyond the first £325,000 there is inheritance tax to pay.'

David was in accountancy mode, doing calculations as Mr Spratt was spelling out exactly what those additional assets comprised of. Not surprisingly he was linking the inheritance to the expenditure needed for the café. Charlotte's chain of thought was at a somewhat lower level.

'The miserable old witch. She never let on she had anything. When she gave the kids £20 at Christmas she made out it was a major sacrifice,' she whispered loud enough for Mr Spratt to hear.

David didn't respond. He continued to tot up the windfall as the solicitor ran through the long and complex list of assets. For insurance purposes the jewellery had been valued. They might decide to keep some, but if they sold it and on the assumption they got two-thirds of the insurance valuation, that would bring in another £200,000. The substantial savings accounts Mr Spratt had mentioned were in excess of £300,000. The extensive portfolio of shares was in British companies; they had been purchased many years ago by their father. He'd known what he was doing because although a few had declined, most had grown to become major international players. David would be able to work out the exact current value as soon as he had access to a computer or newspaper, but they would make a sizeable contribution to the total. Then there was the large house in one of the most fashionable suburbs of Edgbaston which Charlotte's husband would have no problem selling. In all they would be inheriting a pot in excess of two and a half million pounds!

'Just making a quick call,' David informed Charlotte as they left the solicitor's building.

'Me too,' said Charlotte as she stepped a few paces away from her brother.

David dialled Bridget.

Chapter Thirty-eight

Throughout the first three weeks of April they had enjoyed delightful blue skies and the first warm sun of the year. On the day of the funeral the weather turned and it was as cold, windy, and wet as the most brutal mid-January day. The small group of mourners made their way to the graveside, their shoes caked in sticky brown clay. Wrapped in dark raincoats, they were desperately hanging on to unrestrained umbrellas.

David and Charlotte were at the front behind the hearse, walking alongside the vicar. Jane was in the second row with Rachel and Sam. Poor Sam, it was his birthday. Donald, Charlotte's husband, and her children, Crispin and Emma, were next in line. They were followed by Bridget, Andy, and Kay. Next came the few acquaintances of David's mother including Mr Gupta and his wife.

The rain lashed down as the vicar spoke, generic words of kindness followed by the traditional prayer. The mourners watched as the grave diggers turned their attention to filling the hole, shovelling sodden soil onto the coffin. David listened to the harsh rattle of clay and small stones against the wood, reducing to soft thuds as earth began to drop against earth. He looked around and noted there wasn't a tear in sight. His mother's bitterness and harshness had stifled love and affection.

Back at her house caterers had provided sandwiches, cake, tea, coffee, sherry, and wine for the mourners.

'We could have gone for champagne and caviar what with all our money,' Charlotte joked.

'Can we keep quiet about that for now?' David pleaded, looking across to Jane.

‘Sure. Are you able to stay on for a bit afterwards, to start clearing some of her stuff away?’

‘Yes of course. How long have we got the skip for?’

‘As long as it takes to fill it. The cost isn’t based on time.’

Rachel and Sam were unsure where to go. They wanted to be with their father to offer support; they liked Bridget and her children and would have chosen to spend time with them, but were made to feel guilty by Jane who was intent on monopolising them since she was, as she put it, alone and uncomfortable. They ended up circuiting between each party for sound bite chats.

However, after lunch Jane told her children to move away as Donald approached. She’d always got on well with her brother-in-law and now, in the corner of the living room, they chatted away like there was no tomorrow.

Bridget and her children approached David, Rachel, and Sam. They had their coats on. ‘We need to head off. Andy’s got judo later this afternoon and if we get back in time Kay can get to her dance class.’

‘Thanks for coming,’ he said, addressing all three of them. ‘I’ll call tonight.’

Rachel and Sam stood by David’s side as mourners offered their condolences. By the time David had begun a conversation with an elderly lady who claimed to remember him from his childhood days, his children were bored to death. They edged away indicating that they were going outside for a walk – suffering the rain would be by far the lesser of two evils.

When the woman told him her name was Vivienne, memories came flooding back. She had been vibrant and vivacious, now she was slow and listless. She slurred as she spoke.

‘Yes, you were a good boy, that’s for sure.’

‘Thank you,’ David replied, hearing the same claim for a third time.

‘Not like that sister of yours, she was a right little madam.’

‘Oh, I don’t think so.’

‘When she was one of those teenagers she was, I can tell you. All that loud music, punk wasn’t it? I don’t know how the rest of you coped.’

This was going in a direction David didn’t want to follow. ‘It wasn’t like that at all, we loved our childhood together.’

‘I’m only repeating what your mother told me, god rest her soul.’

‘Mother liked to grumble a bit, but she and Charlotte got on fine. In fact …’

‘Talking about me?’ Charlotte was by their side. How much had she heard?

‘I was just saying what a lovely family you were.’ Vivienne might have deteriorated, but a capacity to lie convincingly remained intact.

Jane approached the group. ‘David, I need to speak to you.’

Charlotte hadn’t spoken to her since the separation. ‘Hello, Jane, how are things?’

Jane didn’t reply, she was looking at David.

Vivienne chipped in. ‘You’re the wife who ran away, aren’t you? David was such a good boy.’

Jane didn’t reply to that either.

David faced his soon to be ex-wife. ‘What is it, Jane?’

‘Not here. Somewhere private, please.’

‘OK, let’s go upstairs.’ They left Vivienne and Charlotte together to talk about little madams, coping with teenagers and the social impact of punk music.

David led the way. He headed towards his old bedroom, but this had been the venue of their clandestine sex sessions ahead of getting a place of their own. It would be a poor choice given the circumstances. He did a quick about turn on the landing and they went into his mother’s room. Clothes were piled high in cardboard boxes and the bed was stripped down to the stained mattress. They sat on it.

‘What is it?’ he asked.

‘I think you know very well. How could you, David?’

‘How could I what?’

‘Don’t pretend you don’t know what I’m talking about. Donald’s told me everything.’

‘I have no idea. How could I what?’

‘You were so keen to rush the financial settlement, weren’t you? Now I know why.’

Sitting together on the bed, David could feel the heat of her anger. He stood and walked to the window, looking out over the large garden. The swing at the bottom was still there, though in a sorry state, the chains rusty and the wooden seat rotten. He’d spent many an hour on it as had his own children. The grass needed a mow; the March rain followed by the early April warmth had brought rapid growth. Flower beds housed untidy clumps of uncared for bushes. He wouldn’t miss the place, they should put it on the market as soon as possible.

He turned back to face Jane. ‘OK, I get it. What you’re implying is laughable. Remember, you were the one who wanted things done quickly. In time for a spring divorce and a summer wedding.’

‘You knew your mother had a weak heart.’

‘If you’re suggesting I knew she was about to die, that’s ludicrous.’

‘Is the amount of money Donald mentioned true?’

‘I’ve no idea what he told you, but I’m not prepared to discuss it.’

David walked away from the window, stopping at his mother’s dressing table. There were large opal necklaces and pearl earrings on it. The stones looked real enough, though Mr Spratt had informed him and Charlotte that the expensive stuff was stowed away in a bank safe. On seeing him looking at the jewellery Jane stood up and went across to inspect. David wasn't comfortable with this and moved across to intercept. They stood close, eye to eye. Anger, distrust, and hate had replaced love.

'What on earth are you going to do with all the money?' Jane asked.

'I'm sorry, but that's not your concern.'

'Maybe it is. You've got enough to change the arrangement for how much I contribute towards the children's maintenance.'

'I've buried my mother today, Jane. This is not the time to have a discussion about anything to do with money,' David asserted. 'Much of it will go in tax, then half to Charlotte, and my half for a business venture I'm starting.'

'Your café? I've heard about that from the kids. Why on earth are you chucking in a good job to do something so daft? I don't understand.'

'Well, it's not for you to understand any more, is it? Perhaps more appropriate today is for you to offer your condolences.'

'You never even liked her. She got on better with me than with you.'

'Yes, maybe you were more similar than I ever realised.'

'That's insulting.'

David returned to the window and faced the garden. There was a splash of colour, a clump of purple tulips with petals open wide and drooping. Soon they would be rotting – like his mother.

The impasse continued as they both waited for the other to speak. Finally Jane left and he heard her stamp downstairs.

Rachel came into the room. 'Dad? Everything OK?'

'Yes, fine, Rachel,' he said as she moved closer. He smelt tobacco.

'Mum's stormed out. What was that about?'

‘Just the usual post-separation hassles. She’s tough, she’ll get over it.’

‘I hope so, she was furious. We were on our way in and she brushed straight past us. Not even a bye.’

David shrugged.

‘Would you rather be alone?’ Rachel continued. ‘Shall I go downstairs?

‘No. Actually I’d like you to look at Grandma’s jewellery. See if there’s anything you want as a keepsake. Then as soon as everyone’s gone we’ll get going with clearing out her stuff.’

‘It’s weird. I don’t feel a strong sense of loss, but now you’ve said ‘clearing out her stuff’, like chucking away evidence of her life, I think it’s all very sad.’

When Sam came in to see what was going on, his father and sister were hugging.

Chapter Thirty-nine

David had returned from the funeral with a heady mix of guilt and anger – guilt because of the lack of a strong feeling of loss for his mother and anger because of Jane's accusation.

Any feeling of unease had been replaced within a week by elation due to the arrival of two letters. The first was from his solicitor confirming that Jane had no claim on the inheritance, the second from his mother's solicitor informing him that the transfer of money associated with her liquid assets was about to be made.

And now, less than one week after that good news, this wonderful day – the signing of the lease and possession of the property. They'd already commissioned an architect to draw up plans, and delighted with what she had suggested, the tender had gone out and the builder recruited.

Bridget was making a habit of racing round to David with a bottle of champagne. She'd done so when he'd telephoned with the news of the inheritance, repeated the action when he'd told her about the two letters, and now, having signed the lease and gained possession of the property, champagne was again flowing as they stood in the building, re-examining the architect's plans ahead of meeting the builder. Excitement mounted as they discussed ideas for furniture, lighting, and décor.

It was time to consider colour schemes. They'd decided to go their separate ways to gather paint charts and highlight which colours they thought would work best. It would be fun to see how close their choices were.

They were not close at all. Bridget had chosen light greys and beiges, David had gone for bold primary colours.

'But you love these colours, Bridget. Your house is full of them.'

'But this isn't my house. The café needs to be a place where people feel calm and relaxed.'

'They're like all the off white colours I got rid of in my house.'

'No, they're bolder than that. I've gone for Scandinavian cool – that's very popular now.'

'I'm not sure.'

'I know I'm right. You can't have apple green or indigo or yellow on these vast walls.'

'It would make a statement.'

'Yes, it would do that, but not the one we want.'

The bickering continued for a while, developing into a rare argument. It was six o'clock when Bridget dropped down onto a rickety chair and David followed suit. A period of quiet reflection followed as each of them tried to imagine what the place would look like in their own and the other's choice of colour.

Bridget broke the silence. 'Look we don't have to decide for ages. I'm absolutely shattered, let's head on.'

'Agreed. We've done enough for a day.'

David dropped off Bridget then headed home, desperate to unwind. He settled down to watch the recording of a TV drama about a group of factory workers who'd won the national lottery. The reviews had been positive and this light-hearted production would provide much needed escapism.

The doorbell rang. He waited in anticipation of either Sam or Rachel coming downstairs to answer it, but neither did. With reluctance he pressed pause on the remote and investigated. It was Jim.

The last thing David needed was this. He would not tolerate an accusation that he'd treated Jane unfairly.

'May I come in, David?' Jim always looked earnest and

sincere. Perhaps it came from being a Philosophy lecturer. The rat.

'I suppose so, but I've had a busy day so not for long if you don't mind.'

After Jane had moved out, one to one conversation with Jim had been confined to the confrontation following the accidental burning of Jane's clothes on Guy Fawkes Night. Since then there had been no more than nods in acknowledgement of each other's presence when the children were being taken or collected from their two parents' homes.

'Don't worry, this can be quick, but there's something you need to know,' Jim said. He had a face that exuded his mood and this one suggested the end of the world was nigh. David prepared his answer to what was to come. He had phoned his solicitor and there was no way Jane was entitled to any of the money left to him by his mother.

They sat in the lounge. The TV screen was frozen on a painfully thin, middle-aged lady wearing a factory overall. Temporarily static tears rolled down her cheeks. David was unsure whether they were tears of joy or sorrow because despite the win, not all was going well for the lottery winners.

'Could we ...?' Jim suggested, nodding towards the screen.

'OK,' David conceded and switched off the TV. It struck him that when they had been friends Jim always got his own way. He had a knack of making it blindingly obvious that his preference was the logical one. He wasn't going to win this time. 'What do you want to talk about, Jim?'

'About Jane. Jane and me.'

'Look I know how she feels about my inheritance but I have to tell you ...'

'It's nothing to do with money, David.'

'What is it then?'

'I've decided not to marry her, David.'

David was unsure how to respond. Jim had had what seemed like a wonderful marriage until poor Vanessa had died of cancer. She'd ignored the symptoms for ages and by the time it was diagnosed it was too late to take action. Jane, David too, had been supportive during the last few months of Vanessa's life and then with Jim afterwards. Of course David hadn't been aware of just how supportive Jane had been. Was it now evident to Jim that his love for his wife had been so strong that he couldn't put her memory aside and remarry?

If this was the case, David had a suggestion. 'You needn't think about marriage. Just enjoy the relationship and see what happens in the future.'

'I don't only mean not marrying. It's over between Jane and me, David.'

'What?'

'I've fallen in love with someone else.'

David remained silent.

Jim continued. 'A lecturer joined my department in January. We see eye to eye on everything. Right from the start we've spent hours in coffee bars and pubs chatting away on the same wavelength. It's incredible, it's like we're telepathic. Yesterday we discussed producing a joint paper on free will versus determinism. You see Descartes viewed the mind as pure ego, a permanent spiritual substance. Of course since then –'

'Jim, I'm not interested in that. I have similar ideas about the layout of balance sheets as some of my female accountancy colleagues, but that doesn't mean I have affairs with them.' Mary did cross David's mind at that instant, but he brushed the thought aside.

'Fair point, David. For me and Ursula it's more than that. We're in love.'

'Does Jane know this?'

'Yes she does. She's rather upset, David.'

‘Rather upset! Honestly, what do you expect?’

‘Fair point, David.’

‘Stop saying “fair point” will you?’

‘Fair … yes, sorry, David.’

‘And stop putting a ‘David’ at the end of everything you say. It gets on my nerves.’

‘What do you mean?’

‘I mean there are only the two of us in the room, not a group. When you speak it’s obviously addressed to me so there’s no need to end with “David”.’

Jim called up his hurt look. Head down, speaking even more softly than usual, he conceded. ‘If it bothers you that much I’ll stop doing it.’

‘Good,’ David replied, adding ‘Jim’ for good measure to make it evident he saw through the manipulation. But he didn’t anticipate what was to come.

Jim turned on his ‘deep in meaningful thought’ face as he looked around the room. ‘I’ve not been in here since you changed things. Jane told me how much she liked the new colour on the walls and I must say I rather agree.’ Once again his face transformed, now to an “I’ve suddenly thought of a great idea” mode. ‘You’re incredibly similar, you two. Made for each other. David, would you consider taking her back?’

‘What?’

‘Jane. Would you take her back? I think she still loves you, David.’

‘I have a new partner, Jim. Someone I love very much. And unlike you with Jane, I intend to ensure it’s long-lasting.’

‘There’s no need for that jibe, David.’

‘I think there is. You’ve quite possibly ruined her life.’

‘I don’t think so, David.’

‘Cut out the “David”, will you!’

‘Jane will be fine. She’s an attractive woman and let’s face it, there are plenty of fish in the sea for her to choose from.'

'Including sharks. Fortunately not everyone behaves the way you do. I think you'd better go now.'

'Yes, perhaps I should, David.'

Jim stood. Some people think a handshake makes up for appalling behaviour. Jim had attempted it when he and Jane had broken the news of their relationship and now Jim extended his hand once more. David refused to take it and marched Jim out to the hallway. Jim departed without a further word between them.

David was shocked to hear the news, but there was nothing he could do about it. It was Jane's problem. He returned to the lounge, switched on the TV, and fast forwarded to the point where the factory worker was crying. He was pleased to see they were tears of joy. The drama moved on to a younger winner who had bought a flash sports car and then been caught speeding by the police. Offering them a £200 bribe to let him off was not a good idea. It looked like the police were going to arrest him – which was a bit of a problem because his wife's waters had broken and he wasn't answering his mobile. The drama was hotting up.

Chapter Forty

David told Bridget about Jim's visit as they were driving to the café the following day.

'Maybe she deserves it, but what a bastard he is.'

'To be truthful, I can't help feeling sorry for Jane.'

'That's very generous of you. Oh look, the builder's already arrived, that's his van across the road.'

They waved to the builder as they unlocked the door and he followed them in. Greg Saunders was carrying his copy of the architect's plans together with what turned out to be his work schedule. They walked round the premises discussing the order that things would be done, with Greg checking that their ideas matched his interpretation of what the architect had drawn up.

'Is the architect managing the project?'

'No, that'll be me,' Bridget said.

Greg frowned and looked across to David to verify that this was indeed the case. David was about to speak when Bridget continued.

'I've given up my job so I'll be able to pop in every morning to check your plans for the day. I'm assuming that's acceptable.'

Greg nodded. 'I must say though, this schedule is very tight.'

'The reason we chose you is because you indicated it could be done within our time frame.'

'That's true enough,' he conceded, addressing his response to Bridget. 'But one of my jobs is taking longer than I expected and I've got two decorators off at the moment.'

Bridget had taken the lead. 'That's your problem to

sort. This work schedule of yours shows completion on time.'

'I wrote it only a few days ago, but things change quickly in this industry.'

'What exactly do you see as the bottlenecks?'

'Getting men in to knock down this wall,' he said pointing, 'then the brickwork. I can't do anything until those jobs have been done. After that, like I've said, my problem is decorators.'

'Surely you can get your team to do overtime for the wall and the brickwork over this weekend, they're hardly massive jobs are they?'

'I might be able to do that …'

'I'm sure you can.'

'Then there's the decorating, like I said.'

'Well, again, overtime during evenings if you can't find freelancers to help you out. And we're both free to paint if need be, though if we're involved that would need to be knocked off the bill.'

With agreement about the way forward reached they sat on three chairs that had seen far better days.

'You drive a hard bargain, don't you?' Greg declared, looking across at Bridget. 'You seem to know a lot about the industry for a woman.'

David prayed that Bridget wouldn't explode with anger and sack Saunders on the spot or attack him to such an extent that he'd quit.

To his relief she remained calm, smiling at Saunders as she indicated that her job had involved setting up exhibitions which gave her a good insight into how builders operated.

'Seeing him every day is going to be fun,' she said when he'd left. 'Let's resolve our wall colour dispute, I've got a good idea.'

Driving home David considered whether he had been out-manoeuvred by Bridget, but she was the arty one so he was prepared to give her the benefit of doubt.

He was surprised how exhausting the planning was. After dinner he sank into an armchair and tuned into Film4 for an hour and a half of zoning out before bed.

The doorbell rang. He pressed pause on the remote.

It was Jane and she was in floods of tears. David's good nature came through and he put a consoling arm around her shoulders. She was blurting out the news in between tears as David informed her that Jim had been round the previous evening so he already knew. He led her to the kitchen and offered her coffee or wine. She chose wine; he opened a red and poured two glasses.

'He hasn't come home since visiting you. No doubt he's off to the club again tonight,' she mumbled.

'What do you mean "club"?'

'The club where he met his new woman.'

'No, she's a colleague at the university, a Philosophy lecturer.'

Jane dabbed her eyes with a handkerchief, downed the rest of her wine, and held up her glass for a refill. David poured as requested. She took another large swig before continuing. 'No, she isn't. I discovered the truth. Jim is a regular at *ComeInside*. All this time when he's been telling me he's got to stay on for a lecture or a meeting at the university, he's been going to a strip joint near Covent Garden.'

'Are you sure?'

'Completely. I found out after a work colleague phoned to speak with him, a woman called Ursula who I vaguely know. I'd met her at a university drinks party. The evening she called he'd said he'd be late home as he needed to plan next year's courses. With Ursula, the idiot told me.' Jane started to cry again. 'Got a tissue, please?'

'Yes, I'll get them.'

David rushed up to his bedroom – once upon a time

their bedroom – and brought down a box of tissues. Jane took a handful and dabbed her eyes before continuing. 'Soon after Ursula called, he texted to let me know that the meeting still wasn't finished so it would be best to stay over. That wasn't for the first time. Until then I'd had no reason to doubt what he said. I know lecturers can get a bedroom at the university if they're working late and that had been his routine excuse. Of course, he didn't stay there.'

'How do you know?'

'Because a couple of days ago I confronted him. As calm as anything he came out with it. Full of his bloody intense looks and "you see Jane, this" and "you see Jane, that".' She gave a bitter laugh before continuing. 'I yelled at him for calling me Jane every few seconds. It's a habit that drives me mad. He speaks like he's a counsellor giving me advice. So there he was, fucking someone else, and my biggest complaint when he told me was his use of language!'

'But what was going on if it's not Ursula?'

'He's fallen in love with a woman called Nadine, who's one of the hostesses at the club. "Hostess" is the word they use but if my internet research is anything to go by, "prostitute" might be a more appropriate word. According to him she's different to all the others; a comment which doesn't help because it implies that he knows all the others. And "knows" in a strip joint puts a certain slant on the word. I hope I haven't picked up anything.'

Jane looked across to David, sensitive to the tactlessness of her remark. But thinking about Jane having sex with Jim no longer disturbed him.

'What happens now?' David asked.

'Jim thinks she's different, a "reluctant" worker at the club, gallantly saving to make sure her daughter has a good quality of life. And now that she's found true love, la-di-da, she's going to quit *ComeInside* and live with him.

I suppose as soon as I'm out of the way.'

She started crying again as she stretched her arm out for another top up of wine. David was still on his first glass. 'It won't last,' he said. 'The man's an idiot.'

The children had heard the crying and were standing by the lounge door. David was unsure how much of the sordid story they had picked up.

'Can Mum stay here tonight, Dad?' Sam asked.

David had contemplated that; he was prepared to sleep on the couch.

Jane thanked Sam, but indicated there was no need. Jim had agreed to move out until she found somewhere else to live. She reckoned that "somewhere" might be her mother's for the time being.

There was an awkward silence as the four of them walked to the hall and Jane opened the front door. 'What the hell am I going to do now?' she said quietly as she left.

'I'm afraid that's her problem,' Rachel said after the door had closed.

Chapter Forty-one

WPC Zara Dixon was sitting on a very comfortable couch in a middle-class home located in one of the most affluent outer London suburbs. She was drinking Earl Grey tea served in a bone china mug. The startlingly bright orange walls were perhaps atypical, but everything else was appropriately respectable. The room was spacious with high ceilings; a maroon lacquered Chinese cabinet with big brass inlays stood by the bay window; two bold abstract art works hung on the wall opposite the Victorian fireplace; and a dark wood table in the centre of the room had coasters placed on each corner. She set her cup down on the one nearest then examined the swirling pattern on the Oriental rug that covered most of the polished wooden floorboards.

David lifted the plate from the tray on the table and offered her a biscuit, which she took. Almond and pistachio slices were embedded on a light shortbread base and it was delicious.

Zara had been transferred from east to north-west London almost a year ago and the contrast was dramatic. Back then she'd been involved in life-threatening operations at high rise blocks with their forever failing lifts, damp and blackened walls, and harsh concrete outside terrains. Here she was relieved to no longer have to break up feuding gangs or deal with associated knifings, shootings, and brawls. Her current beat, she'd have to admit, was very easy by comparison. Drunken teenagers, minor drug offences, and dodgy insurance claims were the main demands on her time. And this family had scored for all three despite their comfortable home, delicious biscuits, and the other outward signs of middle class propriety.

‘Why would I want to set fire to my own business premises before I’ve even got started?’

‘Why indeed, sir?’

‘I’ve already told you, I can’t be held responsible for my ex-wife’s actions. We separated months ago and I can’t for the life of me think why she’d want to burn down the café. In fact we get on fairly well now.’

‘Clearly not that well. May I?’ Zara asked as she leaned across to take another biscuit.

‘Yes, help yourself.’

‘You say your “ex-wife”. We have no record of a divorce.’

‘Well we aren’t divorced yet.’

‘So she’s not your ex-wife then?’

‘Technically not, but to all intents and purposes she is.’ David was being made to feel guilty when there was nothing to feel guilty about. ‘The financial settlement was completed a while back and we’re going through the final legal bit now.’

‘To what extent is she involved in your coffee bar plans?’

‘Not at all.’

‘Let me get this straight. You’ve sorted out the split of your finances so she has no interest in the success or otherwise of your business venture. She doesn’t stand to gain or lose any money. So can you think of any reason for her action?’

They were going round in circles. David considered Jane’s jealousy regarding his mother’s death and the subsequent windfall inheritance. Then there was her distress at being dumped by Jim. ‘I have no idea,’ he declared.

At 12.15 a.m. on the previous Sunday morning, two policemen in a duty vehicle had been making their way at no great speed along Muswell Hill Broadway to ensure that the behaviour outside the pubs and clubs was not intolerable. As they reached the quieter end of the road, the officer who wasn't driving glanced down a side street and noticed a car parked on double yellow lines with warning indicators flashing. They stopped to observe. It had been an unusually calm Saturday night and these two young policemen missed the buzz of confrontation.

'I bet there's a party on somewhere and that's a poor parent who's been ordered to collect their little darling but instructed not to park too close to avoid embarrassment,' Robin surmised.

William laughed. 'No, it won't be a party and I'll tell you why not; it's approaching exam season. All the sixth formers are busy revising.'

'What about the younger kids?'

'They've got exams too.'

'Do you think they care enough to stay sober?'

'This is Muswell Hill. Of course they do.'

'Yeah, maybe. Let's do a good deed and see what the problem is.'

'I'm telling you, it'll be a middle-aged lady. Mind you, we could get her because she is on a double yellow line. God knows why she hasn't parked a little further up the road.'

'You know what, I can't be bothered. Let's leave her in peace.'

'Agreed. Turn at the roundabout and head back to the station. If we drive slowly we'll be pretty well off duty by the time we get there. I'm knackered anyway.'

Robin drove to the roundabout, went all the way round, then headed back down the Broadway at a snail's pace. This gave them plenty of time to observe as the woman got out of her car and looked around before staggering up to the last shop on the small parade, an empty plot. She peered through the letterbox.

William prided himself in recognising the potential for

crime, although in this case it didn't take Sherlock Holmes to appreciate something was up. 'Pull in for a minute will you, Robin. I want to see this.'

Robin stopped barely a hundred yards from where the woman was standing. He switched off the car lights and then the engine. She was too preoccupied to notice company.

Unsteadily the woman returned to her car, opened the boot, and lifted out a yellow metal container. It must have been heavy, she struggled to carry it.

'That's a petrol can!' William exclaimed.

They watched in awe as this smartly dressed middle-aged lady stumbled back to the shop, pushed the stem of a large funnel through the letterbox, opened the can, and began to pour out the contents. She was finding it difficult to control the action and some of the liquid was spilling onto her clothes. She set the can down on the pavement and put her right hand in her jacket pocket.

'Enough of that,' Robin declared. 'Let's go.'

'Within seconds their siren was blaring, their lights were flashing, and the car was speeding the short distance towards the imminent arsonist.

On hearing and seeing the advancing police car the woman raised her arms high in the air to indicate surrender. Her dramatic stance made William laugh out loud and he had to bite his lip to stifle it as he stepped out the car. He stopped smiling when he saw a lit match in her right hand. She was in grave danger of setting fire to herself.

'Don't you move an inch,' he yelled as he sprinted towards her. 'Not an inch!'

When he reached her he grabbed hold of her wrist, brought it down close to his mouth, and blew out the match.

'Thank you, that's very kind of you,' Jane mumbled. The policemen's attempt to get any sense out of her was pointless given her level of intoxication. A flustered, incoherent Jane was taken to the police station and locked up for the night with charges of attempted arson and drink driving imminent. On taking the breathalyser test she used the logic of an alcoholic to explain that the drinking had been essential to build up the courage to carry out the arson.

She spent a miserable night in a cell and was remorseful by the morning when she gave David's contact details to WPC Zara Dixon. After a brief interview Zara decided to visit the address provided, well aware she had been there before. Twice.

'If, as you say, you are separated, why would Jane give this as her home address?'

David explained the situation. His soon to be ex-wife had been dumped by the man she had left him to live with. Although she was still living in Jim's house this was only for a short while until she found a place of her own. She probably thought his address was the best bet.

'Though finding somewhere to live clearly wasn't the only thing on her mind last night, was it?'

David decided to keep any further answers brief in an attempt to terminate the interview. 'Apparently not.'

The policewoman asked if David intended to press charges. He'd been expecting this question and replied with a monosyllabic "no".

'No?'

'That's right, no.'

Zara was beginning to think the work in east London, although a lot tougher, was rather easier to comprehend. She waited for David to explain his decision. It was a long wait, but finally he continued.

'She's going through a difficult time. And she didn't end up doing anything wrong, did she? The premises weren't set fire to, no property or person was injured. I'm sure she would have realised it was wrong before taking the action.'

'Sir, the officers were fortunately able to intervene just in time. There was a pool of petrol inside your door, she was covered in it, and she had already struck a match.'

'I'm sure all sorts of things were going through her mind at that point to prevent her doing it.'

'In her state I don't think much could have been going through her mind. We have a recording of her interview. She admits to getting drunk to give her the courage to commit arson.'

'People can say things in the panic of the moment, things they don't mean. The fact of the matter is that there was no fire and therefore no crime.'

'Apart from driving when almost four times over the limit.'

'I thought she was parked when you apprehended her. Did anyone see her drive in that state?'

'Well that's for us to act upon, it's not relevant to this conversation. Are you sure you won't press charges?'

'I'm positive.'

'OK, I'll record that.'

'Is that everything then?'

'I suppose it is. Thank you for your time.' WPC Dixon stood and David led her to the front door.

'There is one more thing, sir. Those biscuits, where do you get them from?'

Chapter Forty-two

'This place is so cool, Bridget,' Rachel said.

David had to agree – whether this was Scandinavian chic or not, the café looked fabulous. Bridget's colours dominated, the largest beige wall filled with an exhibition of paintings by one of her friends, a two-tone grey wall bare but for two recesses with abstract scarlet glassware. Scarlet had been one of his colour preferences and there were bold splashes of it throughout the café – the coffee cups and saucers, the wooden edging around the giant mirror above the bar, all the doors, the aprons worn by the serving staff.

'Yes, a huge well done to you both,' Joe added. David had seen a lot of Rachel's boyfriend in recent weeks and was rather fond of him, even though the knowledge that Joe was sleeping with his daughter wasn't easy to come to terms with.

Regardless of whether it was cool or not, the first night was as big a success as they could possibly have hoped for. The café was jam-packed and everyone was in good spirits, laughing and chatting away. Jabulani's band was well-received and customers were purchasing the full range of food and drink on offer.

'Dad, please can I have a glass of red wine?' Rachel asked, technically for the first time but she'd already requested white wine and beer.

'Stop it, Rachel. You're not having any alcohol. I could lose my licence and get shut down on the first night.'

'I look old enough. Anyway if an inspector came in I'd hand my drink over to someone else,' she said looking across at Joe, who had already turned eighteen.

'Absolutely not.'

'Fun killer. Never mind, we're off to a party now. Well done with this place, Dad. I'll see you later or maybe tomorrow morning, I'm not sure yet.' She kissed him and he could smell alcohol on her breath.

'Text me if you're staying out,' he called after her. He was unsure if she'd heard because at that point the song the band was performing, initially soft and melancholy, picked up pace and volume. For the first time in ages David could let all thoughts of what was needed to be done wither away as he listened to the music.

There was a loud cheer as the song reached its climax. Jabulani spoke. 'Thank you, thank you very much. It's an honour to be here on the opening night of my friend's café. I must say a few words about David – he's been helpful and kind from the first day I met him at work. But hey, I'm not going to speak, we're going to perform our new song called 'David and Bridget's Dream'.

There were no instruments for this song, just vocals. Wonderful harmonies across several octaves. The lyrics brought laughter even though most listeners were unaware of the significance of references to the local council, a lethal underground car park, Queensbury, tea at Harrods, and a tight-arsed boss called Mary.

She wears ethnic chic
Thinks our work is bleak
Keen to criticise
Especially all the guys
It's scary Mary
Yes it's scary Mary

David roared with laughter until interrupted by a sharp poke in the ribs. He turned and faced his ex-tight-arsed boss. She was taking it in good spirits, all smiles as he would expect from the new Mary. The song ended with '*My God, it's scary scary ... scary Mary*' and there was wild applause.

Kanjani had finished their set and Jabulani's brother was thanking the audience, informing them that their first album was about to be released. One of the reasons for such a crowded first night was the reputation that the band had acquired in the local area over recent months.

'Luckily you've resigned, David, otherwise it would be instant dismissal on a charge of gross misconduct.'

'It weren't me, your honour, it were Jabulani,' he exclaimed in mock defence. 'Thanks ever so much for coming along tonight.'

She moved closer and kissed him on each cheek. 'I wouldn't dream of missing such an important event.'

David noticed Bridget looking across at them. She was behind the bar serving drinks – they were taking it in turns to support their staff there. 'Let me introduce you to Bridget.'

'Sure.'

As they headed across the room, Ross approached at considerable speed. He grabbed hold of David's hand and shook it furiously. 'Hello, mate. You've done it, well done.' His attention turned to Mary. 'I hope you're going to introduce me to this beautiful lady?'

The beautiful lady didn't seem to be put off by the crass chat up line. 'I think I'm able to introduce myself. I'm Mary,' her new voice said.

'Well, hello, Mary. I'm Ross, a close friend of this entrepreneurial wizard.' The entrepreneurial wizard needn't have been present because Ross's attention was fully on Mary. He took hold of her hand and kissed it. She didn't mind – in fact she was beaming.

Red alert. *Keep away from him*, David wanted to warn her, but he was already relegated to bit-part player, in fact completely ignored as Ross invited Mary to join him at the bar for a drink. He watched as they walked off, his gaze fixed on the tight fitting purple skirt that Mary was wearing.

He caught Candy's eye and she waved. She had come with a group of friends, students on her degree course. Presumably the relationship with Ross was over since she was sitting on the lap of a more appropriately-aged male. Ross would be on the lookout for a new woman and judging by what was going on by the bar, was already making good progress with Mary. They were sitting close together on bar stools and his hand rested on her knee. David dismissed his gut reaction to intervene. Mary was tough enough to cope and who knows, it might end up as the perfect match. Bridget was serving them drinks – David hadn't got as far as introducing the two women.

And now another woman was on the scene. Jane approached him with a man by her side, who was rather formally dressed for the occasion in suit and tie.

'Hi, David.'

'Hello, Jane.'

They'd had a heart to heart after the attempted arson attack, Jane full of remorse and grateful that he hadn't pressed charges.

'I thought I'd support your opening. I wish you lots of luck.' She looked across to Bridget, busy at the bar. 'Both of you.'

'That's very kind, I appreciate you coming along.'

'This is Rupert, he's a friend from work.'

Rupert extended his arm and they shook hands. What with the tension of the opening night, Mary turning up, Ross chasing Mary, Candy with a new man, Rachel heading off to God knows where, and now Jane arriving, he was struggling to build up enthusiasm to speak to Rupert.

'Go and get a drink. Now the band's finished I need to put on some music then I'll have to relieve Bridget at the bar.'

David led Jane and Rupert towards Bridget, passing Ross and Mary who were laughing away. He felt a tinge of jealousy. He escaped into the small office and chose a Beach House album to play, appropriately gentle end of evening music. They had to close by 11.30, so how to get customers to leave on time was on his mind when Bridget joined him.

'It's beginning to quieten down,' she said. 'I know we want masses of sales but I'm dead beat, I wouldn't mind if everybody went home now.'

They peeped out.

Candy and her friends were still partying, the youngest of the mixed age profile of customers that they had so hoped for.

'Wow, what a great night,' Bridget exclaimed.

'Yes, I think we're going to make it. In fact, I know we are.'

'I believe you could be right. When I first saw this idea on your list I thought it was a wild fantasy.'

'No, you were my wild fantasy! I've been thinking, partner. Now we work together perhaps we should live together.'

'Let's not run before we can walk, David.'

'Yes, but do you think a run might be possible?'

'We'll see, David.'

'Stop saying "David" at the end of every statement! There's no need.'

'What are you talking about? Why are you laughing?'

'A private joke, it reminded me of someone I used to know.'

'Sometimes your humour is utterly incomprehensible. I've got no idea why I'm fond of you.'

'It could be my money.'

'Ha ha.'

They watched the band members pack up and left it to the more conscientious of their staff to collect glasses from the near deserted tables. Jane and Rupert, engaged in earnest conversation in the shadows of the far corner, were holding hands. David was happy to see that.

Candy and her gang were getting ready to leave. Drinks were being downed, coats put on, and the couples were having a farewell snog.

Propping up the bar ever closer to Mary, Ross looked across at Candy. When her kissing ended he laughed aloud to indicate that he was having the time of his life with a new woman. Candy didn't notice or didn't want Ross to see her notice. She waved at David and Bridget and blew them a kiss.

Ross rested a hand on Mary's shoulder and whispered something that made her giggle. 'Who's that woman with Ross?' Bridget enquired.

'Why do you ask?'

'I saw you talking with her earlier. Who is she?'

David reddened. 'That's Mary.'

'Your ex-boss? God, she's not at all what I thought she'd be like. She's incredibly attractive. Don't you think so?'

'I suppose she is, I've never thought of her in that way. She was just my boss.'

'Come on, I reckon it's time we shut down,' Bridget said as she turned off the music. They stepped out the office and observed the arrival of the very late comer.

David was flabbergasted that she'd popped in to support their opening night, presumably having just got off duty as she was still in uniform. He rushed over to greet her.

'Hello, it's great to see you. I'd better not contravene licencing laws or you'll arrest me, but there's just time to get you one drink before closing. What would you like?'

WPC Zara Dixon stood her ground by the entrance as the few remaining guests looked on.

'That's very kind of you, sir, but I'm still on duty. I need you to come with me to the station.'

Zara watched the woman who was by Mr Willoughby's

side take hold of his right arm. Next, Mrs Willoughby, assuming that was still her status, approached Mr Willoughby and clutched his left arm. The man who had had his arm around the maybe Mrs Willoughby's waist followed her, clasping her spare hand.

'The police station?' David asked, the woman on each side of him tightening her grip.

Diagonally from the right a third woman came hurtling towards him at great speed. She yanked away from a man who struggled to retain his arm around her shoulders. To no avail; he stumbled and fell to his knees. Ignoring the cries of the fallen one, she continued her rush up to Mr Willoughby, flinging her arms around him. Their faces all but touched.

'This is fabulous,' Mary slurred. 'Fabulous. I'm going to miss you so much; please promise you'll keep in contact.' Before he could answer she kissed him on the lips and sustained the embrace. He didn't, couldn't respond, because his arms were still pinned down by the other two women. The fallen one shuffled towards them on his knees then stood.

'I know all about you two, you are such a crafty bugger,' he said to David as he pulled Mary away.

The other two women, still affixed to David, looked on in puzzlement.

Unsure who to face, the policewoman addressed a convenient gap to the left of David's ear. 'I'm afraid it's your daughter, sir. She's been apprehended for drunk and disorderly behaviour.'

And not surprising, she thought.

Women's Contemporary Fiction

For more information about **R J Gould**

and other **Accent Press** titles

please visit

www.accentpress.co.uk
and the author's website www.rjgould.info

For news on Accent Press authors and upcoming titles
please visit

http://accenthub.com/

Lightning Source UK Ltd.
Milton Keynes UK
UKOW04f0319060115

244040UK00001B/4/P